what good is this?

also by Keith Mitchell

The Garden Sanctuary

The Law of Attraction

Four Noble Truths

Stage Play - Dream of the Ridiculous Man

what good is this?

a comedy of errors
by **keith mitchell**

Beyond Horizons

First published in the United Kingdom by
beyond horizons

copyright © wgit/kwm13 beyond horizons

ISBN 978-0-9566894-0-5

Keith Mitchell asserts the moral right
to be identified as the author of this work

All characters in this book are fictitious and any resemblance to actual persons,
living or dead, is purely coincidental

All rights reserved. No part of this publication may be reproduced, stored in a
retrieval system or transmitted, in any form or by any means,
without prior permission of the author.

for Jaki who started it all

Prologue   what good is this?

Palm a handful of the smallest sparkling grains of sand on this beach, a trillion atoms in every one. Weightless soft they wriggle away between your fingers, a glistening shower falling back into an ocean. From a boundless night sky the stars proclaim meaning and purpose. Though the evidence of my own place in this majestic order appears only fleeting in moments of wonder.

Be grateful for such insights, for occur they do in spite of our inane flailing about. It's true, no one says you have to be happy all the time. We learn by our mistakes, don't we? In that case, what is a mistake but another learning opportunity. And how do you find the nerve to maintain a belief in that?
They say hope is a good thing, maybe the best. I don't know, I've given it up so many times I'm completely its prisoner. To me it looks more like brinkmanship. Hanging on to the bitter-end with a desperate, dimming faith that surely things must get better..

The Bitter End: A traditional sea-fishing term used to describe there being no more of the rope to pay out. Nothing left with which to land a catch but fortune and what the tide may bring.

So, where to turn for any certainty beyond our frighteningly limited experience? We can get help, read, talk. Sometimes something new arrives just by listening. But meditate, watch TV or go for walk, it's still all about your own judgement. Alone we juggle and decide how and where to go now.

God doesn't play dice, Einstein said. Did he hope for nothing left to chance? All and everything ordered and clear, following solid sequential formulae? Had he been alive today, amidst the spectacular ascent of quantum mechanics, he may have had to admit a few more things to heaven and earth. Granted the reason-obsessed fashion of his time, was he so convinced by certainty? That's certainty not truth. But as that does appear to be our overriding interest, what constitutes a certainty has been argued about ever since. Right now, the cleverest people on the planet, physicists, cosmologists and philosophers, whose forebears have for centuries searched for simple and elegant solutions to describe the Universe, are now saying that what once was empirical truth, is in fact utterly unpredictable. They find evidence full of quantum, random possibility too numerous to calculate, so that Nature itself may not know what it's doing..

And where does that leave us? Any who are left still hopeful. Where? Between the devil and the deep blue sea..

Between The Devil And The Deep Blue Sea: A shipwright's maxim which derives from the arduous task of corking or filling the longest seam along the widest girth of the wooden hull of a boat. This longest seam is so-called 'The Devil', because simply that's exactly what the job is like to make it watertight. But get it wrong and you'll sink.

Chapter One   what good is this?

What good is it to harp on cold, hard reality?
'Who makes the morning fabulous?
Who says today's a fun day?
Why do I feel like sailing again
Honey it's you – Janie Runaway' *

Dreary October. Raining. Almost as much water from the sky as under the barge. Round the back of some factories she sits in a small basin on the Grand Union Canal. Just audible above wind lashed rain splashes, through a skylight atop her low-pitched roof, an early morning alarm bell is exhausting its spring.

..a darkened gale blew around us. Deep foreboding fear took my breath away as we breached and plunged through torment unseen. The cabin walls shook with each pounding. In panic I flailed and beat at every door to get out of my prison below the decks. At the peak of whistling and crashing above, an enormous splintered spar hove through the roof and, launched like some giant's arrow, from top to bottom, narrowly passed my face, forcing my recoil and pierced the floor at my feet. Instantly a fountain of water exploded from the breach and I could feel the boat roll and plunge down as we began to sink. Streaming water burst through every crack. The walls bulged and splintered under irresistible pressure. With huge weight suddenly released the room became a maelstrom of white water which took me up so fast I struck my head hard on the beam above. The pitching ceased and an insulating silence overcame the world as the room filled to the top. The only sound a distant bell clanging on spars above. We are consumed and gone. I knew with the last gasp of air that I would die and be carried down by the sinking ship. In my deepest surrender to inevitable death, I threw my arms open wide crucifixion-like. Then, in some violent ejaculation ready for punishment, there was an huge explosion from somewhere over on the right and a sudden sharp deep pain in the back of my hand. I tumbled over and over in reaction and fell right through a hole in the floor that just seemed to open up beside me..

Adrenaline driven panic threw open my eyes in time to hit the floor and witness bedlam reality in action. The bedside table, the lamp and the alarm-clock on it spinning across the room, arriving over at the bulkhead wall with the most almighty clatter. Sharply withdrawing the guilty arm, I lay there breathing heavily, nursing the pain now entering my chest. In the stillness that followed, the only sound of my new twilight void, the alarm-clock faltering.

How many times have you heard someone say that dreams give portent and meaning to life? They describe the inner workings of our subsumed personality. The stuff our sub-conscious is busy working out for us whilst the marvellous waking mind is out of the way. Thoughts you'll never know you had. Too uncomfortable, too incompatible with hoped for images of an in control self. Rumbling earth-tremor-like they are a Royal Road leading to the really important stuff we've done our best to ignore.

Theatrically flat and spread-eagle on the rug next to the bed, I turned slowly over to look up toward the skylight. Rain is teeming and with gusts of wind, flaying the window. A drip of water splashes onto my forehead. I watched it coming all the way down to impact and then realised the back of my head is in a puddle. Other drips have formed two little pools ready for further rude awakening. Above on the skylight frame it's possible to trace a tiny glistening rivulet that must lead from the leak. I have spent so much time trying to seal those.
'Sinking boats?.. Don't even go there.'

An appropriate sense of drama emphasises my dreaming or even waking incompetence. With a vague lazy urge to get back to sleep I crawled, hands and knees back, but then spied the time. Defiance collapsed and stared irresolute, waiting for the next drip to join its puddled friends.
It took a matter of mille-seconds. 'Oh God!'

It really doesn't matter that much. I mean the drips. It's a boat. Outside of dreams and paranoid fantasy, it floats. And as long as you avoid the water soaking into anything along the way, it all runs down into the bilges. Reaching a hopefully uncritical level under the floor, the automatic micro-switch will turn on the bilge-pump and send it back from whence it came. The switch is powered now. Mains electricity guarantees that we don't sink. A triumph beyond the rechargeable batteries I had before. Not that we'd sink far, the canal here is about three feet deep. Of course, that might mean three feet of water and then ten of sludge made indescribable by three hundred years of jetsam. Sinking through that could take coal manufacturing millennia. Trying to stop the roof leaking is a rather more pressing but a similarly eonic task. Stop one and it comes in somewhere else. The wood expands and contracts with sun and rain. If I'd really known what I was doing when I built it, beyond the Reader's Digest Do It Yourself Manual, things might be very different.

I do love my new shower, so much so I think I can make time stand still. I take on a kind of torpor. Timelessness way longer than washing. Thoughts stray along threads. Sometimes idly, some aggressively tense. Lingering over some choice of direction for the day or the rest of life. Something to grasp there, hovering in the steam. We say stand in the shower, but in fact it's only possible to sit in mine otherwise you bang your head on the beams holding up the ceiling. On a boat though, it's not called the ceiling. That's what you call the floor. I still don't understand this but maybe because on top of the ceiling is the deck? Anyway, the ceiling up there, it's low and the sit in the bath shower is part of my poor man's solution to raising waste water out and over the waterline. To avoid a powerful and expensive pump, my bath and shower are perched high. It's a perfectly good pink bath, saved with its pink sink from a demolition. Mounted high on a set of full length magnificently pink painted plinth steps. Once climbed, a sort of western-roll over the bathside is required to get in between lip and roof. You don't bang your head once you get used to it.

Shower reveries can be meaningful. Sometimes real insights arrive in watery drifting. Fantasies of life journeys that inhabit a special sanctuary. Like some irrigated amniotic meditation, I've made many important life decisions, lush-like steeped in mist.
Not this morning however, the choices already have an unsettled twitchiness. Even a five-minute dream is too long. Hurried, wished for magic an elusive fret. This morning it's survival. No direction or belief in much worth. A quick shower check results only in try this, try that. As ever plenty of this and that but nothing clear. Inevitably I end up thinking my choices come down to the job. And mine often end in complaint. They

last for a while, a pattern in two or three year cycles. Then they pall or something goes wrong or they come to a natural end. I think I've been lucky and without much planning or determination there has seemed themes of a sort, threads of emphasis. But you would mostly say that was by accident and, in any kind of bigger picture, without any real informed choice it all looks pretty irrelevant. Look in the paper long enough and eventually one comes along. I get into it, I'm conscientious. I might even enjoy it for a while. Then like a bad habit returning, I wake up to the feeling that it's all just survival. Motivation starts to crack and before long I'm slinking off in the afternoons. Ending up at the zoo or going for a drive. After a while you don't even feel guilty about it. You're an employee, you have no power, you work somewhere to earn the money to afford to live near enough so that you can get there and earn it. It's desperately inane. Meanwhile, you tell yourself, it could be worse. You're okay, you live comfortably. What more do you want?

A slippery slope for the day and not so different from the last weeks and months. Motivation cracked a while back. Does it matter? I don't know. I don't think many of my colleagues care. Would anyone notice anyway? Would a passerby notice you were slip-sliding? Would friends or office colleagues tell you or, would you become gradually, dimly aware through the day that they were all quietly passing on the other side, avoiding a close encounter with the slipping alien.
'Hail fellow, well met. Is it my imagination or have you slipped a little today? Let me help carry your burden and relieve the weight of your obvious wretchedness.' No. Actually they'll all be as complacent as me or too scared. Too consumed in sliding themselves to notice. No, there's no saving you. If you're going to start sliding off your trolley today, it will be a lonely road.

'And the chance of that'll be another miracle.' It won't be a lonely road. The traffic on the motorway will make quite sure of that.
'Oh God, please. They'll be so mad if it takes another age to get there today.' I have to be there at ten. It's only fifteen miles. Leave at eight thirty. 'God, isn't that long enough to sit in a car.'
We might just make it. But I won't, I'll be late as usual.

As predicted, movement on the motorway comes to a complete standstill where it narrows into two lanes. The traffic jam as far ahead as I can see. Growl and enter here for long-suffering daily patience lessons. Stuck in a mind-numbing dawdle and distracted by rare excitement, the cars ahead have moved on and there's an exhilarating, positively storming ten or fifteen yards.
Listen to the radio, occasionally sing or do your hair and make-up. Get ready to exercise brake and clutch ankles for the next three-quarters of an hour. It invariably ends up like the in-the-shower-dreaming, drifting off into another world, only a bit more polluted with precious time ticking. The rain had barely stopped but comes on heavier again to the rhythm of a thousand dancing wipers. We all return to our impotent laced smoking, nose-picking and dreaming of the next spurt.

I rowed down to the pub the other night. Bored with myself and a bit in desperation for something else to happen. I must say it's more about the adventure and novelty of rowing a boat to the pub, than it is actually being in this one. It's gloomy and old-fashioned. Embossed glass windows and old cream paint. A stand-up affair, they do though serve a good pint of Guinness. It takes ten minutes to row the couple of hundred yards.

Under the road bridge there's a rowboat-sized inlet in the stone bank with a rusty iron ring to tie up. Climb thirty or so worn bevelled steps from the tow-path and with complete surprise you come out into the middle of the clamouring High Street. You'd never know it existed from the tree-lined, isolated calm down below. The contrast is stark every time.

The Scots landlord and his wife are broad and impossible to understand. On an occasional Friday night at its busiest, I've nodded to a local shopkeeper or someone I might have passed in the street. This evening was deathly quiet with only a couple of other Tuesday night refugees, so as on previous visits, I settled to enjoy a quiet Guinness. I'd been leaning for maybe half an hour, sipping through the last half of my pint and wanting to go home, when a group of four weathered elderly men entered the bar. At first they huddled in the door and were speaking in whispers as if deciding whether to continue. In turn they each drew change from their pockets and were calculating how much they could afford. They looked a poor prospect, dishevelled overcoats and battered hats. Old fingerless gloves and strings of hanging thread. Eventually, with common agreement they shuffled over and sat at the table. One, a little man in a dirty duffle-coat and very muddy wellies, came over to the bar. He was many days unshaven and wearing a blue woollen bobble-hat, which he doffed as the Landlord greeted him and then pushed to the back of his head. He turned a very friendly smile to me so I raised my glass to him and took a salutary slug of Guinness. In a strong accent the little man ordered four 'alves o' myauld.

So here we all are for seemingly ordinary purposes. An ordinary Tuesday evening late in October. No outward signs of anything more. However, out of such mundanity, the dull mantle cracks. A chance remark, an irrelevant aside. Some factor out of natural contrast to unimportant things.

As the landlord pulled their halves of mild, the blue bobble-hat character turned to me.

'You from roundabouts?' His lovely agricultural drawl stretching it out.

'Yeh, I live just down the canal a way on a houseboat. This is my local. Just dropped in for a pint to break the monotony.' I chuckled at the end, making light of the excuse.

'Very monotonous is it? What you do?' He leaned one enquiring elbow on the bar and pushed the hat a bit further back.

I looked into clear blue eyes and lied, 'Well, I mean not really, you know, it's just sometimes you have to get out for a bit of a change don't you.'

I'm getting in too deep for a casual greeting.

'Well, you couldn't be discoverin' new oceans, lessen you got the courage to lose sight o' the shore now, could you?'

'No I,.. no I suppose not.' I said lamely, working it through.

'That'll be toow-nainety-toow.' the Landlord interrupted.

And the little man paid in a pile of exact change, gathered all four glasses in his woolly fingers, nodded a smile at me and shuffled over to his companions.

I stare for ages at the dregs of my pint with nothing else going on. No room for anything except repeating over what he said. Then it did strike as an enormous irony as I rowed back to the barge, that both banks of my ocean are no more that fifteen feet away. I tied up to the jetty still repeating the phrase like some kind of invocation.

All of the next day and in the week or so since, it keeps coming back to me. Like some unconscious prompter is making it pop up at opportune moments. It might be just a chance remark by some old bloke in a pub but I can't let go of it and, as these things sometimes do, it keeps striking a chord. It feels shockingly relevant to the way my thinking about so many things seems so stuck.

Speaking of which, our jam is yet going nowhere. We are all so stuck and I bet every one of us knows it. The best I can muster at this point is a yell at the windscreen.
'What the hell is goin' on up there? Jesus, we're gonna be sitting here all morning!'

Chapter Two
what good is this?   I was hot dog shit?

Does road-rage really surprise you? It's all consumed in baser instinct. Sitting in a metal box, stuck in an interminable queue. Can't move forward, can't move back. Would like to be somewhere completely else but powerless with horizons limited. In fact totally obscured by the truck in front. Chance or some external force controls the flow that is no flow. Feel the frustration rise at utter pointlessness. No wonder people react. Call it senseless inactivity that drives.. No, don't use that word,.. That sends you crazy.

And we're all doing it, all stuck. Having been persuaded to travel to work to earn the money to travel to work. Obsessively to buy our security in things, in pleasures, in lifestyles that come to completely rely for their existence on sitting in traffic jams. In gloriously secure comfort and any one of a huge variety of models to delight. Our aspirational engines running, where the hell are we going?

'I cannot go on doing this!' I cried out dramatically at the car roof. It's rarely voiced quite as loud and firm. 'God. I wonder how many hours I've sat like this.'

There's a thought to torment patience and I begin working it out. Two hours in the morning, double that for getting home, that's four hours a day. Times five days a week, four weeks a month, that's.. er,.. eighty hours a month, times say fifty weeks. Plus a bit at weekends for shopping and trips out of town. Say another three or four a week.
'Oh God, that's over a thousand hours a year!..' Let that thought linger.
'No! That's impossible!' I go over the sum again.
'I don't believe it. Divide that by what,.. twenty four.' This sum takes a bit longer. Twenty fours into thirty, carry six..
'No!?' Total disbelief forces further recalculating. And again.
'WHAT! That's nearly fifty days a year!' Now that does have to sink in.
'Streuth! If I add that to the twenty-five days I already get for holiday, you could practically take up residence somewhere. How much is that?'
This time I have to get the calculator out of my briefcase on the back seat. Fumbling about, pulling the case onto the front seat, ignoring the traffic outside, more academic by the minute in contrast to this mounting revelation.
'Ohuh. No!' Chuckling derision. 'That's ten and half week's holiday!'
This takes no time at all to sink in. 'Now that, that would be a proper holiday.'
Visualise travelling for that long, where you could get to. Where couldn't you get to? What you could see in that time. Assuming no traffic-jams. You could plan a really extensive trip. No further bidding needed and involuntary virtual reality starts to make brochure choices. I can see the flight deals in the agent's window.
I've been thinking about sailing holidays. My fantasy's passion now allowed a drunken sense of imagined freedom, floats away with ease. If you were to look carefully from the outside of the

car you'd see an amorphous ghosted figure donned in shorts and fluttering Hawaiian shirt, floating free on the fumes.

Where in the world you can hang out and pretend to be mariners. Sun, sea and mooring in secluded palm-lined bays. Deep azure waters populated by shoals of beautiful silver fish glinting and flashing through depths shot with sunlight. A clear breeze at your back, heeling over as the boat cuts warming swell. Finding a star over the mast-head to aim at. I can see myself sitting at the tiller, wearing next to nothing it's so warm, being gently splashed by flying spray. People have been doing this, travelling like this for thousands of years. Sure there are automatic winches and fancy navigation aids but the artistry of sailing doesn't change. It's as old as we are. From the beginning people must have looked at the sea from the shoreline and played with the idea of it. Played in their imagination with the challenge of floating on it. Paddling on driftwood caught by wind and tide. Then discovering how to build more sophisticated driftwood and harnessing the wind. Full of fear but playing with adventure. The irresistible urge to find out what's beyond the horizon. Sailing away, working the forces of nature with which they were already in tune..
'Beautiful!' Floating away, effortlessly creating vistas in which to cruise. Dream on out of this deadening road.

I've done little like this of course. Read about it, enraptured, swallowing whole books about sailing and the sea. A friend who deals antiques generously gave for my birthday two of the most wonderful old editions. Turquoise leather-bound with gilt-edged pages. 'The Ocean'. 'With Maps and Illustrations', by the romantically named, Elisee Reclus. By his name alone I couldn't wait to get them home. They are craftsmen gilded old, published in 1873, stating boldly in red on the Volume One fly-leaf, 'The Ocean; Atmosphere and Life, A Descriptive History of the Phenomena of the Globe'. You might imagine of that period, exhaustively detailed research and all somehow wrapped in an incongruously mischievous love. Academic but still a child-like sense of adventure. A treatise no less, it describes wave types, the colours the sea can manifest, its movements and cycles. The varied temperatures and how this creates changes in texture and form. The weather patterns from clouds to rain-drop sizes, the wind and its multitudinous effect and, the huge variety of flora and fauna. It goes on to describe particular phenomena in minute detail. The Ionian reaches and their currents, the shallow Zyder Zee, the forming of coral reefs and the danger of Arctic flows.

I say I've done nothing like this. That's true, but my appetite has been wet. Sue and Trevor, friends who live on an old Thames sailing barge on the river at Windsor,.. at least they used to.
Trevor has been a kind of business friend. He's a photographer and designer and, has a small practice which my company contracts for advertising and package design. As a result of the connection we've become friends. At first we met for a beer at lunchtimes and later, discovering our shared passion, we've planned many a voyage. Until earlier this year however, we had singularly failed to make it happen. That is until rather tragically their beautiful sailing barge sunk.

Before I bought Ben Lovell, I had visited them on their mooring at Windsor. It was these visits that encouraged me to think about a houseboat. Their barge was magnificent, wooden oak hull from massive trees, about ninety feet long with a highly ornate superstructure and wheelhouse above fancy balustrade ringed decks. Unlike most of these barges, it was never used to carry cargo but built for pleasure, to the order of some Duke or other. Inside, you climbed down a broad creaking staircase into a palatial saloon. A beautiful glass skylight above, at least twenty foot across, looking like a mini Kew Gardens. Dark oak panelling covered most of the walls and bulkheads and an array of fantastically antique features, lighting fixtures and furniture made the whole place feel incredibly opulent, wonderfully over the top. One evening about eleven I got an anxious call from Trevor saying that the boat was sinking and could I come over and help. I dressed and drove the twenty minutes along the motorway to be greeted by fire-engines and blue lights and frenetic activity along their river bank. Sue, bundles of soaked clothes and trembling tears. Trevor running in every direction, one minute consulting with firemen, the next wading alongside the sunken jetty with handfuls of belongings, dumping them in crumpled piles on a chaotic bank-side. Luckily, they had the keys to a neighbour's boat and had begun to decamp there. At least there was some respite space.

The boat was already alarmingly heeled over toward the bank, which meant scrambling across submerging slippery decks. Eventually, Trevor and I stood halfway down that beautiful staircase looking at four foot of dark water in the saloon. Papers and books, half a stereo and one of its speakers, a couple of chairs and other assorted flotsam of their lives. Apparently, they had returned from their ten-day holiday in Spain to see sets of blue lights flashing as they approached the mooring.

'You never think it could possibly be anything to do with you.' He described how they joked. 'What are they doin' here. Getting water out the river for somebody's fire?'

I rested a sympathetic hand on his shoulder.

His theory guessed that the battery driving the bilge-pump had gone flat or the micro-switch for it had failed and then, as she took on more water and got heavier, she must have settled on a spike or something in the river. When they drove up to the barge the fire-engines were pumping for all they were worth and several firemen were trying to lower a huge plastic sheet over the side so that it might slide over the hole and with the pressure of the pumps, seal it. But it wasn't any good, it was too late. The fire-engines were pumping the Thames through the barge. No-one seemed to know who had called the fire-brigade, a wonderful neighbourly act but it was all over, she'd sunk. Heartbreakingly, with Sue and Trevor's whole life and belongings inside. Loads of his precious art works, paintings and photographs were curled up and floating round the fore-cabin when we waded in up to our armpits. We rescued everything we could from freezing water that took your breath away. Some of the floorboards had floated free in this cabin and as I stepped through a hole in the floor my foot rested on something spongy and soft. I called Trevor over with his arc-lamp torch and we peered through gloomy brown water at the cross-beams and knees that form the main structure. I kicked one and to our horror it just dissolved under the weight of my boot, its fibres floating away in little eddies.

After standing there up to our chests in the debris filled gloom for seemingly endless pregnant moments, I said. 'Look there's not much to do here tonight and in the dark. Things aren't gonna take any more damage than they have already. The Firemen are giving up. There's really nothing you can do. Why don't we have a last look for anything valuable, make the thing safe and let me take you to my place for the night. We can come back tomorrow in the light and start again then. What do you say?'

At first he seemed not to hear but then with a huge resigning sigh said. 'Okay. Let's just get out of here.'

We spent days clearing everything up, sealing the holes as best we could, pumping water and inspecting the barge in detail. What we had found that first night turned out true, she was very rotten. Trevor admitted he'd feared as much, but she was just so beautiful he had put off the inevitable reckoning. He recovered and, smitten as we all are, found another barge in Yorkshire near to where his family lived. An even bigger Humber Keel, a hundred feet long and twenty-five wide. It's a monster and this time, like Ben Lovell, it's built of a more reliable five-eighths thick iron and steel. Not so aesthetically attractive perhaps but in my dry-dock experience after I bought Ben Lovell, in the very worst places, I picked off maybe a sixteenth of an inch of rusty metal. Then happily covered it all over with some wonderfully protecting thick black gloopy paint. You can sleep a hell of a lot easier even if it doesn't look quite so beautiful. Earlier this year then, Trevor wanted to bring his new barge to London and put it on the Thames mooring. He invited me to join him and help crew it for the journey.

We left one misty morning, with a bargeman Trevor hired as an expert skipper. We chugged our way down the Humber River and out into the North Sea heading south. Intrepid stuff we thought, on a one-hundred year old barge, its ancient huge truck-sized diesel engine and the three of us.

Trevor is a stoic Yorkshire man. You imagine he must have been a great boy scout. He was so well prepared and efficient. List upon list got filled. During the week we spent together in Hull before leaving, he must have spent a small fortune on all the bits and pieces we subsequently needed. Holes in the water that you put money in, they say. Surely that's for the pessimistic. If it were ever possible, this barge epitomised steady Yorkshire. Incredibly heavy and well built, you could easily imagine her stoicism. Inside the huge hold was empty and austere but a womb-like feeling inside the strength of her. For the journey, we spent little time there, decamped in one corner, our dampening possessions and voices echoing on bare metal.

In two and a half days, with only small mishaps, while inexperience made for some tricky emotions, we made it through thankfully calm weather. The first night we stopped in the port of Great Yarmouth on the Norfolk coast and the second we spent taking turns at the wheel, prodding each other to stay awake. On the third morning, daylight just breaking, we triumphantly entered the Thames estuary within an hour of the incoming, predicted high springtide. The next few hair-raising hours were spent careering along with the rushing torrent. On a turbulent tide and with frightening breakneck speed, we stormed up the river to London. One hundred and twenty tons unceremoniously racing past all of those famous landmarks and us praying to avoid them and anything else that might get in the way. I was convinced we could never have stopped and many times on that journey, feared until the last possible moment, some heart-rending miss. My previously unshaken confidence in the bargeman wavered at his cavalier insistence that everything was perfectly 'true'. That aside, for the whole journey he was a guide and stalwart. In an unsung area of seamanship, the flow is everything. Anticipate and don't panic! We learned immensely from his brave wisdom.

Other water-borne adventures have been tame by comparison. Plenty of fun dinghy sailing, on the river and at a south coast club who will rent you something bigger. And importantly, because it started the whole idea, but only for the amusement of telling. A girlfriend and I took a narrowboat holiday on the Grand Union canal. In two weeks at the required pace we made it from London to Hemel Hempstead, an impressive forty miles. At the time we were living close to our holiday journey's end. We were highly amused then, on returning the boat to London, we walked round the corner to Marylebone rail station and covered the same distance that had taken two weeks in less than half-an-hour.

It's a representation of everything I like about the water and the canal. Like some metaphor for life in another time and place, separate from the frenetic lives through which it often intimately passes. Right in the heart of many cities this once vital highway flows, neglected and unnoticed but for the rare passage of a few enthusiasts or holidaymakers.

What a contrast to this high way that thousands of us are now hopelessly astride. You might begin to cherish the thought that these concrete bastions of our insanity might yet fall quietly into oblivion.

I wonder if gridlock ever happened in the heyday of the canal. It's ten past nine and in forty minutes, my car with a top speed approaching a hundred miles an hour, has made a mile and a half. What other choices are there? I couldn't get off now even if I wanted. Although the idea of just getting out, perfunctorily closing the door, walking off and leaving it, is hugely appealing. If you did something like that, to get to that fit of pique, it would have to mean much more than just leaving the traffic jam. Unless you had also given up all the other accoutrements of suburban life, eventually you'd just have to go back and get it. Or more likely be summoned to the car-pound or the courts to pay a massive fine and answer their intrigued but bullying question. Why?..

'Well, your Honour, because I couldn't stand my gridlocked life any longer!' Just imagine the magistrate's reaction.

'You horrible little reactionary man, what do you think would be the consequence of us all behaving in such an irresponsible manner?'

'Well, paradise actually, mate.'

No doubt, the only one that can do anything about any of this is me. With no resistant little needy thoughts of waiting around for someone else to feel the same. By their action and attitude it's pretty obvious they won't. I've always held a fantasy for a group who through common inspiration would stand up together and decide to begin some life project. Moving energetically forward, sharing the vision, the plans, the work, a sort of safety and motivation in numbers. It's a great fantasy but it hasn't happened. It is almost certainly me alone if I want anything to change. And I've been around this merry-go-round so many times before. Change to what or does it matter what? Maybe it's just change itself that will do. Change anything. But how do you find what to change first? You can't seriously expect to make a list of all of the things you don't like and then just cut them out. Yes, but maybe you couldn't cut them altogether but you could surely limit their effect? At least there might be some satisfaction in the attempt. Otherwise what? Carry on without a commitment to this life or any other. That makes no sense at all. I do know that whilst I cannot or will not decide, there can be no peace of mind and no satisfaction in anything.

There are weighty issues about such radical change. Inevitably, some kind of fait-a-comple about money and security. Like not having any.. If we were really to let go of our dependence though, we might find a lifestyle as rich and secure hidden just around the corner.

Maybe the change doesn't need to be as radical as I think. It's just about settling on something or somewhere that I want to be. You'd expect to be more successful naturally, if your skills are nurtured in optimism. Vitalised and motivated, love it and you can't help but do well. It's the only thing that makes any sense. If truth and strength are born in the heart, then this is the bulwark against insecurity.. 'You'd have to forget security.' 'And what? Invent faith? No.' The only answer is to accept that it's going to be like jumping off the edge.

Before you made a jump like that you'd have to know that it's a breeding ground for fear. Feel that fear and all of us are so

safety obsessed, so conditioned by averse habit, that risk is considered practically immoral. Facing the taboos of such aberrational behaviour you wouldn't be at all surprised at feeling alien.
'For God's sake, you are what you love, not what loves you.'
Nice sentiment..

We move on another few yards and stop. I can feel tolerance beginning to fail. What on earth are you supposed to do in traffic jams? Keep calm and distracted from an overpowering urge to drive over the roof of the thousands or however many cars there are between you and your destination. I suppose if I were more organised there are all kinds of things. You hardly need to concentrate much on driving. But I don't feel like distraction this morning, I need more. Some stretch of imagination, reaching out to a new horizon.. I roll down the window and mischievously want to bellow down the road or at least at the back of that truck.
'A great chance with Fed Ex filling three-quarters of the view.' I yell inside my head.
Then irresistibly out loud. 'The World On Time... Oh Yeh? Just the bloody office 'ud be nice!'
In a sharp glance over her shoulder, a woman in the car a few feet away looks surprised and smiles a silly grin at me. I make back a thin sardonic smile.

I've surely been making this journey long enough to have come up with something better. Although it's far too wretched a thought to want prepare for this, despite creeping inevitability.
You can't help fiddling with things in the car. A switch that needed gluing ages ago falls onto the floor. I give up trying to find it and getting rattier, search around impatiently but too aimless to find anything. There's some pages from a magazine article in my open briefcase on the seat. Roy, my narrowboat

neighbour, gave it to me the other night. He invited me for a drink on his boat and I told him about the old guy in the pub. As I was leaving he gave it to me saying, 'You should read this. It's exactly what he's talking about.'

The article is headed like it's from a New-Age magazine. Next to it are ads for workshops about finding your voice. I know he's into that sort of thing.
'The Parable of the Trapeze.' For perverse theatricality I start to read it out loud but as it gets more interesting I fall silent.
I think my jaw might have started to drop.

'This is a parable or a story in metaphor as a way of looking at your life. In particular, how we learn to deal with change. The Parable of the Trapeze suggests that one of the ways of looking at my life is as a series of trapeze swings. At any one moment, as this metaphor describes our experience, we may see ourselves hanging on to a trapeze bar and swinging along with its arc.

So here we are, hanging on, swinging to and fro, either enjoying the ride or freaked out by it, it doesn't matter, it's still the ride. This is our life and this is how it is. We may be learning the lessons that we are supposed to learn or not but whatever the condition we understand that this is it, this is our life and this is the trapeze bar that we are hanging on to now.

When we are starting to feel comfortable, accustomed to the ride and the idea that this is the sum of our life. Often at the point when we think we are in control and know the answers. We look out there and in the distance see another trapeze bar and it's coming our way. And in that intuitive place that knows these things, we know that this new trapeze bar has got our name on it. We also seem to know once we have seen that trapeze bar coming into view, that somehow, we are going to have to get from this old trapeze bar across to that new one. Because to not do that, to stay hanging onto this old trapeze when we have recognised new experience in the offing, means psychological death, putting a stop on any possibility of growth or learning. Somehow, someway, to properly embrace life and, in our heart that's what we want, we are going to have to get from here to there.

Now, of course, our hope, our prayer is that we will be able to get over to that new trapeze whilst somehow managing to hold onto the old. That somehow we will be able to perform some neat dexterous switcheroo, little manoeuvre thing that will allow us to grab the new trapeze. We will have convinced ourselves that there must be a way to hang onto one whilst reaching out and seamlessly grabbing the other. Then and only then will we leave this nice old security blanket of a trapeze and we will never need to experience what it might be like to have hold of neither.

Well, that might be our prayer, but also in that place that knows these things, we know that this is not how it is. We know that to get from here to there, we are going to have to release our grip on this old trapeze, reach out, swing across and grab the newness with both hands. We can plan it, thoroughly investigate all we need to perfect the technique. Ultimately there is no way that we can continue to hang on to the old and still, at the same time, embrace the new. In short, we are going to have to let go. We are going to have to experience the middle, the void, to be out there in what looks, from this perspective anyway, like nothing. The chasm where for sure we will be dashed to pieces on the rocks below. Believing, that it is only through some unattainable faith experience that we will be able to let go of that old trapeze and grab onto the new.

The point of the parable is to suggest to us that this middle ground, this place with no trapeze bars to hold onto, where we have released our death grip on the old but have not yet reached out to grab the new, is a pretty important place. Too important you will understand to fake, with one little finger gripped fast. But if you do let go, if you did experience that in between, that void dark place where the old questions and answers don't make sense anymore and the new ones haven't yet appeared. You will see that it is out there in the middle that the real ground of being for change exists. Out in the middle, with no guarantees of a net below, no insurance policy that says you will make it to the other side. Only the knowledge that this is where you need to be now, not on the old and still not yet on the new.

Easy to say, easy to write and to read, I don't know what it does for you but for me, it brings up real fear. To be without crutches, without familiar things to hold onto, somehow letting ourselves surrender to the unknown. The silly thing, of course it is not really unknown, we have all been there, perhaps hundreds of times but, each time we do it's just as scary, just as powerful a learning experience. What we need of course is practice, so that eventually, we'll begin to get the idea that we are okay. That not only will we make it to the other side but in the process, we might get a chance to sense the liberation that we are not tied, not fixed or condemned to stay hanging on to old trapezes. The suggestion is that by getting in touch with other, new parts of oneself, it is then that you start to live. Not by fending off or denying the experiences presented but by embracing them.'

'Wow..' Is all I can manage.

Chapter Three
what good is this? Good is that wish?

I'm immensely pleased to report that I didn't make it to the office. I bunked off and called in sick from a telephone outside the Greenwich Maritime Museum. About ten o'clock as we crawled off the elevated section of the motorway to enter town proper, there is a large sign offering the usual choices of all-points east, west, north and south and at the bottom of the mostly resistible list, the Woolwich Tunnel and Greenwich. Put down cars all you like, this is why we are so addicted. Take off when you like, go anywhere in your own little living-room, snack-bar, bedroom. As soon as I made the decision it seemed like the day and the mood changed. The rain cleared and a hazy autumn sun turned everything to colours that make you notice. I couldn't say that I shook off the angst entirely but the trapeze inspired me to at least go looking. Did I spot another trapeze? I didn't think so but I spent a lovely day searching or, at least in a mode of displacement more open to the possibility. For the want of anything better we surely have to believe that.

The morning passed thoughtfully, wandering the Greenwich lawns down to the river. Walking the zero meridian and experiencing a wonderfully expansive sense of the world. A visit to Harrison's sea navigation clock, an archetype of a pretechnological period, when adventure had a more understandable goal. Everything now can seem as though it's already been discovered and you have to work harder to find things to explore. Stirring images at one and the same time superfluous yet meaningful in some imagined bigger picture. Out there, willing yet incomplete. Will it ever be so?.. We gather so much information. So many minute pieces of a jigsaw that may amount to coherence. I wonder if it is the surfeit that simply serves to confuse. But you can't stop the gathering. An inevitable symptom of sentience. Suck it in and see.

On that day, my head filled with busy threads racing for conclusions, what did I do? I mopped up more. More threads and possible lives. At a critical point of confusion but with an urge for pursuit, I spent the afternoon driving the north bank of the Thames, out to the east. A silly pursuit. Experimenting with how close little roads and turnings might get to the river's edge. Pointless but engaging, a game where the rule imperative is to uncover what's around the next bend. I've a fond childhood memory of a first family car. We would go out on Sunday afternoon novelty adventures. With no thought then for the price of petrol, we'd play turning first right-first left. Just for the entertainment of seeing where meandering got you and what prize may await. This afternoon I had pretty much the same idea, to play until my enterprise or patience ran out. And on this day, the lucky journey's end turned out to be a little creek at Grays in Essex. Here the river widens in estuarine mud flats and salt-marsh channels. Too difficult for roads to traverse, most end in rutted wasteland still miles from anywhere. A odd land of disused docks and derelict warehouses. Flat and exposed, a refuge for austerity. The memory of a lost or yet to be discovered purpose.
Full of similar undiscovered purpose and just at the point of giving up, a final and indecisive turn of the day led down a long

lane. From and to nowhere, an age of winding bends eventually resolved in a cul-de-sac and a very ram-shackled boat yard. Dilapidated corrugated-iron and low wooden sheds form the boundary to a gravelled circle of variously rotting and under-repair boats. I backed the car, parking on the verge outside. Standing for a moment, breathing familiar musty mud-salt and diesel smells. Not a soul in sight I wandered into the yard, drawn to the creek beyond the buildings by the sight, over their tin roof, of a couple of tall traditional looking masts hung with wooden spars and rigging. Through a gap between the sheds a path led to a short quay with a dozen or so boats moored alongside. Most were small and unremarkable, an assortment of flapping canvas covering decay. In stark contrast at the far end stood two regal sailing barges with tall masts and brightly coloured flags fluttering aloft. I made eagerly for a closer look, excitement rewarding the afternoon's persistence. Close-up, despite subtle differences between them, a shared character of hard labour oozed from heavily worn smooth wooden forms and polished brass. They were quite beautiful, heavily muscled weight-lifters, a mix of graceful, earthy strength and humble utility. They'd obviously been lovingly restored. I ambled admiringly, running my hand along the gunwales, feeling grain and long weathered deviation. Looking over the decks, thick darkened planks and fresh painted iron winches. Polished seems speckled shining copper rivets. Hung at the mast and decorating their full length, each had rolled and roped red sails lying furled on the boom. Surely the most corny of fantasies, but try to resist hailing a sunset for them to sail into.

A sign at the quay's end read, 'Mary Ann and London Pride. Property of the Gray's Creek Thames Sailing Barge Restoration Society'. In small letters at the bottom, 'All Enquiries to Site Office'.

'God! Where's that?' Nothing in the local dereliction suggests anything approaching an office. But I'd love to talk with someone who knows about these treasures. What does it feel like sailing under those red sails? I want to applaud and appreciate the dedication. Some of it might rub off. I might get invited for a ride.

'Hello! Anybody home!?'

Rope-creakings, flags and slapping lines reply. Windy echoes from rattled loose patchings.

I wonder how far you could go in one of these.

'Hello, is anybody here!?' I noticed on one of the barges a heavy padlock and chain between the locker door and its huge steering wheel.

'That's a pity.'

I sat down nearby, perched on a pile of sleepers and rolled a cigarette.

The yard and quay were still quiet and rain began from new and darkening clouds. Retreating to the car, the rain growing heavier, I was still hanging it out and wondering if someone might turn up. Eventually, having to switch on the wipers to see outside felt like a conclusion. With a last salutary nod to the masts and their obscured treasures, I headed for home. Needless to say I caught endless rush-hour traffic but somehow the time passed in a haze of cruising dreams. I arrived home late. In the kitchen and waiting for the kettle to boil, there was a message on the answer-machine from Trevor, so I called him. He was still up and art-working.

'Look, I need to ask a favour.' His lovely Yorkshire colour elongating the vowels. 'Me broother and his girlfriend want to move down from York. He thinks he can get some work in town but 'e's not sure and they really just want to try it and see how it feels before they commit. I'd promised them they could come and stay with us, but now we've been told we've got to move out of the neighbour's houseboat and I'm still way not ready with the barge. For us it's an immediate move to Sue's parents but for them, well here it comes.. Do you think, and I know this is a big thing to ask, that they might come and stay with you?' He paused, gauging the tone. 'I mean, you know you can say no if it's too much.'

'Sure of course.' It was sprung and I could do with time to react. 'I'm,.. I mean I've got the space for them, Trevor. That's no problem. You've seen it, it's all pretty much finished bar the polishing. I can even boast two bedrooms. They could have the master suite.'

'Well I wouldn't want to chuck you out of your room.'

I could visualise them. The younger brother, we'd met at a family dinner before the barge trip. I liked him, arty and scruffy, a youthful, less polished version of his brother. And she was a sweetie.

'When do you need to let him know? Well no I mean, when do you need to know?'

'Yeh, that's it. Actually pretty quick really. Sorry, that sounds awful. But I do need to work it out for them. He says he wants to come next week. It would've been fine except Graham, you know, who owns the houseboat, wrote to say he's coming back from Spain and wants to move in asap. I knew it was coming, I mean we've been here seven months or more. It's all entirely my fault and dreadfully last minute. Sue's been having a right go at me. And I should've anticipated somethin' like this. I should have got on faster with the barge. But you know what it's like. We've had tons of work pretty much since we got here. And I'm not complaining about that, it'll dry up anytime. Make hay and such. Look, I'm sorry. Tell you the truth I haven't even thought of anyone else to ask. Do you want to think about it?'

'Doesn't sound like I've got much time, ya bastard.'

'O' God I'm sorry. Look why not..'

I interrupted him. 'Shut up Trevor, I'm pulling your leg..' In for a penny etc I thought, like it's fated. 'Okay, look there is

absolutely no problem. I can put 'em up easily and I'm happy to help. How long d'they want to stay, any idea?'
'Well not really, but I mean given this new situation I can't expect you..'
'How 'bout a month? Would that do them? Long enough to get their bearings?'
'Oh God. Yeh, I'm sure that 'ud be great. A couple of weeks, p'r'aps a month. I mean plenty. And that's what I'll tell them. They can stay with you for a month, max. And actually by then I ought to 'ave sorted something. If I don't sort a bloody home for us now I'll crack-up anyway.'
There is a pause while he thinks about it. 'Trevor?'
Yeh. Sorry. Listen that's amazing Will, thank you. That's really generous. You're a mate. Thank you very much indeed.' He really did sound relieved.
'It's a pleasure, Trevor. Especially for you.'
'Hang on, Sue's yelling at me. Yeh okay. She says can we come over to dinner next week or when they arrive. Yeh alright. And if the answer's yes, she'll come and do the cooking.'
'Phfff. Well, you better tell her the answer's definitely yes. What are we having?'
'He says what are we having.' Their voices back and forth. 'She says she doesn't know yet,.. your favorit.'
'Marvellous.'
'Well, okay. Are you sure you're okay with that? Shall I call them and then let you know when they're coming.'
'Yeh. Absolutely. I'm sure. I'm out Tuesday and Wednesday but apart from that I'm here every evening.'
'No it won't be before that. I know he's got to finish a job up there but their tenancy is up and,.. Oh, it's complicated. Okay. Look, that's great. You're a good man. You don't know how much of a relief this is. Speak to you in a few days. Bye.'

It took a while to process. Over a bedtime cuppa I walk around and begin to happily visualise them here. By the time I got into bed, the idea of company is warming.

Within a week, five of us are sat around my table tucking into a great co-operative effort. Tom and Barbara, I discovered since their arrival, are kindred spirits. Following the call with Trevor, I hadn't realised the urgency. They moved out of their house and arrived within days. We'd already spent a long evening around the fire discussing the world and prospects for them in the big city. Now, with Trevor and Sue, it's a thoroughly congenial rapport.

'Tom's got a boat in Selby, did he tell you?' Trevor asks, his mouth bulging with Sue's mum's home-made ice-cream.
'Yes,' to Tom, 'You mentioned it the other evening and said you had some pictures.' I was inviting.
'I'll get 'em, shall I?' Like he needed encouragement.
While Tom skipped off to the bedroom we congratulated one another on surpassing a superbly creative dinner. Glasses were filled with more plonk and as Tom returned I offered a toast.
'Well look, here's to you two and to health and fortune in the Smoke. I hope it works out for you both and your wishes come true.' We clinked and quaffed. Tom followed it, ceremonially clearing a space of plates to lay out a row of ten large photographs of the most beautiful of old sailing barges. A little one!

'If I'm going to set up down here, I'll need to sell this. She's my second most important baby, but I can't afford to keep her.' He and Barbara exchanged a wistful look. 'If it comes to it I'll put out some ads but if anyone's any ideas or know of any likely candidates..' His Yorkshire is delightfully broad of Trevor's. He gave a short history and sales pitch whilst passing the pictures around.

'I've done these Trev with a sort of guided tour in mind. I thought a bit of a portfolio might sell her.'

'Good idea,' approved big brother and then, as expert photographer. 'You've done a good job wi' these Bro, they're great.' He turned them on edge, inspecting the pile or something. 'Nice finish too. It's good the matt, isn't it?'

Tom smiled at an obviously important affirmation and turned again to me. 'She's a mite special this one. She's the very last of the Queen Mary's lifeboats. As far as we know there are no more of the originals left. We've been in touch with the Cunard archives in Liverpool and the history department at Long Beach and they can trace 'em up to the point when they were changed to a newer design in the fifties. These old ones were offered for sale or they broke 'em up. They've only got paperwork for two that were bought, this one and another was found at a breakers in Felixstowe. So I mean, let's say it's very likely, she's the last still afloat.' He took a long draught of wine as we admired his baby.

'I bought her off a Polish guy in York, five year ago. You can see he'd done a real conversion job on 'er. Large kind of mezzanine wheelhouse, which is a great protected space from the weather, complete with decking all round and a new main mast in a tabernacle on the deck. The mast is one bit I'm not sure of, I'd like it to have gone right through to the keel, just for a bit more strength, but you know, you pays your money.. See originally, there'd have been no mast, no sails, she'd have been an open boat but for a small quarter deck in the bow with a cabin underneath for casualties and a big diesel in the back. They'd pull a big tarp along the gunwhale for shelter.'

'She's got a very smooth hull, Tom. What's she made of, is it steel? I can't see any rivets.'

'No. She's all timber. She's double-diagonal mahogany. That's like two diagonal skins, one on top of the other, with oiled canvas like a sandwich in the middle. Laid on oak frames, it's beautifully done. Strong and flexible. You hav' to imagine the specs. She was designed to be put down int' middle of the Atlantic with fifty-odd people aboard and keep 'em safe until they were rescued. I've seen an old painting of the ship with great rows of 'em hanging from the davits. They say they kept them half-full of water so the boards were always tight. Amazing eh? Imagine the weight?'

'How big is she, Tom. It's hard to tell from these pictures, those buildings in the background could be any distance.'

'Ay you're right. Well she's about, I say about, I mean she's just over forty-five feet and twelve foot six in the beam. She's almost double-ended, well you can see, it's like she's got a stem-post at either end. But the stern's a bit more shapely, a bit transom like, but not much. She's so broad she's a bit like a bath-tub really and she only draws about three foot six with bilge keels that the Pole added. You know about draught, don't you? How deep she is in the water?'

'Yes I do. This barge draws about eighteen inches 'cause it's practically flat-bottom.'

'Yeh right.' He continued. 'She's a complete bastard to sail, she'll go almost as fast sideways!'

'I was going to ask you about that.' I said. 'But love those red sails.'

'Mmmh..' He is very attached. 'That's the most serious work I've done on her, her sail-plan. Sail-plan? It's a bit of joke actually. Her gaff-rig is a bit small, she's a motor-sailer really. But she will go quite nicely without the engine, just not very fast. I took a sail-makers advice and put another temporary mast behind the wheelhouse. It's even smaller, just a stick of a steerage sail that you can haul up and down, but it helps. If ya want to be snotty you could call her a ketch now. I didn't put it up for the pictures, I thought she looked nicer just with the gaff. She does sail a bit better though. Well, in more of a straight line anyway. The only other major works is to open her up inside. When the old guy converted her he put loads of stuff in. I mean his work were beautiful, a real cabinet-maker. All in this dark rich red mahogany. But it were too much, big sideboards and tables and a real old-fashioned galley. It was really dark in there. So I've opened it up, taken out some of his stuff and then painted a lot of white on the bulkhead walls and the roof. Here look you can see in this one.' He showed a picture of the interior. 'Oh, and I've completely refitted the galley too. Here.' Another photograph showed stainless steel and white with a cooker and shelves and, what you could tell from a picture, a good size space. 'We've lost two bunks because of my changes, but she still sleeps five, six at a push, but really comfortably. She's big inside, it's like there's ample room. You know, it's important, you can all sit roundt' table and move around easy, it's great.'

'She looks beautiful, Tom. You'll be sad to lose her won't you?'

'Ahuh, but it's gotta be. I can't move down here and manage it. I wouldn't want to leave her in the water without checking regularly, so I'd have to store her dry and the expense of that, in and out of the water, I couldn't afford it. She weighs seventeen tons so it's a bloody big crane each time. I've tried to think of all the ways of keeping her but it just doesn't stack up. Yeh it's gonna be difficult. She's in beautiful knick, not a bit of rot anywhere. They certainly made 'em to last, and when I got her I'd visions of sailing round the world. Bit optimistic, me with no money, but she'd do it.' He paused, his expression full of pride and disappointment.

'You know, I thought of bringing her down here and we could live on her, but she's a sailing boat not a houseboat. She needs to sail not sit in a canal basin. Moorings down here within reach of the sea 'ud be stupidly expensive and she'd still be too far away so I'd still have the same problem. No she has to go. And perhaps to someone who'll use her properly.' He paused again and Barbara put her arm around him.

I had a row of pictures in front of me. 'How much will you get for her, d'you know?'

'Well, I've thought around twenty-five thou, I'm not sure. I mean I think she'd be worth that easy but she's old, wooden and most people are scared shitless of that, they want plastic and tin or concrete, and she doesn't have any of the modern gear either. She is old-fashioned but I mean I think that's proper sailin'. You feel the ropes in your hand and the tension of the wind, not some alloy and plastic winch-handle you just twiddle and wank all day. But you know, it 'ud have to be someone that takes to that sort of thing.'

'Funny, that's what they tell me this is worth, now I've finished her.' I chipped in irrelevantly.

Trevor jumped in. 'I should think so, now. It's a great houseboat with everything you'd need. Bigger than a house. It's worked great with all that reclaimed stuff too, it's got a real character with the panelled door partitions,.. clever. I'm sure it's worth that.'

'And your bathroom is like a pink wet dream.' Sue joined in.

'Really?' Tom looked around the room, like it was an appealing coincidence, and chuckled. 'P'r'aps we could swap?'

I didn't reply. But in that moment recalled the sailing barges. He didn't look serious, but I couldn't help the thought.

The next days and then a couple of weeks passed. Tom and Barbara were into a routine. His work was secured and Barbara had made something of a momentous decision to begin nursing training. Apparently there's a shortage and she can get on the course within a month. As usual I'm to-ing and fro-ing, sitting in traffic jams, getting pissed-off, arguing with the boss and generally feeling a steam valve under pressure. We ate together most evenings, exchanging the day's events and traumas. They were wonderfully positive to have around, quite a tonic at the end of the day. One evening at dinner they wanted to discuss in more detail where to live, what they could afford in rent and so on. We had touched on it but now as they seemed to have made their decision, it was more pressing. As the conversation progressed, it was going to be tight for money. Rents are ridiculous and forget buying. Unless you earn fifty thousand a year you'll never get a mortgage. I'd been through it and whether I could afford it or not I felt certain I'd be ripped off whatever I did. And then the idea of houseboats. It is just a matter of exposure that makes you find these things. I had Trevor and Sue, who lived in a floating palace. Alright, so they did have a not insignificant hiccup, but that was later.

'You've got it great.' Barbara said. 'I mean this is perfect really isn't it. You are so near town, but you'd never know it down here. And from what I've seen in the classifieds, you'd be lucky to get a shed for your mooring rent. I think it's fantastic, don't you Tom? What about us finding a boat to live on?'
'Yeh. Be nice wouldn't it.' He's staring through the skylight, agreeing but elsewhere.
'The trouble is, they don't come up that often. I mean, I wouldn't discount it but there are still not that many nutters who want to live like this. And when they do appear they're getting expensive. It worked for me because I found just the hull and then could do the work myself. Finding this mooring was a bit of luck. But, as I say, don't discount it. And if you did find one there's plenty of room here, we could be neighbours.'
Still looking skywards, Tom said. 'Yeh, I was scanning boat magazines the other day and you're right. There were only three, one at a quarter of a million in Chelsea and then the others were sixty and eighty something thousand. And it looked like only the one in Chelsea actually had a permanent

residential mooring. I suppose we might find one but it's a lottery.'
'Well I certainly think it's worth looking.' Barbara was taken with the idea.
'It is but don't get excited, luv. We're never gettin' anywhere near that kind o' money and, I'm not sure we've got the time to look. I don't want to overstay Will's welcome.'
'You don't need to worry about that.' I said. 'It's working out fine, isn't it?. I'm enjoying having you here.'
'Yeh, but still. Thanks so much for that, but we've got to get ourselves sorted.'
The conversation went on and around the subject for several hours. Deposits and rent in advance mean easily needing to find a couple of thousand just to get in. They were great though, their approach was really positive but you could see that the costs were beginning to dawn on their enthusiasm. Another few days passed with similar conversations and reports. After another week they were beginning to get discouraged. It may have continued but for an event of mine that decisively tipped the scales.

I went to work, as usual, sat in the inevitable traffic, as usual and, was three-quarters of an hour late to the office. On arriving at my desk, the boss was sitting there waiting and looking like thunder.
'Where the fucking hell have you been!?' The immediately combative tone was usual too. He was always freaking out about something, but this time it had a different edge. He continued. 'You must have been late here every day for the last six months. Work starts here at nine-thirty. And if you can't get here on time, I suggest you look for another fucking job!'
I know it's true but still was surprised by the tone and a little victim hurt. I hadn't even got my coat off.

'Hey hold on.' I protested. 'I regularly work here 'til seven or eight at night to make up for the time it takes me to get here, you know that. You get plenty out of me. If I took off all the extra time you owe me, you wouldn't see me for months!'
'Well that would suit me fine!' What is wrong with him. Before I could finish thinking it, he was off again. 'And anyway that's not the point. We all work long hours, it's part of the job. What I expect from you is that you work the same hours as the rest of us. There wouldn't be much point if we all decided to work different fucking hours.'
'O' come on. It's hardly as bad as that.' I whined.
'Yes, it is as bad as that, Will. When I get here in the morning I expect to be able to meet my staff and discuss the day's work and schedules. If I can't do that 'til eleven o'clock because you can't get it together, then as far as I'm concerned that time is fucking wasted. And I won't put up with it any longer. Is that clear?'
'Yes that's very clear, Don.' I said in monotone. 'And something else that is clear, Don, is that you have been on my back for months now. Nothing I have done has been good enough for you. Look at the Mills campaign, I finished it last week. They were over the moon and everyone was gloriously happy except you. It wasn't good enough, I should have done better. They paid three-quarters of the bill upfront and the very next day delivered that case of champagne addressed to me, which you kept, and you still complained. You went on and on about it and it was more and more obvious that your criticism had nothing to do with the job, you were just pissed off at me.'
'Are you surprised?' he retorted. 'It took you twice as long as it should have done because you're never fucking here until midday!'
'Look Don, that is not true and I'm sorry you feel like that.'
'You will be fucking sorry.' He was about to go over the top. 'And had it slipped your fucking stupid mind that we had a

meeting at nine this morning? Or did you forget your fucking diary. Again!?'

'No Don. I do not have a stupid fucking mind. I did not forget my fucking diary and as you will see..' I reached into my case for my diary and opened it at today's page. 'There is no meeting marked here for nine o'clock.'

'Well that's presumably because you weren't here when it was arranged!'

'No Don, I expect that is because you forgot to tell me.' That was always happening.

Now his face started to redden and he shouted for all to hear. 'Look, I've just about had enough. You think you can do just what the fuck you like. You always have. Ever since you started here you've been nothing but a fucking pain in the arse! I'm sick of your attitude! You think you're so much better than everyone else. I'm absolutely sick of you! In future if you can't be here by nine-thirty then don't bother to come at all! Is that clear?'

At that moment something in me flipped. Why do we grit our teeth? Is it to stop the words coming out?

'And likewise. I've just about had enough of you, Don. And your bloody job! I've done great work for you, despite the fact that you're far too dumb to realise it. And no, I will not be here by nine-thirty. I could never guarantee it because of the traffic, which I am also heartily sick of driving through to get to work for someone who is as much of a cretin as you are! So Don, I think you can just go and hang yourself by one of your shrivelled neurotic balls and whilst you're doing that you can shove your job right up the pain in your arse! I hope that's very clear to you!'

I dramatically threw my diary back into my case, spun around and stomped towards the door. And just before slamming it..
'And you can send my P.Forty-Five to my address, because I certainly won't be coming back here to collect it, nine-fucking-

thirty or otherwise.' As I clattered down the stairs to the street, the little gremlin figure that appears on your shoulder at such moments was busily mithering back 'So there, mmtheeerrr!' and sticking his tongue out.

I had driven some few streets before I'd slowed to anywhere near legal. My accelerator foot directly linked to my temper and I kept speeding up as I ran the conversation over, thinking of better and better things to say. As I hit the motorway there was hardly a car to be seen. I must have got home inside twenty minutes. On arrival I made a cup of tea and sat at the table.

'Oh God, I certainly have done it now, haven't I?' Puss, the cat arrived on cue to commiserate. 'What are we gonna do now?'
Somewhere half way through the couple of hours or so I sat there drinking tea, scanning the myriad of consequences, expecting at any minute a cold draught of panic to seep through the cracks,.. a pool of sunlight that had started over in the middle of the table reached me. Even November sun is warming through the skylight glass and, corny though it may sound, I felt comforted and with it the morning's jarring crap began to dissolve. A soothing sedative smoothed the harshness and vulnerability.

I felt as though maybe, just maybe, I could handle whatever the fallout. I needed more reassurance and so lingered quite purposefully enjoying the bathing, feeling every inching of its movement until it passed on into the kitchen. I did nothing more, for the first time in months. Something in me had grown since I last looked and this had a potential to create. I began to feel I might hold onto it if I nurtured and drifted with the feeling. In the pool of sunlight, a trail of thoughts was warmed.

But this late in the year the sun sinks quickly. Steadily crossing the living room, the pool eventually arrived at the coffee table where Tom had laid out his photographs.

About five o'clock Tom and Barbara arrived home and the spell was broken. Suspended I thought, at least until I can pick it up again. Their mood was immediately disruptive. The day had not gone well, viewing more prospective flats. Barbara described dirt, peeling wallpaper and extortionate rents. Exhausted and looking dark, in unison they flopped onto the sofa. Like something automatic, I jumped out of abstraction and into recovery mode.

'Want a reviving cup of tea then, you two? I'll start some dinner.'

I busied quietly in the kitchen leaving them space.

One of my famous ten-minute, half snack-half dinner preparations and a drawn teapot later, we sat together at the table.

'So come on. Is it all awful?' I began.

'Not so much.' Tom returned. 'But I don't think we're making any headway. Really. We've seen, I don't know Barbara, how many, maybe twenty plus places now, and it's just really depressing. I don't think I could live in any of 'em. What about you, luv?'

'No, I know, I feel the same. I know we've got to find one, but I don't feel we're getting anywhere near. What do we do? We can't afford any that we've seen, even the really awful ones. Do we keep looking or just settle for one of those grubby bedsits or something, and say it's just temporary and hope to find something better in time? Or do we just say it's not possible and go home. I know that would be awful for you and work and everything. But right now, I'm sorry, I have to tell you, that would suit me fine.' Her head bowed.

I'm still in calming mode. 'I've made more tea, but would you prefer a glass of wine with this?' They both took tea and I continued. 'I mean perhaps you've got the most sensible way to look at it. Maybe it's a bit optimistic to think that you'd have landed on the perfect spot so quickly. What is it, three weeks

and a bit only? Perhaps you need to be more patient.' A fine one to offer such sense.. 'Once you're settled, you know, perhaps roughly in the area you want to be, then looking will be easier and you can take your time.'
After a pause Barbara responded.
'You're right, I know you are. I don't really think we've any choice and we're probably being too impatient and expecting it all at once. It's just a bit hard having our hopes dashed when we felt so good about coming down here.'
'I know,' I sympathised.. 'But you know there really is no hurry, you can stay here whilst you look and that's fine by me.'
'Thanks Will.' They chanted together and smiled at one another for their harmony.
'We're going to look at a houseboat this evening.' Tom chimed in lighter. 'It's just down the canal at Brentford. That's just before it comes out into the Thames, isn't it?'
I nodded with a mouthful. 'How much?' I asked through chewing.
'Yeh. There's the thing,' he paused for the coming effect. 'They want fifty-five grand. I mean it sounds great. Well, it sounds like a caravan on a pontoon actually. But it's a residential mooring with services. Seventy-five a week for that, plus we'd have to borrow to buy it even after I sell the boat. Anyway, we're takin' a look. Nothing ventured..'
Barbara sipped tea and said with a watery smile and sigh. 'It just goes to show, Will, what a great situation you've got here. I don't think we'll ever find anything like this.'

The rest of dinner passed slowly almost in silence, our own thoughts churning. Mine over today's events muddled with theirs.

'I've got a bit of news,' came out. I didn't seem to be driving the words. They both looked expectant. 'I quit my job today.'

Two pairs of eyebrows rose. Tom said 'That was sudden.' Barbara said. 'What happened to make you do that?'

'It's been building a long time. And this morning we had a fight.. The boss behaved like a jerk and I told him to stuff it. That's it really..'

'Is that okay? What will you do?' Barbara is there with an instant sympathy. She is asking for something with meaning and I decided not to disappoint her.

'Good question.' I chuckled. 'The short answer is, I don't know. It's a bit fresh, a bit raw, I guess. But I think I've been asking for it for some time. I seem to have presented myself with some sort of crossroads. P'r'aps the opportunity to grasp what I've been asking for..'

'What is that?' she gently interrupted.

'God. I don't know that I know. It might be as simple as freedom.'

I hesitated so that I could hear myself saying it. They were both smiling quizzically. I felt encouraged. 'It's a long story. I've been wallowing in this for ages. I don't know how to tell you, really, it's such a long story.' I pushed the plate away and both of them looked intent. I had their attention that's for sure. I jumped in, both heavy feet. 'I'm just pissed off with everything really!'

They listened attentively and patiently as I went into when, why and how much everything pissed me off. I rambled in and out of sense for an hour or more, actually discovering for myself in this chronological telling, a palpable decline matched by an ascent of anguish. And, however vaguely or muddled were my thoughts about it before, when telling the story, by the time I eventually ran dry, I grew surer that here, right under my nose was an answer. And now with them, prompted by them, it was as though some thick, weighty mist is dissolving and one thought is rising. I felt I was teetering on the edge. A new trapeze hove into view and the chasm opened.

If you have a clear choice between continuing to beat yourself to some inevitably destructive point or to be presented with the chance to do something that only scared you, what would you do? It's never difficult to draw the scariest conclusions either way. In the momentum, something yet unknown is breaking through to the surface. As though from somewhere deep, some permission is being granted. To be free of a sticky trapeze? It was unconscious this morning. I don't quite know how but I feel on a bit of a roll..

'Look, this might be a bit of a jumble and it's not a complete idea by any stretch, but I'm just gonna say it and see how it comes out.. That night a couple of weeks ago you made a sort of flippant remark about swapping this boat for yours. I know it was only a passing aside, but actually I think,.. I mean, at the time I thought part of you meant it. I caught the sense of it and actually something in me really liked it too. But, you know,.. it could be a fantasy and,.. you don't jump at those things, do you? And maybe there was, for all of us, some water that needed to flow under the bridge. Since then the idea has been,.. what? I don't know, just hovering, playing around in some quiet corner. Out there. Now, with today's events, which actually don't feel half as bad as I thought they were going to. In fact I've really surprised myself, I think somewhere I feel quite good about it. And so now.' I hesitate on the brink, the trapeze looming. 'Look, here it is flying across the table,.. I'm suggesting it back to you. Should we do it as a temporary solution, swap a temporary lease or what, I don't know. But what I'm going to suggest is that we do it. You come and live here and I'll take your boat and,.. sail off round the world or something. I don't know about that bit yet. That's gotta sit in the stew. I think, I see I've got a fascinating choice. An opportunity being presented,.. even just in this moment, like some obvious gift. Do I ignore it or wake up and grab it? It's so tempting and now the more I think about it, it's calling. And even though it's not like a plan in any detail, it's offering more than that..' I pause and let the jumble of thoughts and ideas cascade.

'What d'you think?'
I'm not sure when they looked more exhausted, when they came in or now. But certainly bemused.
'Are you sure this is not just the result of quitting your job this morning?' Barbara was sensible. 'I mean that's quite an event for one day.'
'You might be right but it isn't just today. I've been saying,.. this has been coming a long time. What Tom said so innocently happened before today and it struck me very strongly. But maybe I didn't really see it this clearly until today, maybe even until just now. When I string all the events together, seeing those sailing barges and the same day Trevor asking if you could stay here. Then you coming and us getting on so well and, all the difficulties you're having. It all strikes me as some sort thread of something meaningful that holds a possible solution. A win-win for us all, wouldn't that be nice?'
Tom answered. 'I don't know that I was serious when I first said it. It did have some sort o' legs, but you know, it's just like one of those things you say and then you think about after. A little fantasy like, wouldn't it be nice if,.. but I didn't know you'd be interested and, it could all have seemed a bit far-fetched.'
There was a long pause and then Tom let some resistance go and turned to Barbara. 'I think we should explore it, luv? I mean it would be a fantastic break for us. It could solve everything' He's gaining momentum. 'It can be flexible if we work it out. As Will says it doesn't have to be permanent if we don't want it to be. We can just swap and then swap back if we choose. What've we lost?'

'Yes I know. I just don't want Will to make a decision like this in a,.. in a fit of pique. He already means too much to me to do that. I haven't known you that long,.. but you know what I mean, you're already special to me.' Turning her warming smile on me just seemed to affirm it more.

'I don't think it's a fit of pique, Barbara.' I suddenly felt very clear and level. 'But it could be a,.. excuse me, a peak of fitness.'

We each in turn look intently at the other.

'Look, for the moment it's a suggestion. I'd like us to think about it. We don't have to decide anything now. But what I am just seeing, the way it's come about,.. it feels like it might be such an obvious solution for us both. When I think about me, it's that just maybe, that if I don't do something now. It suddenly feels a bit like a test of courage. That I might never give myself,.. or be brave enough, or even perhaps, spot another chance like this. I've been running through little images of chances and choices since I got home. But you so easily dismiss things as though they are impossible. But why are they? You know, as options go this is a very nice one to play with. And just playing with the idea, now it feels kinda real,.. tangible, possible even. In my imagination I can touch it. Not every part, okay. And Yeh, it's probably that dangerous too,.. but from my point of view, it's like it's being presented, for our approval..'

We fell silent. Feel it sinking in. Running through pictures of little virtual passages, snapshots of red-sails, the sea lapping and rolling. Little insecurities hover. What about money, what about earning? But almost as immediate, that this is new. It won't happen overnight. Who knows when you're accustomed, what possibilities there might be. Eventually I arrived back in the present and wanted resolution.

'Okay. Look then, how about this for now. I like you two. I really like you two. We're not getting in each other's way here.

In fact quite the opposite, it seems really natural. How about if I say, stop the worry about flats for now and stay here as long as you like. Meanwhile, I'd like to move in the direction we're talking. Whilst you're here we can still change our minds. But meantime, I can go and see the boat. I can make my plans as if I'm going to do it. And see how it feels. I mean, as I think about it now, we none of us have anything to lose. At any time we can come to one another and say, this is not working for me. And perhaps we should say that for an agreed period, if either of us does that it's off, okay? And we've lost nothing. Nothing ventured, nothing gained.. I'm just as afraid, as maybe you are for me. That I might get carried away with this, but you've got to admit, it seems like a perfect solution if it works. But look, we don't have to decide anything now. Let's sleep on it. Let's see how it sits over the next few days?..' I laughed at it and us, the feeling of rightness and the relief it seemed to hold. Infected, they began chuckling too.

In the following days I couldn't temper my excitement and that was infectious too. The relief is palpable. Every time we're together we can't help but create an air of increasingly dizzy celebration. I think we lasted almost two days in the limbo. Eventually as the climax rose on the second evening, we arrived from separate places within minutes of one another and stood at three corners of the table. I went for a bottle of wine and could hardly get it open fast enough. We giggled until it started to make sense, then we toasted and toasted the idea, each time wilder and more imaginative. We were installing elaborate engines in order for the Ben to take off for luxurious weekends. I was taking rides on the Seine in Paris and navigating the Suez Canal. Fortunately I had a wine stash as two more bottles disappeared in very short shrift. I told them about the trapeze and we toasted letting go. It felt amazing. I was flying.

Chapter Four
what good is this?   Wish toad hogs it?

The sense of sheer elation is hard to describe. Like a kid being let out of oppressive school. It's been going on for days, skipping around the barge. Tom and I danced a little jig and an arm linked twirl in the middle of the living room this morning after breakfast. We had said to each other that we couldn't imagine being happier. How great it was to have met one another and been given the opportunity to really do each other so much good. What a sentiment. When was the last time that you were able to say such a thing to someone you'd only just met? Beyond our celebration, the sense of mutual service seemed so completely life affirming. We agreed that the overwhelming feeling of rightness was so strong, as though we had been lead to it. I understood real gratitude. And more, as though we were synchronised, for once in tune with something. Like some aid or guiding hand that so naturally was aligning itself to our purpose. Or we to it. Then it was like letting loose a frisky young animal. We did a bit more frisky dancing round the table!

Night and day I devoured the images in Toms' photographs. Several times I woke in the middle of the night and snuck out to the table, a little altar to adventure. I dreamed the most exhilarating dream. I was somewhere at night gliding across a dark ocean decorated with breaking phosphorescent waves. A warm gently gusting wind filled huge white sails ahead and above me. Beyond the mast top a bright constellation in view. My sole purpose to aim at the apex star. I leaned relaxed and confident against the tiller, placing one foot over the side into the rushing water so that streams of phosphorescence cascaded into the boat. An assuaging ride, driving exalted flight across the waves. Then one puzzling element appeared. Off to the left on a far distant island, a volcano erupted plumes of orange glowing stars. In the pall created by the eruption, a beautiful pink but foul smelling dust was blown toward me. The dust descended and choking thick it turned the whole boat including the sails, an iridescent red.

I never know how to interpret these things. Do you gauge them by the feelings when you wake? I woke confused with a silly thought. I already have the red sails.

I am on the road but this time for a pleasure journey. Hopefully it will lead easily to a village in Yorkshire most poetically named Scrumston-on-Ouse and beyond it to who knows what yet undreamt worlds. There, Cirkus, the last of the Queen Mary's lifeboats is moored on the river and waiting on me. I have to find George Falley who keeps the local yacht club moorings. He has keys and apparently any other assistance I might need. Tom suggested I stay on board and do as much as I feel I need or want to acclimatise. The whole journey, mile by mile consumed by increasing anticipation. This may be racked up by anxieties about my sailing skills on such a large boat. But, for the moment, it's a holiday. There need be no serious excursions. Simply idle aboard and explore. If I'm feeling brave I can pootle down the river. I'll read manuals and sailing books with which Tom says the saloon shelves are bulging. And consider future voyaging.

It's a beautiful day, heavy traffic is flowing and that prompts an enticing thought. I wonder if when I am clear and happy with my direction the traffic seems to flow. Might it be that clear thinking equates to a clear passage? Silly thought perhaps but you can imagine it might be true. I wonder whether all those traffic jams I sat in on my way to work were actually a result of not wanting to get there. How many people who don't want to get there does it take to make a traffic jam? Surely not. But you do get those mysterious hold ups on motorways that apparently have no cause. Good enough, I've not been stuck in one since.

I arrive in Scrumston in the early afternoon, following a river for the last twenty minutes. Tom's directions are perfect and I find the Shipton Yacht Club exactly next door to the pub. George Falley sat at his desk in the office resplendent in string vest and shorts despite the cold. I introduced myself as a friend of Tom and Barbara and he is charming. Leaning back in his chair, he lit a large cigar and pierced a quizzical grin.

'Young Tommy phoned, so we 'ad her down t'yard,' he said, gesturing somewhere out through the window. 'And fill her up wi' diesel. Loovly girl. She'll be ready to go out whenever yo' like. Will yer be needing any 'elp to get her gooing?'

'Well I might.' I said. 'Tom's given me pretty detailed instructions, but can I call on you if I get stuck?'

'You can that, lad. There'll be som'ne here if I'm not here mesen. And we know 'er well. I knows old Carvic who used to 'ave 'er, as well as young Tom. Fine lad. You be stayin' long?'

'I don't know, as long as it takes, I think. I'm gonna have a bit of a holiday and if I can get it all working I'll run up and down the river a bit.'

'Well, you take care, lad. And watch for t' tide. It bain't strong up 'ere but downstream she gets a mite shallow when she's out so don't you go getting stuck. 'Cause ifen you do you'm have to wait 'till she'll cum back. You'll be alright, you'll just 'af to wait.' His sizing makes him reasonably content. He got up from the chair, across to a cupboard on the wall, producing a set of keys from one of many hooks.

''Ere yar, lad.'

I'm sure he'd have talked more but saw I was itching to get to the boat. He dismissed me with a back-hand wave and I thanked him and left the office, clutching keys. Unable to walk demurely I broke into a skip as I followed his directions the few hundred yards along the towpath. She is plainly obvious in the middle of a row of ordinary cabin cruisers. The largest by far and the only one with a mast. At the very top flew a blue and white pendant fluttering welcome and I couldn't resist a call back.

'My God, you are magnificent!' From this angle she is tall. The mast top against a cloudless sky and, with sunlight glistening water, the impression is literally dazzling. She is exactly like a mini version of one of the sailing barges. It's that same kind of old but polished worn grace. Like a reminder of something grand, despite being barrel-like, she has a sleek line. I feel a mix of pleasure and pride. She's bigger than I imagined. The deep and heavy hull, with almost no visible seams, contours with steam bent precision. Brilliant glaring white, dappled with bright dancing reflections. A lipstick red rubbing-strip at the gunwale, runs her whole length. This broad red strake is carved and ornate as it hugs her shape and accentuates a sweeping curve rising to the bow and stern. Above it a heavily varnished cabin side is pierced with three evenly spaced brass portholes, burnished and gleaming. She is delightful, a proper little ship, grained with character and dignity. A testament to her pedigree.

From the towpath the back deck is a short hop and after the longest pause to take it all in, I clamber over her mooring rope and slide on board. With each turn catching little breaths of excitement. 'Yes!' Stepping onto the small deck at the back of the wheelhouse, instantly drawn to the paraphernalia, neat coils of braided rope, cleats and shackles. From up here you see broad beam and ample. Clasping a brass rail on the wheelhouse roof I measure steps slowly around dark wood, past windows and a sliding door, up a large step onto the main deck, wide and open. Just right for sunbathing.. Silver stanchion posts thread tight cables around the deck edge. In the centre, smooth and tall, a mast is draped with hanging ropes coiled and tied in bunches. From its top to the deck a three-point pyramid of heavy cables stretch from the apex down to ornate bolted clamps on the deck and off to a large iron ring at the bow. Another cable tensioned from the top stretches all the back across the wheelhouse roof to the boom's end, tracing the shape of an invisible giant sail. Cleats wound with rope and shackles hang limp, their purpose unknown. Right on the front of the main deck, a huge winch with greased winding gears looks strong and invulnerable. From a perfect place leaning against the mast and boom, I look back along her length, breathing a myriad of powerful impressions.

Imagining how all this fits together will take a while. And there is everything to imagine. Around the wheelhouse to the stern, the door has a heavy hasp and padlock. The first of the keys fit and the door slides smoothly open on greased rails. Inside a set of cute varnished steps climb down into the room. Large windows make it wonderfully light with great visibility all the way around. Varnished mahogany beams divide crisp white panels. Two more sliding doors open onto the little decks either side but most prominent in the room is a traditional spoked steering wheel with a brass central ring. A sprung circular seat below the wheel is hinged to the wall. This is a large room at mezzanine level in the boat. A wide facia shelf in front of the wheel, set with dials and a compass, looks out ahead through the windscreen along the shallow dome deck outside. Adjacent to the wheel is a cute little rack with thirty or forty tiny compartments. In each is neatly folded one of an assortment of highly coloured material. I pull one out and it's a perfect miniature flag complete with a wooden toggle in one corner.

'These must be signal flags. Like there's a whole alphabet here.' I pull out another couple and roll them up again into their nestbox. 'Oh God. Fantastic.' In the middle of the room is a large rectangular varnished box. I lift one corner of the lid and it opens easily revealing a huge engine below. Disappearing four feet under the floor, six cylinders, injectors and workings around the edge.

'That's huge. I bet you've got some power! And it's all so neat. Look at those beautiful little boxes built around it.' Long wooden boxes in the bilge either side of the engine, full with spanners and nuts, washers and indeterminate engine parts. A row of compartments have swivel locks and finger holes to pull open each door, revealing shelved lockers below the decks. Each shelf filled with ropes and oil cans, engine spares and tools, cables, fenders and lifejackets.

My head inside, 'It's Aladdin's seafaring cave in here!' I slide out and close the door. Put the lid back on the engine and stand up to look out the windows.

'Everything you might ever need, neatly stowed.. Ready to go..'

On the opposite side to the wheel a step down leads to an ornately carved narrow door. I try the keys and the last one fits. The door opens awkwardly toward me in the space at the bottom of the step. You need a back-shuffle before walking through. Two more steps lead down a narrow passage opening into a grand little saloon. About twelve feet square, high enough to stand tall in the middle. Sunlight streaming beams into the room through a little angular skylight above my head and opening brass portholes on either side. It is exquisite, a black japanned table and padded benches on one side and a full-length plush green sofa on the other. Behind my left is an open entrance to the galley kitchen. A prism-glass light in the roof and another brass porthole throw more light beams on shelves of cups and plates. A tiny many draw cabinet next to the cooker and little work surfaces around a miniature sink, emphasise the neatness. Such unusual and impressive function in miniature. Across the saloon is another narrow door where beyond I can see beds in a torpedo shaped cabin in the bow. Between this fo'c's'le-cabin door and the table is the smallest Number One Arctic stove without its chimney. Tom's instructions tell how to set it up. A neat little box on one bench-end full of perfectly fitting cut logs. Around the room and another door opens to an antique-looking toilet with mystery paddles and levers. 'I'll read your instructions as necessary.' Above it a shower head is angled as though, so naturally, you'll sit on the toilet and shower at the same time.. A porthole glass is beautifully embossed with a star for privacy.

'It's like a wet-room. Just gorgeous!' Stepping back into the saloon. 'This is a fantasy come true.' A long sigh turns slowly, savouring all and more than I imagined as my part in our swap. On the sofa, stroking the nap and gazing up through the skylight, sunlight pouring in and filling every corner, I felt unbridled pleasure and release.

Tom made me promise that as soon as I settle I'll find a bottle of vodka and some tonic in the fridge. The cupboards in the galley are so beautifully made, finding a glass is a treat. Old Carvic was a patient craftsman. Each drawer and cupboard has the smallest dovetail joints, every edge finished with tiny brass corners. I drain the glass with a series of homilies to everything.

My first night aboard followed a sublime wake of the day. Spoilt for a choice of beds, I chose the sofa in the saloon which surprisingly opens into bunks. Her gentle sway against the mooring soothes. Ben Lovell is too large to be so easily moved. While here is a stretch of rural river and, unlike the canal, the water flows a continual trickling under the boat. I found the chimney, lit the fire and climbed into bed. Gently rocking I lay listening to new sounds. Creaking fenders and ropes ticking stretch and slack. In the early morning we must have touched the bottom and the change in movement woke me. I got up and went outside to see the deck behind the wheelhouse now below the bank. Grabbing a blanket against the cold, I sat for a while on the top step inside the wheelhouse, watching frost clear stars fade against the advancing light. I grew too cold and went down inside, closing all the doors behind. I rattled and stoked the Arctic and it burst easily into life. Within a few minutes warm filled the room.

During the first day I did little. I just want to get the feel. Walk around opening and closing doors, looking in cupboards, sitting on deck, making tea and lunch and playing in the galley for dinner. I laid out the pages of Tom's instructions on the saloon table and prodded and probed.

Instructions for starting the engine are dutifully approached. That I am sure, needs preparation and there'll be time enough. I siesta-ed after lunch and lazing in the saloon, made a start on the Cirkus library. The subject matter is very specific to manuals-the sea, manuals-navigation, manuals-boats, manuals-birdspotting, manuals-fishing, plus three unheard of well thumbed novels. I began with the sailor's bible, the Reeds Almanac. Unfathomably full of completely useless information for other lives but essential for sailors. Charts and graphs, tide times and port entries, instructions for protocol between ships, collisions and salvage at sea. Surprising facts and pages to dally over. A section on multi-coloured international signal flags with examples of conversation. Weather lore and sea states. Another wonderful volume from the shelf is Sail and Motor Cruising, a vintage Lonsdale Library 1935 edition. It has drawings naming every part of a motor sailing cruiser, on ship handling, anchorwork and mooring, making a passage and navigation. I'm going to have to practice all this essential stuff. You might pootle up and down rivers and cover a good distance without it but if you really want to go anywhere, you'll need to learn about the sea. How to navigate and not get lost. How to pilot a boat! A lot to learn and tuition is expensive. Courses in sail magazines spread over months. If I'm to begin this adventure I'd like it to happen soon. Maybe like Trevor, I can hire a skipper to initiate me.

The following day, the book of local times and heights tells the high tide is at midday. Mixing impatience and trepidation, after early breakfast I decide to prepare a first solo. Are we going anywhere, I don't know but one thing at a time. Tom's instructions are a generous step by step idiots guide. He's even drawn little boxes for ticks on task completion. Getting underway has quite a list. Secure everything, the fire and chimney, turning the cupboard locks, close the toilet intake. In the wheelhouse and on deck, ticks are required for engine cooling water coming out and what to do if it doesn't. Fenders, ropes and a myriad of seaworthy minutiae.

At about eleven, with five or six hours of sufficient water, I pushed forward the gear lever, opened the throttle and eased her away from the quay. Out in the middle, pushing the throttle again, she powerfully surged forward, the bow rising alarmingly. Heart pounding adds to the stress. Throttled back we settle for a more gentle chug to acclimatise. The running checks allow for calm procedure. She responds to the finest adjustment and we begin to cruise smoothly. A calming breeze through the open doors and windows, I sat at the wheel, leaning out onto the deck. Confidence growing and settling to the chug, we drew past rolling fields and farms and a view of Yorkshire moors in the distance. She is heavy, moving slow and deliberate. An old limousine used to dignity. No hurry and standards to uphold. Passing a couple of cruisers they salute appropriately. A man on a bicycle shouted, 'She's beautiful!'

I wondered if I should pinch myself to check the euphoria. After a couple of hours though, the foray ended more abruptly. A sharp bend in the river was followed rapidly by the appearance of a low rustic bridge. In the sightline ahead it's obvious we are not going there with the mast still upright. And I have absolutely no idea how to take it down. With this kind of advance notice, it's completely out of the question! I had several times tested our brakes by pulling the tall gear lever back to reverse but there followed a important lesson in how much she weighs and, how long you can expect to go before it stops. At the very last perilous moment I feel bound to point the bow at a reed-bed before the bridge and we grind to an undignified halt. Recovering composure I check around for witnesses to amateur agonising. Hanging down over the prow to look for damage or need for further panic. Eventually, in the wheelhouse and slowly, with little throttle spurts she backed out to the middle. Sighing huge relief and a multi-point turn is enough for one day and we head for home.

And I spent an age mooring on our return. Slow, slow motion shunting back and forth under the prying of a bemused passer-by. Eventually his sympathy took my rope. Stress calming and in spite of novice antics, Cirkus was easy on me. She is big but handles beautifully, turning efficiently in the confines of the river and, despite my anguish, giving me a maiden voyage that felt like a gift. Each docking task ticked and finally turning the key to silence her engine, gratitude spilled over, 'Well done, girl. Thanks for looking after me.'

Over the next days, more relaxed in holiday mode. Living aboard Cirkus is already a happy habit. I really feel at home and begin to rehearse determination. I wonder how Tom and Barbara are doing. This new mobility exactly suits me. I have no idea how far I could go but a sense of freedom in potentio sets imagination alive. Here, at least for now, is the perfect solution. I might even earn a living by working her, taking rides or charter tours or fishing. On climbing into bed each night, surveying her by candlelight, the prospect for a life with Cirkus seems so much better than anything before. If I can keep hold of courage and confidence, that surely more experience will bring. As the days pass it seems increasingly possible.
'Keep answering yes and it'll happen.'

I'm becoming quite proficient. Beginning to feel a bond as I find my way into more of the things that make her work. I love the routines, rope winding, cleaning and checking. Still out of my depth but believing I can. Keep cleaning, winding, neatening rope coils.
We ventured out more and away from low bridges. Time to try taking down the mast though she looked undressed without it. Two hours of working it out, completely the wrong nuts and bolts, lowering massive weight inch by nervous inch down to rest on top of the wheelhouse. I stepped onto the quay and wanted to put it straight back up. A quarter of the work was actually necessary. I should have used the winch to lower it and there were only three nuts needed to undo it. I read that sailing barges would step their masts, sails and all, in a matter of moments before a bridge without stopping or slowing and, having passed beneath, immediately put them back up. No doubt a heavily muscled crew, years of confident practice and serious optimism.

On the final day, again through the lists, I closed and secured everything and, stepping down to the towpath, doffed a symbolic cap in salute to her. Still a little faltering but it's simply a matter of the courage to leap.

Within half an hour on the road, I'm deep in the conversation ahead. There are plenty of loose ends, not least in me. Working to reinforce the positive, asking over again why give space to fears that surely are ninety percent imagination, ten percent fact. What is it about us that makes doubting so much easier? Secure atrophy can feel like a blessing next to taking a risk? The what-have-I-got-to-lose measurement long and sobering. And the illusions we create about things we're sure we'll lose, end up being the very barriers to finding new ones. Pull it apart and they're just crutches. What do you want? If this doesn't work you'll do something else. Nothing is set in stone.
'Yeh and how bored do you want to be?'
Round and round in circles, every so often I picture old-bobble-hat leaning at the bar.. How'd it go..?
The shore still close.

Chapter Five
what good is this? Good is that wish?

Tom and Barbara are so happy with their new life. In ten days they had settled and everything is falling into place. They were at home on Ben Lovell. The whole atmosphere is changed from former best behaviour, staying in someone else's house. Cast-off coats and washing-up, unfamiliar things in the bathroom. Quite as though it were no longer mine. I felt uncomfortable but, when we talk, the feeling served to spur and they were very clear. Barbara's nurse training is about to start, Tom already has work and more in the pipeline. It makes complete sense to them and, if only I can calm my doubts, all is obvious. They are moving into a home and I need to beat insecurity by moving away from one. As far as our swap, there's no doubt we're already there. When we sat together over the next days there was an irresistible momentum. Far from preparing to make a conscious choice, it has been made. So surf the wave or impossibly try to stop it. We invited Trevor and Sue to dinner a couple of nights later and, with their blessing and witness, we agreed. Tom and I had written each other letters stating the agreement and we ceremonially signed and exchanged them while Trevor toasted our future. Signed, sealed and practically delivered..

I decide to collect all my fears and put them in a box marked, ever unresolved. Is it the thing itself I fear or is it the habit of fear itself. Something is shifting, becoming at least more aware of the habit. Difficult to describe the process, like sloughing off a heavy overcoat, but I think it mostly happened while sleeping. In truth I had made the decision within the first few hours. I'm going to make the boat ready. Tom and I have agreed it won't take much. Clean and paint her barnacled bottom. Overhaul the engine, rigging and workings, winches and pumps and, having put her in prime condition, get her a survey so that she can travel insured. The process will teach all. Once re-launched, as I try to think it through, a short journey with a crew will get us down the North Sea and into the French canals. After that I'll be able to handle her alone. Navigating the relatively safe canals, sailing slowly and sublimely south through France. What happens then? I've no idea and will have to wait for what presents. I'll certainly be 'out there' pitching. Beyond that, fantasies meet imagination.

It won't cost a lot to travel. Beyond fuel and sailing, I have a few ideas about earning. Maybe carry a sign offering rides or fishing trips. A beautiful old boat and little adventures. All sorts of people might pay for that, don't you think? Anyway, it must all stew and tumble in the pot and it's so much more than money. I need growing courage to explore and experiment. And building it from warm winds and tantalising adventures. How else can you do it? Okay, study and learn. And round and over it again, in one breath everything to lose, in another nothing. I only know what I know now and have an overriding urge to know something different. I know that could let in almost anything but what is it exactly that has me at its mercy?

Down the North Sea will be the real initiation. For that I'll find experts or a crew with the right skills. If we pass that test, I'll continue. If not maybe I'll moor up next to Ben Lovell. At least to know that I tried to create something. Who knows, perhaps with Cirkus there are opportunities here. I'll be an inland pleasure-boat captain and take rides up the canal. Make some attempt and it must lead where it will. That's my best strategy. That's my only strategy. As the days pass, I feel better. Treasured optimism creeping into thoughts and days. It's beginning to last, feeling steady. That's a first!

The sea, the sea, how full of mystery and guile is she. 'Cold but containing the hottest blood, the wildest and most urgent.' I think Lawrence was talking about whales but, although we're beached, the blood is up.

Think of sailing and I am transported, passing islands and azure bays through tossing waves. Last year's calendar picture hanging in the galley is our closest yet. Azure or in the present reality, greyish water laps the edge of my new car park residence. From a rain sprayed vantage overlooking the river Ouse our view is heightened by breeze-blocks and timber supports. But grey or otherwise, watery escape is but a few concrete yards away. The Starborough Sailing Club, my own beachfront bar is just beyond the picket fence. A busy road is somewhat closer and the last quarter of one side of the hull, covered in barnacles, is closer still. My hands are red raw in delicately patterned sore cuts. Canny little crustacea, they are unbelievably sharp and gloriously impervious to hammering, chiselling and any amount of cursed threat. Slow progress is thorough and if all goes well with remaining skin on my knuckles, I should have finished picking and sanding by tonight. Painting of this final piece can begin in the morning. Cirkus looks comical like a backwoods shack. Smoke belching from the arctic and a draped skirt of tattered blue tarpaulin around the hull, reaches to the ground enabling work undisturbed by rain. The deck, similarly clad and covered in canvas, is littered with paint pots and tools, six grades of sandpaper and gooey half-dried filler. The inside is similarly limboed. Like the rest of the dream, a temporary frozen kinesis has the engine in as many bits as I dare, cleaned and oiled around the wheelhouse floor. A diesel mechanic is coming tomorrow to check it and hopefully, help me put it back together. It would be more sensible once we're afloat, as we can't start it without water but I'm behind schedule and it's the only day I could get him to come. I began to think he's afraid of turning into a pool of vampire-grease in the sun if he ever had to leave his workshop. Eventually his palm got enough greasing. Another guy, I had to lever and persuade, is down there since this morning. He's an auto-electrician trying to make sense of the spaghetti that feeds power to lights and pumps and starter-motors. Be sure when you switch the switch that says bilge, it does actually pump bilges rather than start the engine or flush the toilet. Graciously entertained over many cups of tea and a hearty lunch, he has managed non-stop to complain about 'jobs like this,' when someone 'didn't know his electrical arse from 'is elbow'. He'd just about exhausted grace when finally appearing, groaning in triumph and rather too gratuitously presented me his invoice. It should all work now and I should notice a complete change in performance.

Should?! I exhorted privately, writing the cheque. I want a gold-plated guarantee after three hundred and some odd quid for less than four hour's complaining. He smiled benignly oblivious. I wished I'd invoiced him for tea. I flicked all the switches and happily, the right lights lit and dials flitted response. For a bonus finale, a previously unlabelled switch

shocked us both as the siren wound bellowing octaves to blasting pitch.
'Told you it'ud work', he said, a broad grin pocketing the cheque.
'Ay. Get nauticed wi' that one, mate.'

Most of this will satisfy the insurance company of her seaworthiness. By a visit from an assessor, apparently accredited. He arrived unannounced on Tuesday, a week earlier than agreed. With curt introduction and unwrapping a highly sophisticated tool kit consisting of one long screwdriver. Duly he attempted to make holes all over the hull both inside and out. Each time he failed with much straining to penetrate the screwdriver blade more than a quarter of an inch, he marked another box on his line drawing of a boat that couldn't have looked less like Cirkus. Peering into cupboards and lockers, tapping everything as he went. He rattled the anchor chain, pulled at the propeller and stepped in a tray of white paint. It all seemed cursory and I used none of my prepared excuses. After he left I spent the rest of the day repairing his gouges and feeling anti-climactic. This morning an eight page survey report arrived by post, accompany a letter saying that Eagle Sun Insurance would be prepared to insure the boat for £45,000 in UK waters only. For the meagre charge, read: Super Introductory Bonus Offer; a premium of £1997 for one year. A result I guess. One that everyone I asked for advice had said, was completely academic and not worth the paper it's written on. I shouldn't try to claim because, such is the insurance industry, they'd be unlikely to pay under any circumstance.
I read the report several times over breakfast and, quite complimentary in its legalese. She is well-founded of sturdy construction with no visible faults. Down on page whatever there are several caveats that this document, not being a full survey and the company not being liable is,.. not worth the

paper it's written on. It does say things require maintenance, the stern-tube where the propeller comes out, the steering wires and sheaves that link the wheel to the rudder and, the rigging stays. All moving parts, it seems obvious would need regular maintenance. I'm in the middle of greasing and everything cited is on my lists. However, the minimum asked is the minimum given. The bottom line, that I now comply with something. However minimal or in favour of insurance company profit.

Well past dark, I had finished barnacle scraping and emerged only a little more blooded from beneath the tarpaulin. I decide to reward myself with a beer at the sailing club. Accumulating aches make for an awkward straddle over the picket fence but the lights are shinning bright and with a prospect of Guinness, I open the door and step into the glow.
Against the bar a group of six or seven elderly and middle-aged men, almost all wearing identical club-badged blazers and captain's hats, turned an unfriendly glare.
My 'Evening all,' generated low mumbles.
'You a member?' the bartender's brusque took me by surprise.
'No. But you remember me? I've been in everyday at lunchtime. I'm working on my boat in your car-park. Mr Falley introduced me.'
'We only serve members.' It had been quiet previously and he was jovial and accommodating. Now he's subservient to the troop of captain's blazers and shot a glance at them.
'Yes, but you served me only yesterday,' I persisted. 'And I've been working hard on the boat today so I thought I'd come in for a pint.'
'We only serve members,' he repeated with another look down the bar. I felt resistance and thirst rising and we stood for a moment unresolved.

'I'll buy him a drink.' A rather urgent and squeaky feminine voice cut through the pregnant impasse.

A tousle-haired scruffy young woman alone at a table in the corner stood up. She put down a book and came over to the bar smiling a broad if skewed smile.

'Would you like a drink?' She ignored the collective mute objection. Standing boldly close, a fiery expression overwhelmed her young freckled face, dark tired circles around piercing eyes, she intimidates.

I should have walked out but I've a real thirst and my fridge is empty. I looked at the captains, the bartender and then my interloper. There was no doubt she and a pint of Guinness were the most appealing.

'I'd love a drink,' I said, spreading my smile amongst all. 'A pint of Guinness, please? Thank you very much.' Her glare flickered.

'Join me?' She softened and then from a pocket drew some change and theatrically slapped it on the bar. She grinned at the captains and with a swagger, returned to her table.

I stood uncomfortably waiting for my pint, remembering the shop that might still be open.

Avoiding contact the bartender placed the pint. And out of politeness but also to satisfy the intrigue, I had to join her. Despite her assertive intervention, as I cross the room she now looks suddenly uncomfortable.

'God, what we do for a pint?' The joke fell flat.

She is dark but almost pretty, unkempt red hair. She fidgets, clasping and unclasping her hands. Her whole demeanour is disturbed. I decide to be polite. A little chat, drink my beer and go.

'Thanks very much. I'd like to pay you for the beer,' I said, the Guinness wonderfully cutting barnacle dust. 'And thanks for sticking your neck out.'

'They're such jerks,' she returned. 'Tired old little horn-blowers.' A venom twist in the corner of her grimace. 'My father used to sort them out.'

'Well the bartender was fine yesterday. He served me and we chatted.' I tried to lighten it up.

'I hate them.' She was determined. 'Stuck up pretend captains. None of them's got anything like a boat. They come in here and pontificate, pretend to be important expert sailors. Just needs someone who really does know to tell 'em what's what.' Her faint smile looks like an appeal.

'I don't think it'll be me. I'm just here for the beer.'

'Your boat's beautiful. I saw you working on it yesterday.'

This subject I can handle. 'Yeh I've got lots of work to do and only the day after tomorrow before the crane comes to launch her. I think I'll get it done though, it went well today.'

'I saw you working yesterday'. She repeated.

'Oh right. What do you do?'

She thought about it. 'I read books.' She said to the one open on the table.

'Oh Yeh. Read any good ones lately?'

'This one.' She held it up.

'P.D. Ouspensky. In Search Of The Miraculous. Mmm, sounds good. What's it about?'

'It's about symbolism and sexuality and transcendence.'

'In that order?'

She ignored me. 'It's about love and higher-consciousness and illumination. All the things we need to live authentic lives.'

'Sounds great.'

'He embarks on a long spiritual journey in a search of new ways to overcome this thin film of false reality.' She gestured to the room.

'Really?'

'Yes, and he finds the answers in the practice and teachings of the ancients. By tapping in to the cosmic-consciousness that's all around us but we don't see it.' She taps the page.

I look around the room. There's only mock-captain's conscious as far as I can see. They're now in a loud argument about yachting technology.

'Oh don't talk rubbish man. Men have been sailing the oceans for thousands of years without all that new-fangled what-not. These modern namby-pambies couldn't navigate their way out of a paper-bag without their GPSs and their RDFs.'

I'm inclined to agree with him, especially since Cirkus doesn't have any. I keep seeing them in sailing shops, priced well beyond my pocket.

'He meets a man called Gurdjieff. An Armenian who learnt everything from a secret brotherhood in the Gobi.'

'Does he know how to navigate without global positioning satellites?' It seemed to me the two conversations should meet.

She turned suddenly angry at my flippance.

'This is very important.' She demanded, tapping the book cover. 'The kind of lives we're leading are stupid and ignorant. We are all asleep and without any kind of purpose.'

'Well, I'm inclined to agree with that too. I'm sorry, I didn't mean to..' I took a long draught of the pint. I'd like to go now.

'Will you show me your boat?' She smile-appealed and loaded it with coy.

I took another long draught, whilst trying to imagine what kind of planet I'd emerged onto. 'I don't think so. I'm very busy working on her and it's a terrible mess inside, all the floorboards up and you can't move for all the stuff everywhere. Sorry.'

She slumped dramatically, elbows hitting the table loudly and sighed. Several of the captains looked across.

'I only wanted a look,' she pouted. Her eyes tracked deliberately across the table and on up until they met me.

Something shudders. Do this politely. 'I'm sorry. I'd love to show you.' Pause for effect. 'But it's really not convenient just now. I'm sorry. Another time perhaps.' The hairs on the back of my neck are curling.
She continued to look intensely into my eyes and then, without a waver in the stare, reached to the back of the chair for her coat. Closing the book she stood up, picked up her glass and drained it. Without a word, she flicked hair aside, strode across to the door and left.
I put my glass to my lips to have something to hide behind. What shall I do? Finish and look like I'm following her or sit it out. I decide to sit. Isn't there a hole with a passage to the boat that I can crawl down. Nothing to do but prolong the torment. Eventually, an appropriate age passed. As graciously as possible thanking the gentlemen, I measured my way past the bar to escape. Welcoming fresh air and impersonal stars. All reminders, next time go to the shop.

Once inside, the saloon is friendly. There is actually hardly any chaos. I made a special effort to leave it and the galley as together as possible whilst the work is going on. It's important to have one calm and ordered space. Not only the boat needs preparation.
Slumped on the sofa, staring at the ceiling, indistinct thoughts roll a jumbled passage. A feeling of cold grubbiness got the better of me. I riddled the Arctic and took a tepid bedtime shower. It's April cold and so, warmed by a cup of tea, refuge is found under the duvet. I had only just begun the thought that sometimes bed is a wonderful place and fell instantly asleep.

I have no idea how long I slept but woke with a start to the sound of stumbling and crashing in the wheelhouse. As I jumped out of bed the saloon door opened and standing in doorway completely naked was the girl from the bar.

'What are you doing?' I said inadequately
She said nothing, staring blankly at me from the step.
'What on earth are you doing here?'
We stand facing one another gripped like rabbits caught in a headlight. I scrub the association to rabbits. In the half-light she began to look nervously around. Seeing the toilet door ajar she fumbled for the handle, yanked it towards her and with a look of panic, jumped inside, slamming the door behind.
'What the f...!' Only half-awake this is surreal.
I moved to the door and she found the bolt inside and snapped it across. I stared at the door handle. Is she nuts? Seriously, she must be disturbed. There was something peculiar about her performance in the bar but this is too bizarre.
After an age of silence, both listening intently either side of the door, I decide to try to take the threat out. Let's be normal. I rattled the kettle in the galley.
'I'm going to make tea. Would you like some?' She didn't reply but having embarked on the strategy I continued with accentuated noises of cups and water and cupboards opening. Tea made and getting cold and all possible words of encouragement did not elicit a single response.
'I've put your clothes by the door and your tea's getting cold,' I try again. Looking at my watch,.. it's three in the morning.
Disguising impatience. 'Look, I've got masses of work to do in the morning and it's getting ridiculously late. How long do you think you're going to carry on with this?'
'I just wanted to see your boat.'
At last! Why the hell is she naked then? This is insane.
As calmly as possible I said, 'Well, all right, come out and put your clothes on, drink your tea and I'll show it to you.' Silence again. Is she thinking about it. Please!
I made more tea and sat at the table staring at the door. How on earth did I attract this? How nice it would have been to meet an attractive woman. I need love too. I've got a woman in

my bathroom, naked! And she's a basket-case, for crying out loud..

After an age, I said in my calmest voice. 'Look, I'm falling asleep here. I can't carry this on. I don't really know what you want,.. but I'm going to go to bed in the fore-cabin. I'll make the bed up in here on the sofa and you can stay and we'll talk in the morning. Okay?'

No reply. I thought about valuables and began collecting camera, wallet, walkman. I gave up, took them with me and closed the door. There's no lock! But she surely can't be that dangerous? I lay there thinking about knives in the kitchen and aberrant scenes. Eventually I must have fallen into exhausted sleep.

Dawn light vapour in the porthole, it must be early. No sound above or below canvas flaps and slack rope. Relaxed hissing and new-day thoughts floating in. I had heard nothing, lost to the pillow. Perhaps it was a dream. That would be nice.

I opened the door slowly, peering into the saloon. She's there on the sofa, a body wrapped in covers. Little sleep breathing noises.

'Thank God.' I'll just creep about and hope she stays that way. I dressed and made tentative tea. Occasional roll-overs paused the action. I put a second cup on the table and went up into the wheelhouse, closing the door behind me. Up and out on deck, mug in hand, descending the ladder to the ground. The painted hull is still sticky. It looks good, bright white smooth above the water-line and red-oxide below. The last de-barnacled bit, sanded and ready for paint. I sip tea and gather gratitude. With touch-ups, another couple of hours will see it finished. Nearly three weeks and she's really looking the part.

An hour or so into work and I hear movement inside. What shall I do? Confront her, chuck her out? I wonder where she lives. Oh God.. I should carry on with my normality. That's it,

nothing unusual here. I'm ready for breakfast and a chat.. Show her the boat and then she'll go.. Purposefully I climb the ladder and drop down into the wheelhouse. Pausing for doubt at the saloon door, I decide to knock.
'Good Morning. Are you decent?' No reply. With a deep intake of breath, I opened the door. 'Hallo!'
She's standing in the middle of the room, dressed thank goodness. She looks nervous, white knuckles clutching the bag hard to her chest.
I raise gesturing palms. 'It's all right. Just relax.. It doesn't matter about last night.. Why don't we just sit down and have a normal cup of tea and a bit of breakfast. I'm starving.. I'll show you the boat if you like,.. and you can go when you're ready? Okay?'
She doesn't move, wide-eyed and cornered.
'Come on, why not sit down and relax?' I gesture this time to the table. There's a tiny flicker.
'Do you want a cup of tea?' My eternal solution. She lowers the bag slowly, looking across at the table.
'Go on, go and sit down and I'll make us some tea.' This time she complies stiffly clutching her bag.
'That's better.' I glide into the galley and pumping the floor stud, fill the kettle.
'I'm having toast and marmalade. Would you like some?' When there's no reply I peer at her around the bulkhead and she nods without looking up.
I carry on in the kitchen and call over my shoulder. 'Come on, talk to me. What's your name?'
After a long pause. 'Lucy.'
At last! I peer again around the bulkhead. 'Hi, Lucy,.. I'm Will. How are you? Are you okay?'
'Yes,' she says coyly.
'Yes what? You're okay?'
'Yes, thank you.'

Kettle's boiling, toast is done and in a couple of trips I take everything to the table. She's held in.
I love this little table, its short cushioned benches either side. It's cosy, intimate. I bring tea and toast.
'Here, help yourself.' As I sit down there's a nervous flicker and suddenly it's too intimate. That's okay, work with what you've got.. 'Tea?' I slide the cup toward her deliberately.
'How do you take your tea? Sugar, milk?'

'All right, so tell me about yourself? I know you read books, what else do you like?'
'Don't like anything else.. Boats.' I offer toast.
'Toast?' I pass the butter and marmalade. 'Do you have a boat?'
'No.'
'Oh. Have you done much sailing?
'No.'
As we munch she looks like she might relax. 'But you've been on a boat before?'
'Yes.'
'Really?' Oh God..
'Yes.'
'ermmm...and er..where was that?'
'My father.'
Grasping at anything. 'He had a boat? What sort of boat?'
'Small.'
'And where does he do his sailing?'
'The river.'
'Oh. What, this river?'
'Yes.'
'..More tea?' How sad am I? Interminable pauses twixt question and answer.
'So,.. where do you live?' This time there is no answer because my timing is off and she has a mouthful of toast.

'Do you live nearby?'
'Mmnno.' She spits a bit of marmalade onto my plate and jerks a hand to catch it.
'So, where?'
'York.'
'Uh Huh.'
I have to think about that. York is a long way. 'Have you got a car?'
'No.'
'How d'ya get here then?'
'Walk.'
'You walked!? But it must be twenty miles.'
'Twenty point five two kilometres.'
'Pardon?'
'Twenty point five two kilometres.'
'Yeh. I should think you would know it that precisely if you walked.' She's dead serious.
'That's incredible. You walk that sort of distance for a drink?'
'Yes.'
'Oh. Come on. You're pulling my leg.'
She looks under the table. 'No,' she says, looking indignant.
'So let me get this straight. You walk twenty miles...'
'Twenty point five two kilometres.'
'Yeh. I get that. You walk twenty odd kilometres...'
'Point five two.'
'Yes. And you have a drink in the sailing club..'
'Two.'
'Okay. You have two drinks in the sailing club. You then hang around until two o'clock in the morning. Come on to my boat. Take all your clothes off and then spend half the night in the toilet. Why?!'
'One forty six.'
'What?'
'One forty six.'

'What's one forty six?'
'One forty six.'
'What, precisely?'
'Yes.'
'I don't understand. Is one forty six important?'
'Yes.' She says it very earnestly.
'Why?'
'Venus conjunct Jupiter.'
'What!?'
'Venus conjunct Jupiter.'
'Yeh. I got that. What's Venus conjunct Jupiter got to do with it?'
'It was the right moment.'
'The right moment for what?'
'For love and joy.'
I have to think about this. Mmmmh oh dear! 'But hang on. What's lovely and joyful about spending the night in a toilet?!'
She held that for a long time, and then just said, 'Don't know.' Her head dropped with the down-tone.
I can't do this. I want her to go. 'Well, if you don't know, I'm sure I don't.' I stare at her and then realise as her face greys, I'm intimidating her. I look into the porthole.

'So it was in the stars that made you decide to do this? And then, what, you chickened out?'
'You frightened me.'
'I frightened you!?'
'Yes.'
'Look, I was asleep and you woke me up in the middle of the night. And when I got up you were standing there with no clothes on! I think I was the one who might be expected to be frightened, don't you?'
'No.'
'No! Why not?'

'It was the right moment.'
'For who?'
'You and me.'
'You and me to do what!?'
'Make love.'
'Oh. Hang on. You don't know me. I don't know you. We'd only met for a few minutes and you walked out. What kind of grounds is that for making love?'
'The aspect.'
'What. So you asked the stars if you should come on to the boat at one forty something...'
'Six.'
'Yeh. And take all your clothes off and make love to me?'
'You don't ask.'
'How did you do that!?'
She took her bag and fumbled inside. Out came a huge book which she placed on the table facing me. 'Twelve Year Planetary Ephemeris 1980-92 Key to Geocentric Observation and Planetary Aspectarian.'
'What's this?'
'An Ephemeris..'
'Yes I can see it says that. So is this what you consult to come up with your plans?' I pick it up and flick through pages of indecipherable charts and graphs. 'This is complicated.'
'No, it's easy.'
'Well it might be for you, but for me it looks like gobbledegook.'
'It's easy.'
'Alright. So aside from the fact that your plan went a bit wrong, what else can you tell from this?' I tap the book.
'Anything.'
'Well, like what?'
'Anything.'
'Yes you said that, but what exactly?'
'Anything.'

'Okay.. So you've got these charts and things. How do you know what they mean?'

'I know.' How did I know she was going to say that?

'Yeh, but how do you know? It's just a matter of interpretation, surely?'

'No.'

'Yeh, but last night you were wrong.'

'No I wasn't.'

'Surely you were, it went wrong. It didn't happen, did it?'

'You frightened me.'

'Oh right, so it was my fault, because I didn't know what the plan was or what the stars were saying?'

'Yes.'

'Oh, bloody hell! I've got to have a cigarette.'

'You shouldn't smoke.'

'I know.'

'It's bad for you.'

'I know.' I light one.

'It's bad for you.'

'Look. Let me get this straight. You say that you can tell what is the right thing to do by looking at the star charts in this book..'

'Yes.'

'Okay, I've heard of that before, the stars in the Daily Mirror and so on.'

'It's not like that.'

'Yeh okay, but these are really small things, like last night, how do you know it applies to those sort of things?'

'It does.'

'Well, of course, that's because you believe it. But it doesn't apply to me, does it.'

'Yes it does.'

'But you said because I didn't know it was my fault that it went wrong. Didn't you?'

'Yes.'

'Alright then, why didn't it apply to me.'
'You frightened me.'
'Oh Right! Alright then. Why did I frighten you and not do what the stars wanted me to do?'
'I don't know.'
'No hang on. Look, why didn't I want to? Because I didn't know?'
'Yes.'
'So had I known, it would have happened?'
'Yes..'
'I thought so! Alright. I suppose so.' Let's try again. 'If I know what the stars predict, I can somehow make it happen?'
'Yes.'
'And if I don't know, I can stop it, or somehow get in its way?'
'Yes.'
'Okay, how will I know?'
'You can't.'
'Why can't I? If I've got the book?'
'You can't.'
'Why?..'
'Study.'
'Oh Right. How do I do that?'
'You can't.'
'Why not?'
'You haven't got the books.'
'Oh right. So I haven't got the books so I can't find out. So what do I do?'
'Ask me.'
'Yes, but how do I know you know?'
'I know.'
'Yes, but how do you know?'
'I studied.'
'Oh of course. Why didn't I think of that? You've got the books?'
'Yes.'

'At home in York?'
'But I don't need them now.'
'Oh right. You just remember.'
'Yes.'
I don't really believe we understand anything.
'So,.. if I want to know when is the right time to do something like launch a boat.. And when is the right time to sail out to sea. You can tell me, right?'
'Yes.' We both nod.
'And if I don't do it at those times, what will happen then?'
'You could die.'
'Oh that's cheerful!' Maybe this is not such a good idea. 'And I suppose I need you to tell me?'
'Yes.'
Suddenly there's a creeping inevitability. Do I dare think about where we're going.
'And I suppose that means you have to come along?'

She stayed. I've asked her to leave five times. I don't know how she stays through not so subtle discouragement. The astrological stuff carries on remorseless, defeating all rationale. Unlike the stuff you get in tabloids, this is an intellectual art. She believes it's possible to predict favourable and unfavourable circumstance. To aid some potential if not entirely guarantee its outcome. Call me vulnerable, when I may literally be out of my depth. And, damn it,.. the question of whether she is the best guide is academic. She is the only one presented. I keep asking how I conjured her. She tries to be helpful. Painting, although painting herself as much as the boat. I tire regularly in exasperation and want her to leave.

Appropriate celestial appointments fair, my crane arrives on a sky-blue and bright morning. We who are about to float salute you! Not quite the romance I had in mind. A lumbering caterpillar-tracked muscular arm strop, lifted her with awful sounds of cracking and creaking. Difficult finding moments of ceremony during brusque, construction-site efficiency. The hurried surly crane driver did stop briefly for me to spill champagne on her stem. Amid engine noise and shouts of instruction and palpable paranoia that she'll drop at any moment. A few precious words invoked her fortune and the womb-like safety of all who sail in her. She looked beautiful. Shinning, graceful and portly. Motherly lines dashed by the water and regal on return to her element.

A vacant space on the yacht club quay, along from the car park, is reserved for two days. We carefully haul ropes until she's alongside. Another glass of champagne and long sighs of relief. On with engine and watertight test boxes to tick.
Two days before we leave for Hull. Two days of checking and trying, mast up, mast down, sails up sails down. Maybe sailing will be too much alone but feeling the wind even in the confines of the river, rigging and feathering, is too exciting not to try. Engine on engine off, cooling water running, gears forward, gears reverse, ropes and new dinghy, anchors and winches, everything including me, needs the workout. And beautifully smooth, we all work well.

On the night before leaving I tried another serious attempt to get Lucy to leave. I don't want responsibility for her but she will not go. Bar physically carrying her out or calling the Police. Persuasion stretching into anguished hours, she would not go. I decide I could wish all I like for someone more sane. But then they probably wouldn't be here in the first place. Crew is crew for fending off and pulling ropes.

With a last look back at the car park, we set off early. Slowly, gently cruising through widening waters and on into the tidal race. There is plenty of time before the rendezvous in Hull. Dallying, getting used to her again, through placid and spring garnished lands. Putting the sails up, taking them down. No low bridges so no mast stepping, everything seems to work. Optimism and confidence in my captaincy is growing. My crew, having fully found her voice is prattling nonstop. There is a particular moment, the first time I sense the sea. A breeze from somewhere ahead across flattening land and, ready or not, a brief perfume of destiny calling.

Chapter Six   what good is this?

The Humber River in full spring flood is an awe inspiring sight. Such an impressive gesture. The breadth of the rushing ocean, the North Sea anyway, confined to a narrow gorge. When you feel it under the boat for the first time, it is absolutely terrifying. On a good tide, and to those that call it such that means high and fast, it's possible to release an unpowered barge weighing more than two hundred tons, straight into the torrent. Precisely aiming, it is let go from the speeding rafted group mid-stream, travelling entirely unassisted, propelled purely by the current. An arrow true manoeuvre, the barge arrives in a measured glide, to stack neatly alongside another rafted group at the quay.
The skill of the bargemen who perform this many times daily, is an inspiration to any mariner. Timing and pace, never forcing but delicately deft. Intuitive knowledge of the dynamics and weight of travelling water. Try to drive a boat at the quay and you'll certainly crash, putting gashing wounds through your hours of sanding and scraping. Fine judgement, anticipate and measure.

There's no getting off or turning round. Steering wheel paddles spin alarmingly, wrist crunching vortices at the moment a direct line is deviated from. Everything happens at break-neck speed, such that you have to foresee the course way in advance or find yourself overshooting the target. A naïve casualty of hasty wishes passing rapidly behind. To slow down as an essential for turning, you keep pointed direct into the surge, with minute deviations veering like a whip.

Obstacles are dangerous, the land even more. Many other perilous things you're supposed to avoid are marked on a local chart. Mine is not that good, though even if it were, you'd never have time to read it and look where you're going..

In a favourite house, we had graffiti-like, scrawled on the low ceiling of the attic stairs. 'It's Easier To Ride The Horse in the Direction S/he's Going'. I passed it every morning, mostly not seeing it. Occasionally a little insight would strike a few steps from the bottom.. It's all about aligning and synchronisation and symbolises perfectly this rushing elemental ride.

Sit up and take notice. Good, bad or anything else in the ride of our lives. Whatever the outcome, it's all precarious. Imagine wider contexts and we soon have to admit we are simply not equipped for stewardship. The only chance, to tune in, to go with it and find a way to enjoy the ride. Only by skill and confidence, are we able to truly meet its embrace.

An early morning feeble sun lights the fore-deck of the motor-sailer Cirkus. Sitting on my ropecoil, cup in hand, ready to embark, there is now no choice but to leap and feel that embrace. Everything done, or as much as the lists and paranoia dictate. Uncertain fear visualised through a fogged blanket of detail overload and cranked by anticipation angst.

Albert Dock in Hull is quite a place for a departure. Since we arrived yesterday, Cirkus has seemed insignificant against a backdrop of serious tankers and coasters. The bustling commerce barely stopped for the night. A squeal and clatter of cranes and trucks began again before first light.

It took an age to find this mooring when we finally arrived on the incoming tide. I could see nowhere that I wouldn't be in the way amidst intimidating professional hubbub. After cruising up and down, some bargemen spotted me passing for the third time. They directed me into this little tidal cut off the main dock. Where all the pleasure craft and small boats moor, the amateur quarter.

I made a pretty amateur arrival too, trying to get too close to the quay before there was enough water. Handling a large old-fashioned boat without modern winches and steering gear was never going to be easy, but only an idiot would run aground in this tiny channel. In the effort to refloat us, I put her so fast in reverse that once released from the glutinous gripping mud, we catapulted across the narrow canal, stranding on the only sand bank. In full public view I sat waiting for the water, which is what I should have done in the first place. After an age and ignoring my embarrassment, the same two bargemen took the warp ropes and hauled us in.

We won't have that problem for a while. I now have the makings of a crew with experience of jumping off and yanking ropes. Pete and Sally and their dog Bubbles arrived very late last night. They are asleep down below in the fo'c's'le. Pete is a major third of the working crew, our engineer. They were new arrivals on the canal mooring in London and in the short time of our friendship, over some oily Saturday morning coffees and arc-lit late nights, I saw him perform minor miracles with their old narrowboat engine. He's the man for me if anything breaks fifty miles out to sea. On our first meeting there was instant rapport. We seemed to have so much in common. Later, when I told them about Cirkus, Pete was immediately engaged. When I said I needed crew for the first part of the journey and particularly an engineer, he made quite a pitch for the job. At first Sally looked doubtful. I thought she was suspicious of me but, it turned out she had never even been on a ferry until they got their boat. Pete pressed and persuaded that they would surely have an exciting holiday.

Trevor, the important other third is late. Rushed because of some last minute client. He was supposed to arrive last night. I need his confidence and some of the journey south will cover the ground we made on our previous voyage.

Trevor is the navigator. When sailing and studying charts he is wonderfully meticulous. In fact, with a perfect anal aptitude to the equations and calculations that make for sensible navigation. Annoying that may be at other times, for this job he gifts confidence. Trevor will guide us from buoy to buoy, along charted channels and around sandbanks. I spent almost eighty quid on the new charts from Hull to Calais. Very expensive four bits of paper, they are important wonders, vital for sailing near the coast. Where mud flats snake and channels dissolve, here dangerous shallows are laid bare in colour and contour detail. Fascinated, we pawed at them for hours, chewing over minutiae.

Trevor is nothing if not consistent. Oddly he's always late. I've laid everything ready on the wheelhouse chart shelf. A comfortable workstation, vacant and waiting for him.

'Turn up, Trevor,' I whisper a plea.

Cirkus is almost dry, leaning on the dock wall. The tide has been at its lowest since the small hours and must be well on the turn. Not much change since I got up for the Shipping Forecast.

'It'll be coming soon.'
In a little more than an hour it will flood, the top of the tide in four. A big one, full moon just passed and the spring season too. The peak tides are nearly always higher in spring and autumn. Racing into this little cut it will herald the most dramatic transformation. By the time the tide has turned again, going out and south down the coast of England, we'll be well on our way. At first, the tide against us will make progress slow but help our control in the river. Once it turns we'll take full advantage of the fast flowing ebb to carry us out into the North Sea. It could take three hours to get down there and I want to be on time. Crucial to the whole the journey is to be at the estuary by the time it turns. Tide and wind behind us, a North West four to five the forecast predicts. I could wish for no better and held the image of a plump-cheeked cherub blowing us south.

'Yes!' South, that's the object. Out and away down the North Sea, into the French canals, leisurely sailing along. Heading ever toward the sun. Living aboard, finding little jobs along the way. Pulling alongside in Paris, putting out the sign for rides on a Queen Mary's lifeboat. Up the Seine to Notre Dame and back! Find a little sea-port that I like and do some fishing charter. Buy a bit of gear, a few fishing rods and tackle. As much about entertainment as fishing. Plenty of drinking and eating to supplement vagaries of the catch. She is superbly set, I can feed six and roomy deck space lounging. Day sailing and lunch in a deserted bay..

Movement!.. A rush of new sound and something other-worldly arriving like a wave of new energy. The first penetrating rivers skate and stream. Under the boat bubbles, rattles dissolving fluid mud splash the length of us. Already a foot up the wall and the rudder starts to creak, its shaft dividing the stream in twin surging runnels. I get up and walk her length, leaning over the stanchion wire, watching the water surround us. Time stops to watch for tides. We shift, bubbles rising to the surface. Small shudders run the length of her as the keel disturbs muddy sand. And then we're afloat..

It prompts another checking and tugging of ropes. Running attentive hands along the boom from the mast to the wheelhouse. The red sails are reefed and ready. I hop up onto the wheelhouse roof and stand for a moment, high above it all surveying the scene. The deck ahead is full of stuff that we must check is tied down before we go to sea. From up here, that wonderfully broad, perfect sunbathing space. However unlikely today, late April and coming on predictably, waves of cold north wind, piling over grey cloud. Perfect English and, looking across the arc of the sky, I turn and see Trevor standing on the far quay.

'Hi!' I yell. My relief winging its way across the seventy foot of dock.

'How do I get across to you?' he yells back.

'You have to swim now, you bugger. You're too late for the ferry'.

'I know, don't nag me'. He turns to walk in the direction I'm pointing. Up toward the road and bridge across.

'You have to go around and over the lock, there.'

I cross the deck and this time have only three steps up to the quay. We are well afloat and rising. I lean in to the wheelhouse hatch calling to Pete and Sally.

'Trevor is here! Stick the coffee on someone!'

In a few moments he's up to me. He drops his bag and we hug.
'Hi ya.'

'I'm sorry I'm late', he says with disarming comfort. 'How you doing? Is she ready?' And without a pause. 'I just had a job to

finish last night but delivered it on the way this morning. Was still doin' it at two o'clock and delivered it at five. They'll be impressed but I'm knackered!' he chuckles 'It's a good job I stayed. It's worth a packet, and I need one of those right now. Got time for a snooze, have I?'
'No you bloody haven't!' And then I thought about it. 'Well actually of course you have. Listen, do a quick check around with me first and then Pete and I can handle her down to the estuary. You could have a couple of hours at least.'

I take his bag and motion him to step on board. We hop the couple of wooden steps on the dock wall and down over the guardrail. Trevor is tall and confident, reassuring. With both hands smoothing the edge of the wheelhouse roof, he takes stock.
Nodding he fingers a bit of polished brass. 'She looks good. And God, I'm glad to be here.' He let out a long breath. 'Feels like I've been driving forever.. You okay?'
'I am now you're here. I was beginning to get a bit twitchy.'
'I know, I'm sorry. There was no way to get in touch, though.'
'Well you're here now. That's enough for me.' I wipe pretend sweat off my brow and we chuckle together, exchanging a warm, broad smile. 'Come on in, kettle's on.' And then over my shoulder. 'We got maybe half an hour max. We're going to have to move. Look at that water.'
We climb down into the wheelhouse and Pete is standing in the saloon doorway, tousled hair and genial if sleepy smile. Bubbles is squeezing past him and arrives, whole body-wagging furiously to bound up onto the engine cover.

'This is Bubbles, a vital member of the crew.' He strokes her gyrating nose. 'Hi, Bubbles!'
'You remember Pete? He came to your party to christen the barge.'

'Yeh, I do. Hi Pete. How you doing?' They shake hands with Trevor continuing. 'Yes, we spent several pleasurable hours discussing the merits of putting concrete in the bilges of old wooden boats!'

'Yes, yes, well thank you both very much. That'll be quite enough of that. Cirkus is thoroughly seaworthy, I have a brand new survey that says so and she's certainly not gonna need any of that kind of treatment.' They both laugh, Trevor winking at me. 'And I'd appreciate it greatly if you didn't insult my girl, gentlemen. Especially when she's listening. She's got to get us a long way today.'

We duck through the saloon door and down the step.

Sally is at the galley stove, pouring hot water onto coffee. 'And Sally.. Sally, this is Trevor. Trevor, Sally. Sally couldn't come to your party. So she's come to this one..'

'Hi, Sally,' he smiles, kissing her cheek.

'Hallo,' she returns quietly, looking a little embarrassed we've disturbed her wake up. Sally is feeling the most nervous. This is her school holiday. She talked about scary last night, never before in a small boat at sea. Lucy hadn't helped, launching into long declarations of full-moon and esoteric aspects, making it definitely the worst possible time. Pete dismissed it as 'complete bollocks' and I, more subtly stressed favourable tides and wind direction and how safe is the boat.

She shuffles over to the table with her coffee. There's not exactly anywhere private when you've just got out of bed, so not the best for introductions. Lucy meanwhile on the sofa, is completely dead to the world.

'That's Lucy, I told you about. As you can see,.. I'll introduce you later.'

'Hey Lucy.' He grins, raising an eyebrow. She is unmoved.

'Here, let me show you to the quarters.' I move his bag into the fore-cabin. 'I'll put this in the fo'c's'le for now, and we'll sort out the sleeping arrangements later. The three of us can sleep in the saloon so that the women can have some modesty in here. Pete and Sally are using it but we'll put everything we don't need in here for now. Is that okay, you two?' Bubbles pushes past to sit on the bed and confirm it. 'Make yourself at home Trevor, there's loads of food in the cupboards. We'll have breakfast once we get underway.. You better have the grand tour first, so you'll remember where everything is.' Sidling around Pete and bags on the floor, I lead him around the boat, with broad gestures, we open the doors and point. 'How long is it since you've seen all this? Toilet head and shower, all working now.. Oh, and the locker with all the batteries, electrics, bilge pumps etc.' He sticks his head around doors and peers into cupboards.

'She's looking beautiful, Will. It must be two years since I've seen her and I'd forgotten that wonderful shape, these heavy timbers. She's really built, isn't she?'
'Yeh. She is. A proper little ship. Did I tell you, I got onto the museum in Liverpool. They couldn't tell me very much more but apparently they've dug up some old drawings and shipwright's plan. They say we can copy them if I go up there. I don't know if I'll get the chance but maybe if anybody's passing we could pick 'em up.'
He's still opening doors and turning over contents. 'Yeh. I was always impressed, but hey, doubly so. She looks great.'
We move up into the wheelhouse. Like everyone he immediately fondles a signal flag. 'That's such a nice touch, isn't it? Have you used 'em yet?' He grins and passes on.
'Yeh. Didn't you notice the Blue Peter up the mast?'
He looks out through the windscreen at the top of the mast. 'Nice touch. Is that for me?'
'Of course. All aboard.. for lucky departures.'
'Radio work now?' He moves over to it, hung on the back wall.
'God, it's such an antique, this thing, Will. Is it working?'

'Yeh. It works. Take a look up the mast. I've had to put up another twenty foot aerial on top. We'll have to watch it in a high wind. It's so long and bendy, it'll poke your eye out if you're standing on the back deck!'

'Good old Pye Cambridge,' he taps the casing. 'These things shouldn't still exist. I bet it cuts across every frequency there is when you start transmitting. It's illegal now you know?'

'I know, I know.' I'm defensive. 'But listen, I'm not interested in having social intercourse. If we're in trouble and want help, I don't care who hears!'

'Yeh, I guess so,' he agrees. 'Bet it needs a small nuclear power plant to run it though, doesn't it?'

'Yeh, the lights really dim when I test it. It's amazing what you can pick up though. I got some ham broadcasting from Thailand the other night.'

'And you could've answered him too..' Then to Pete, 'Some people have satellite navigation. Will has an aerial that'll touch passing ones.' With a serious edge, he turns a sardonic grin at me. 'Well, as long as it works if we need it.'

We step up the four stairs through the rear hatch door and onto the stern deck. Trevor continues to look around, checking and asking,.. does it work, is it okay? I'm happy he does. I need to share the responsibility and the butterflies rising. It was late last night when Pete and Sally arrived. Too late and too dark. Instead we sat by the fire, catching up. That seemed better anyway, I was happy to relax and forget about it for a while. Everything has tested over long hours but that's nothing. The next few down to the sea will be testing. It's one thing pootling about in rivers and estuaries, the sea is something completely else. An element you can't predict. Things break and that's a risk you have to,.. no,.. want to take. Alongside very present agitation, keep checking, keep urging, grease this, prime that. I'm sure I'll get used to it. Departure cranks the pressure. Have I done this or that? Lists are pinned everywhere, bright red ticks almost complete columns. That must mean something! But there's always something else? We have to have something to worry about, don't we? If it's not practical it's time. Though that must get better, I'm free and can go whenever I like and take as much time as I like. It's not the same for them and getting a good crew is vital for this first part. I have to fit in with their schedules. Pete and Trevor are two of the very few I know have the right stuff. But they both work full time. I've got them now because it's Easter holiday and that's for four days clear. We have to do it now or wait months to get them again. I thought about paying someone, a skipper like the guy we hired for Trevor's barge. I've decided, if it comes to that, I'll do it.

I glance at my watch. 'Come on then, let's get ready. Are you okay, Trevor? D'you need a rest? 'Cause I don't need you to start with. Pete and Sally can cast off and get us underway.'
'No, I'll be fine. Plenty of time for that. I always like this bit anyway.'
'Okay, I'm sorry to rush you but we have got to get off. And now.' Water is rising along the far dock wall. A creamy strip of rubbish particles marks the last tide and the water is more than half-way.
'It's coming up fast.' On our side it's one step to the top of the quay. I call down through the saloon skylight. 'So everybody.. Underway in ten minutes, yes?'
Pete appears, his head and shoulders out through the fo'c's'le hatch. 'I'm ready, skipper.'
We walk back along the deck with Trevor tugging at the stanchions. 'We're gonna need a safety line of some sort between the mast and the wheelhouse. Just something to clip onto if it gets rough. Have you got any harness?'
'Yeh, I made some up with rope and shackles. I'll show you.'

'Are you seriously going to tow that dinghy all the way to France, Will?'
'Oh heavens, yes. Shit, I'd forgotten all about it. We'll have to bring her on board and put her on the deck. Pete!' He's yawning and stretching in the hatchway. 'Will you come up and help, we need a bit of hauling muscle!'
'Comin', guvnor! Just let me put me workmen's gear on.'

I untie and bring the dinghy alongside. Using the boom, we rope lift her up and out of the water, over the stanchions and onto the deck. Upside down across the deck she looks redundant, taking more space than I imagined. It's crowded up here, ropes, dinghy and its little mast, my bicycle and the sail canvas. Quite like a proper working boat. The dinghy tips to one side as I tie it down. You imagine a place for stowaways aboard ship. They always pick the lifeboat. A safe and dry hideout under the tarp, in a lifeboat, on a lifeboat. How safe do you want to be?
Sally appears with two mugs. 'This is getting cold you two. Do you want it up here?'

Exactly on cue, Lucy is standing on the back deck, coat and hat, little rucksack on her back. 'I..err, I'm just erm,.. just going to the shops,' she stuttered.
I don't believe it. 'Lucy, you don't have time for that now, we're leaving, it'll have to wait.'
'No, no, can't wait.. must go now.'
She is impossible. 'Lucy, don't do this now. We have got to go now to catch the tide. We've got to leave now.' Surely this is convincing but she just stares. 'What do you need? We've got everything here. Can't it wait?'
She's confused, furtively looking to us and around the dock and the water. Then without warning she makes a leap for the quay, tripping hard on the top step, scrambling the last half-

metre up the wall. She looks hurt and I skip the deck to help. She is picking herself up and running, shouting over her shoulder. 'I've got to go to the shops!' Within seconds she has run the quay and disappeared over the lock bridge.
The others look bemused. 'I don't believe that girl. She is impossible.' It takes a few moments to collect my thoughts. I should grab the opportunity but has she got money, can she get home? What on earth was I thinking. My watch says we've less than three hours to get down to the estuary. We can't wait. Eventually I say, 'Okay. Look we'll wait fifteen minutes. Sally, how about another coffee? Pete and Trevor, let's do a last check. Make sure everything is stowed and locked away. The dinghy's okay now,.. I'll put up the safety-line. If she's not back in fifteen, we're leaving without her.'

Coffee and checks and every few moments I looked to see if she is coming. Even as we cast off, the engine pumping as we drift to the middle the dock, I can't quite believe it.

SHIPS LOG - MV CIRKUS - 19.4. 07.15. Hull - Albert Dock.
Everything Done. Everything Checked and Ready. Crew installed, one missing gone to the shops?. Navigator and Engineer Happy. Embarkation – Humber estuary next.
06.00 WEATHER: All Easterly Areas FAIR. FORCE 4-5 N.WESTERLY OCCASIONAL SHOWERS. SEA: MODERATE GOOD VISIBILITY.
COURSE: HumberReaches/Estuary/SpernHead/120°North Sea/little bit South!
COMMENTS: Tide and wind in our favour. Set fair. Odd feeling about Lucy. What else to do?.. Except go. Tally Ho!

Chapter Seven
what good is this? Oi tight shadows?

Out and under the Humber Bridge the world is very big indeed from the deck of a forty-five foot motor-sailer. The one hundred and eighty degree sky is accentuated just at the moment you pass underneath. We are dwarfed by the structure, so narrow and high, a pencil line drawn on the cloud. Our perspective makes the white, arrow straight strip warp as if to fit the curvature of the earth. Completing my rope coiling labour of love, I marvel at the sublime highway. Stretching my arms up and out, I measure the scale. It feels like a gesture of homage to the god of civil engineers who dreamt of spanning huge expanse. Dreams of life on a small boat, insignificant by comparison but even our vulnerable floating dot might appear grandiose to some.

The tide is full and high already, the river more than a mile wide mass of surging water. Our chart shows broad hidden sandbanks and a deeper channel winding through. Pure theory out here. With the exception of an occasional marker-buoy, there is little indication of safe depth. The river moves as one enormous body limited only by far away banks.

We're a little late and the tide has turned. The outgoing ebb following the full moon highs is an unstoppable force, carrying us like so much flotsam in a race toward the sea. With what little steerage is possible in the torrent, we stick to our estimate of where the deep channel should be. The red echo-sounder flashing dots, joined in a vertical strip read over ten fathoms. Sixty plus feet of water to tempt temporary faith.
'Good job we're not trying to go the other way.' Pete peers from the open wheelhouse door.
Trevor is crouched on the deck at the door on the other side. 'It's amazing isn't it. The current is so strong it's creating a kind of flowing swell like it's overtaking itself. Look, you can see the surface contorting into wavelet eddies just by the speed of it.'

We are careering along at the edge of control. Pete, at the wheel, is being forced to keep up the engine revs, constantly adjusting the throttle back and forth, simply to maintain a faster flow of water over the rudder. It feels crazy, it's fast enough but to steer you have to go faster. Without it we would swing and slew like a piece of driftwood. Already the bridge is receding to an angle where I can see dinky trucks and cars in a slow motion crawl.
Closer down below, a more pressing sight looms into view. A coaster I spotted in the distance behind us a few minutes ago, is now passing underneath the bridge. She is a big ship and, with some tonnage aboard, deep in the water and making heavy headway behind a huge bow wave.
I duck into the wheelhouse. 'Have you seen this, Pete? Coming up behind.'
'Yeh. What d'you think we should do?'
'It's coming so fast, she'll overtake us in a few minutes. I don't think the channel's wide enough here for us to stay safely out of the way. Look, you can already see the wash she's making. I

don't like the idea of getting hit by that. We've enough to stay in a straight line as it is.'

Staring hard through the back window of the wheelhouse I watch the ship gain on us. 'I'd like to pull over as far as possible. She's making a hell of a lick and I bet they've got no control in this either.'

'We could put the sails up to make 'em give way'. Pete is naïve.

'And what could they do? It won't make any difference to them. Wouldn't fancy our chances, would you?'

Sitting on the deck by the wheelhouse door, intending solidarity next to him inside. The channel ahead is marked unevenly spaced green and red pylons. They seem to show a large bend to our left. We've so little steerage in the torrent, our best course might be to miss the bend and carry straight on out of the channel. You have to suppose that the coaster, because it needs deeper water, will have to stick more closely.

'Well listen, how about this? When you can, just before this bend, pull over to the right. Let's get right out of the channel. There's plenty enough water here. Look, you could do it past this marker. And then the beast can pass. We just keep an eye on the Decca for the depth.'

Trevor puts his head in through the opposite door. 'Not too hard though, Pete. This tidal race'll swing us right round.'

'Yes, if that starts to happen, Pete, turn away more to the right and come about completely. You'll have to open the throttle hard and point her directly into the flow. Against it we'll have good steerage and more control and we can probably almost stand still until the ship passes. There's plenty of room if it goes wrong. Just make sure it goes wrong over there out of her light!' I point in a broad sweep over to our right. Looking back along the deck to the coaster she is making on us fast, probably still a hundred yards but it's difficult to tell how far. We are so low on the water, perspective makes her look huge.

Pete begins to steer us starboard and we pass out of the rough buoyed line, our eyes fixed firmly on the red wavering dots.

'Seven Fathoms!' Trevor calls. Unnecessary since we're all watching but an irresistible habit. 'Plenty of water here!'

The coaster is closing and increasing in size. Faster as she closes, her bow wave looks bigger than we are.

'Get a move on, Pete!' He opens the throttle at my urging and immediately and awkward we slew sideways.

Feel the vibration as we rise to the coaster's displacement. The noise of her engines amplified through the water. They're not slowing for anything even if they're able. She is bearing down on us at three of four times our speed and even seems to veer toward us as we move out of the channel. It looks like she might not take the bend and from our position having swung around she'll be coming straight for us.

'More throttle, Pete. Come on, get us out of here! Over there..'

He pulls the handle fully down and in the last inches of its arc the engine responds loudly, increasing its bass revs to a high pitch. The bow rises immediately and we surge forward. Crab like moving away from the coaster's line, time stands still. We begin looking up to see her superstructure. From my place on deck I squint hard to see if I can spot any signs of life in their wheelhouse. There's nothing, no acknowledgement, no friendly hands waving, only a row of faceless dark windows staring cold straight ahead.

We rise on their bow wave as she thunders past. All too quickly the next wave of her cresting wake hits us broadside with a loud slapping against the hull. A sheet of water sent across the deck rocks us violently. I stand up to grab the handrail on top of the wheelhouse as we spin against the direction of these new waves. We pitch into four or five that strike hard and easily bring more water on deck. Gushing rivers weave back toward the stern. Everything accelerates as the Doppler sucks our motion around. She passes and we are rocked but safe.

'Ignorant bastards!' Pete yells up at them out of the door, his voice quickly lost in the noise of engines and rushing water. The wheel spinning briefly from his hands with the shock of another high wave of her wake. 'I thought they were supposed to give way or move over or something if they were overtaking. What happened to the rules of the road!?' he shouts after them, and then a relieved smile breaks across his face. 'The fucking bullies never changed course once!'
As the washing rollers calm, Cirkus settles to an even keel and we sigh collective relief.
While Pete yells a few more abusive rants and I drop my forehead to rest on the rail between my hands.

Trevor, hanging on to the opposite rail above the wheelhouse intones across the roof. 'Here lies the body of Michael O'Day. Who died maintaining his right of way. He was right, dead right, as 'e sailed along. But 'e's just as dead as if 'e were wrong.'

'Very nice, Trevor,' Raising my head I cast a wry smile at him across the roof. 'A lovely recitation. What's that, The Old Man And The Sea?'
'Well it wasn't Hemmingway. I don't think anybody knows. Famous Anon, I should think.'
We rock more gently, up and over the spreading wake until it dissipates. Slowly Pete steers us around full circle and we continue slewing sideways in the current, crabbing our way back into the channel, narrowly careering past a red pylon and resuming the course.
The tension broken I examine my soaked jeans and look up to meet Trevor's smile.

'Well, I've got my own bit of doggerel to summarise the thirty-one rules and Regulations for the Prevention of Collision at Sea. And it goes, the only rule of the road I know, if 'e's a bigger bugger 'an you, you can bet ya life 'e's comin' through!'

Passing the roof-rail hand to hand I walk around to the stern deck and drop lightly down the steps into the wheelhouse. Inside, Sally is standing rigid in the corner, arms up and white knuckles showing how hard she is still gripping the ceiling rails. At her feet are two of the red melamine cups and a pool of coffee on the floor. Bubbles is paddling in the coffee, tongue flapping and wagging her tail.

The sky is brighter, clouds breaking, allowing the sun to cast deep misty rays to race across the water. The coaster, receding fast and weaving its way through the last channel markers, is the only vessel on the wide estuary opening before us. As the expanse of sea grows we shrink smaller. On a faraway shore now to our right and behind, chimneys and factories just visible. Pretty soon any sense of human activity gives way to low dunes and salt-flats. Through the binoculars there is little or no feature. Bleak and windswept, fading to indistinct above rising waves. Somewhere over there a sound like hidden hordes of geese chattering arrives broken and mixed in the stiffening breeze.

We decide that putting the sails up will help the steering and make the most of the wind. Trevor and I set to unfurling them along the boom and the forestay. Pulling on the halyard ropes to raise the red canvas is such a magic moment and the wind immediately rises to magnify it.

It happens like that, in imagination or just fresh awareness of power. As the sail tightens Cirkus leans smoothly to the weight. Feeling the acceleration as the bow dips and the first plunging spray climbs over the guardrail. Then, at last, the engine shut to idle reveals a focus of wind and water, flapping topsail and creaking rope on timber.

Sailing. Flying, skimming the tops. Really for the first time, feel her take to the wind. Truly wonderful and we relax into it, the tensions of the morning beginning to slip away.
Trevor and I play at shortening and lengthening the halyards to the boom and the foot of the foresail, maximising the wind's effect. Creaking and stretching, dipping into the waves, leaning with the force and picking up speed. There is space to manoeuvre and freedom to play.

Far out into the estuary, the prominent landmark of Spurn Head with its lighthouse is visible to our left. A long land spit trailing from the north bank, a marker where the river ends and the North Sea proper begins. Here impossibly the world gets more flat and the sky more enormous. Safe from shallows and into deeper dark green water we sail into waves growing in stature. White tips stammer and break throwing tiny clouds of spray in the air. Cirkus plunges and hops, her jaunty lean with the wind buffeted by the new swell. Tom was right, she sails like an old bathtub really, crabwise according to the wind direction, but now with the wind almost fully behind, we begin to turn out in deeper more determined sea. A new feeling like an arctic ocean cold and a driven blast is hard and constant. It fills the strong red sails to bursting and she fairly flies.

Solid and heavy, charging the water with her four tons of ballast, she steers like a bucking bronco. Low in the water, almost round at the front, round at the back, what would you expect? However lumpy, sailing out on a day like today, with a hard wind and scudding clouds.. And just then the sun breaks through a gap once more. All of our own, a shaft with defined edges, highlights us, making it perfect.

The blustering wind is right on our tail as we turn a little more south-east. The water is thicker and heavier, darker green to cold blue and grey. White wave crests splash our quarter and we heave through a swell beginning to feel like real open sea.

There are no other vessels in sight, the coaster having long disappeared behind the headland going north. A flock of geese put up over sand-flats in the distance. Flying low arrows above the waves they eventually pass in front of us, stragglers trailing away until we leave them behind. A couple of seagulls come for a look, hovering around the mast-head with tumbling acrobatics. One lands momentarily on the very top but the freshening swell bouncing us makes the perch impossible, pitched and toppling, until its spreading wings catch up-draught. The two of them turn away and as if wishing us goodbye head inland along our wake.

Beyond the margin, the estuary astern and the tidal flow that bore us, dispersed into spreading sea, features on the land become distant impression. Occasional floating plant streamers, a fading evidence. Coastal spits, fringes and sandbars recede.

Trevor calls the course for Inner Dowsing, a weather station tower twenty miles out to the east. That will be our first seaward mark and when we make it we'll turn firm right and head due south. Once there and far enough out into the North Sea, the course we set will allow us a pretty straight southerly track to avoid the shallow waters of the Wash. The next land we should sight after altering course, will be around Cromer on the eastern edge of the north Norfolk coast. If all goes well, we'll decide then whether to stop for the night a few miles beyond in the port of Yarmouth or pass by and continue through the night, down the east coast. We do have everything we need to go all the way to Ramsgate, ritual embarkation corner of England. There to re-fuel and check everything again before hopping the channel to France.

That is three optimistic days away. I suspect that by dark tonight, having been sailing since early this morning, our inexperience will be telling. We'll be tired and more than happy to tie up to some land and stop.

SHIPS LOG - MV CIRKUS - 19.4. Midday Humber Approaches
Made Spurn without difficulty. Little longer and more exciting traffic than anticipated

Course 120° – Just South! Inner Dowsing next mark. Everything working; Engine ancillaries working well. Cooling water pumping in and out in a nice regular gush! Sails and rigging working - a treat!

Navigator and Engineer happy.

WEATHER: FAIR occasional squalls. Wind FORCE 5 North West & VARIABLE 6. Occasional blustery rain in the wind. Baro 998 falling slowly

SEA Moderate to swelling and choppy.

Visibility   Good

Chapter Eight
what good is this? Who aids to sight

There is rain in the wind mixed with spray flying up and over the bow. A faint rainbow arcs over where the land and estuary are far behind. Our heading is good, we are making excellent progress, everyone seems relaxed and enjoying the cruise. Low level cloud breaks over us firing a shot of sunlight on to the deck. Sitting in the pool of sun, leaning back against the wheelhouse windscreen, expansive and optimistic, I haul and pay the halyards. Each pull and release affects our speed and the rake of our heel to the strengthening wind. Trevor comes up on deck, this time with his camera and Sally joins in, fur collar turned up and bobble hat donned against the cold.
'I think I can I do that too?' she smiles.
'Yes, look, you can sit here with your back against the windscreen. It's okay it'll take your weight. And just slowly pull in or release the rope. Watch the top of the sail, there, and if it begins to flap or feather,.. look you can see it now,.. look it's just flapping at the top there.. If it does that, just pull its rope in a little. Here I'll do this one for the main and you can do the foresail. Gently though, look you can see the effect if I pull it in too much.' I pull it quite hard and Cirkus heels, leaning against the weight of the wind as the threaded rope tightens the sail, pulling the boom across. She leans further and we cut a

cresting wave. A delightful cascade of spray fountains up into the air over the bow, showering Trevor in photographer's pose. He is still for a moment, surprised and dripping and then climbs, hanging onto ropes, balancing up the sloping deck to a new secure position.

'Would you like to warn me if you're going to do that again?' He laughs, runnels trailing from his oilskin.

'Sorry, guvner. Just schooling the crew.' And then back to Sally, leaning in close against the windscreen out of the wind. 'If we wanted more speed we'd keep it like that, but it's not very comfortable so we'll just release it a bit.' I slowly inch out the halyard and Cirkus comes back almost to the level, the Gaff and shackles chattering release from tension.

'Here, are you ready to try with both?' I pass her the other rope. 'So this one is for the mainsail, it goes back to the boom behind us, and that one is the foresail.' She takes them, smiling the instant she feels weight through the rigging. Pete at the wheel, smiles in unison, joining the intimacy through the glass.

'Say Breeze!' Trevor snaps the moment and we smile obediently, Pete waving frantically through the windscreen.

'Isn't it easy? I didn't think it would be this easy.' Sally sounds full of naïve surprise.

'Well, the wind is making it easy. It's very favourable coming across the quarter from behind. It's not always as easy as this. If we were going against it we'd have a bit more work to do.'

We sit close together, Sally growing in confidence, pulling and playing the ropes, me nodding approval.

After a while, I said, 'What do you think? Can you manage if I go and get us some lunch?'

'Well, nobody's very far away, are they,' she says genially. 'What do you think?'

'I think you're doing wonderfully. If anything happens that you're not sure of, just release that one and let the boom go. And shout,.. shout for help. One thing you do have to watch though, is that no one is in the way when you do it, otherwise the boom might hit them and they'll be over the side. It's a big heavy bit of timber and with the wind blowing hard it'll swing fast. Just yell out before you do it. Boom Hoe!, or Look-Out or something. Okay?'

'I'll try,' she says, an edge of doubt. I'm sure she'll be fine, Pete is watching closely from inside, so I walk around the deck to go below. Once down in the wheelhouse I see Trevor cross the deck and sit down beside her.

'Great, that's the crew organised. I'll go and have a snooze now.'

'Don't you bloody dare,' Pete playfully asserts, grinning. 'Who d'ya think you are, the bloody captain?'

'As the bloody chef I'm going down to make us some lunch. Just you stick to your duties, you scurvy crew-dog.'

'Yeh. Well get down there, ya swab-bastard.' He feigns a kick at me as I open the door.

Downstairs in the galley, the wheelhouse door closed behind, the atmosphere is instantly tranquil. A separate world, insulated by heavy timbers, almost disconnected from rushing wind and water. Sympathetic rattles with the dampened beat of the engine or an occasional wave shudder. Sunlight shafts through the skylight and portholes swing smoothly back and forth across the room, leaping on random waves.

I'm immediately aware how tense I am after the morning's action and breathe a deep sigh, filling my cheeks and blowing air in a long slow release. I stretch up my arms in the middle of the skylight, cracking shoulder blades. 'This is better.'

Opening a couple of cans of soup into a pot on the cooker, I set to preparing lunch. Fresh bread that Trevor found on his way, salad and glasses of wine. The first of which is definitely for the chef. There's time before the pot boils to savour tranquillity and smoke a fag.

Once at the saloon table, wine glass and cigarette alternately to hand, the tension subsides. I lean back into the cushion and gaze lazily around the room. I'm growing to love this space, my home. There is no other and here in its element there is something special about this mobile home coming into its own.
'Love that new carpet too.' I lean down to pick up a bit of mud from the corner, feeling a wave of house pride and then at the incongruity of such feelings as the bow slaps another wave outside. Settling back again, a day dream passing. Probable passages, moorings and dinners at this table by the fire. Summer is coming too and more life on deck. Outside on starlit nights, the hammock strung under the boom, softly swaying to the motion. 'Oh yes..' My reverie is almost complete as the lid of the pot clatters and I scurry to the cooker in time to save it.

Thoughts about Lucy keep entering. Did she really miss the boat or was it intentional. That look of panic as she left was real. She must have woken up and decided she couldn't come. Only she could do it that way and on evidence of her, you'd never find the real reason. Those few days together were pretty weird and I don't regret her passing. Like taking on a hitchhiker with no sense of where they are going. Some ideal of being open to new encounters made it possible. Nevertheless there's something unresolved. Never to be so, perhaps.

In the midst of lunch, taking shifts at the wheel and halyards, we sight Inner Dowsing ahead. Though still tiny on the horizon but unmistakable and we raise our glasses, filling them to congratulate ourselves on making the first mark.

'Well done, Trevor. Spot on, as ever.' We clink and tapping mine on the windscreen, Pete and Sally, windswept on the deck outside respond. Pete, struggling to balance, passes the bottle back around the door.

'We've made good time. One-thirty. We'll be there by two easy. Another five or six hours and we could be near enough to Yarmouth. By seven or eight this evening? That'll be all the light there is, but you remember we found Yarmouth at night on the barge. It's really well lit.'

'Yeh. No problem,' Trevor replies. 'As long as the weather holds we'll be fine.'

'Looks okay at the moment.' I take a long look all the way around.

'Yeh. But there were some pretty ominous looking clouds over there in the east whilst you were down below. They've cleared a bit now. It is changing a lot though,' he is craning to look out the window. 'I don't like the look of it that much and it's so unpredictable.'

'I can see blue sky over there.' I point toward the closing weather tower.

'I know, but we want to keep an eye on it. I mean look over there towards the land. There's something pretty heavy happening over there now. Look at those clouds, you wouldn't be able to see more than a mile in that. We haven't had one of those yet but in this wind, one could hit us any time. I think it's picking up a bit too, it's gone round a bit more north west.' He sticks his head out the door, looking up at the sky. 'I bet it cuts up really rough in the middle of one of those squalls and we better be ready to batten everything down if we spot one,.. 'cause it'll be on us in no time.'

'Okay, let's just keep our eyes peeled.'

As if to emphasise the point, the bow dips more heavily, catching the crest of a large wave, which sends a good sized bathfull of water flying up and over the deck, recharging Pete and Sally's glasses to a light rosé. I switch on the wipers to clear the screen. Amid much drenched laughing and giggling the two of them raise their glasses, toasting one another and us inside and then they toss the contents Cossack-style over their shoulders. We all laugh at the joke.

'Well listen, Trevor, if you're not happy, say so. This crew is supposed to be democratic, right. And anyway I need your input, you know that.'

'No it's okay, I just want us to be sharp that's all. Let's not relax too much. I don't have to tell you, you know what it's like out here and how quickly it can change.'

Inner Dowsing is coming up, maybe another half mile. It's so tall and standing isolated in the unbroken seascape. Even at this distance we see detail clearly. An odd structure, solid concrete like some huge monolith sentinel. A stack of Martello-towers, completely alone at sea and miles from anywhere.

Trevor is busy, the chart for this sector of the journey, laid out on the wide shelf in front of us. He is marking on it the ideal track from Inner Dowsing, south. Laying off the actual heading, taken account of wind leeway, our speed over the ground and the tidal direction. South and in these conditions, with the wind almost directly behind as we turn, we'll make little compensation for the course. The tide goes north on the way in, south on the way out. For today, it will affect speed rather than direction. I read in the navigation manual about its effect on the east-west tidal stream in the English Channel. A high tide can alter a ship's position by twelve miles in four hours. That'll get you pretty lost.

With our new edition of the Reeds giving minute detail of every buoy and tidal stream, the charts and tools, compasses, parallel rules and compass rose, the shelf in front looks set for seriously academic exercise. A millimetre out on this scale would find us off target. Trevor is wonderfully boffin-like, almost to the point of tedium. I love him. That said, he is soon happy with completion of his work, watching in anticipation our approach to the tower.

'It's quite mysterious, isn't it? Looks like a hybrid of an H.G.Wells nineteen fifties space rocket and one of those Buckminster Fuller cities at sea.'

'Yeh. I wonder what it's like living out here.'

'Pretty bleak.'

The thing grows proportion as we edge nearer and finally, as near as we dare, we're almost in its shadow. It towers high above, the sea crashing into enormous legs disappearing below the waves. I step out on deck to close-haul the rigging as we begin to turn away. With Trevor taking the wheel, Cirkus rolls hard as we change tack, the boom swings violently against the force and weight of a new wind. The red sail ripples slack, resting suspended for the briefest moment until the next blast snaps it taught. The foresail likewise feathers and flaps until I rethread the halyard through the blocks and across the other side of the deck. Back at the wheelhouse door, readjusted ropes in my hand, I stand for a moment looking up at the edifice. After the anticipation of reaching it, it's surprising how boring it is. Taking on the track south that I have been wanting for so long, I'm happy to turn away and forget it.

Just as we begin to pull away though, I spot someone, a figure high at a balustrade, waving at us. Picking up the binoculars from the shelf inside and tying off the ropes, I lean onto the roof to steady my arm, looking back to focus on the lone figure.

He's waving, making large arcs with his arms fully extended. Maybe we are his main attraction of the day, a friend a long way from home. I return his wave and for a minute or two we stare at each other, an anonymous compliment across grey and swelling sea.

Chapter Nine
what good is this? Gosh what idiots?

The hollow Winds begin to blow
The Clouds look black and the Glass is low
Last night the Sun went pale to bed
the Moon in haloes hid her head
Look out my lads! A wicked Gale
with heavy Rain will soon assail.

No one would question the supreme importance, when undertaking a sea voyage, of at least a passing knowledge of weather lore and more, to recognise and appreciate change. Former mariners had to rely on their eyes, their instincts and the result of bitter experience. They composed wonderfully explicit tales and limericks to preserve their art. Red Sky at Night,.. there are a many more, lost and redundant.

Frequent radio and television bulletins, daily synoptic charts issued by the Met Office. If I had a Fax I could get them sent. With such a wealth of information, there's little excuse for ignorance. That's what the manual says anyway. It should say, however, that the conditions defined in these bulletins ostensibly refer to past and present. Satellite views and computer models predict and only estimate future trends. Meteorologists often take stick for inaccuracy but it should be said in their defence, even if they are unwilling to admit, that despite all the technology, they are still confined to educated guessing.

What does all that mean? As the march of science doesn't filter down. In the family home I remember we had a strange, unfathomable device hanging on the wall by the front door. With great weight and expectation my father would rap his knuckle on it every morning, saying 'Glass is going up!' or 'Glass is going down!' I'm not sure what he thought he would glean, other than some sort of security-blanket habit. Perhaps he did know something and it would help him to decide to take the umbrella. All my tender age understood was that somehow if it was going up, that meant good, if down, that was bad. Good or bad for who or what, I had no idea. Until I bought one myself, now hanging in the wheelhouse, this was my only encounter with a barometer. Out of necessity, I understand a lot more about atmospheric pressure. I have also understood, however, that the accuracy of this instrument to impart vital future form depends entirely on where you hang the thing. Hang it in the wheelhouse in winter, when the engine slowly warms the room. In streams of condensation it's amazing how much rain it will predict. Hang it in the saloon, where the arctic stove throws warm and dry and you'll be on the deck in a blizzard whilst the barometer predicts lazy hazy days. The range is everything..

When the weather is fine and the winds blow fair
sudden changes may well come to pass
Then let no security lull prudent care
But watch well the range of the Glass

Okay but, where to hang it and glean this truth. Would it have changed the prospect if my father had left the letter-box open? Someone thinks they're valuable. When I decided that the only answer was to hang it outside, it was there for no more than a week and got stolen.

Forecasts cover a large area of land and sea, whereas a voyaging mariner in search of immediate weather news requires precise information concerning a relatively small patch. And that will also be influenced by local topography of which those bulletins take no account.

Ultimately, you are back to relying on the evidence of your eyes. Safe passage afforded by clouds and sky, sun and moon and a few anachronistic anecdotes. Have a look out of your window now. Could you say what it's going to do in a couple of hours? I bet if you can, it's already doing it..

The light is changing, heavier cloud almost touching the surface of the sea arrives rapidly, bringing a squally shower. In the midst of it a sudden freshening gust whips at the water, mixing rain and spray to lash the wheelhouse windows. There is even a bite of sleet and I slide the port door closed.

'Damn! What time is it? Switch the radio on, quick! We're missing the Shipping Forecast!'

'It's five to two.' Trevor pushes past Pete, reaching for the corner to switch on the Pye.

'Shit! We've already missed half of it!'

As the valves on the old set slowly warm up, we fade into the BBC voice.. CHANNEL LIGHT VESSEL AUTOMATIC NORTH BY EAST..

'Damn! We've missed the east coast reports, let alone the bloody forecast!'

..SCILLY. NORTH BY EAST SIX. SIX MILES   NINE NINE SEVEN FALLING MORE QUICKLY.

'Damn! Damn how stupid!' I bang my fist down onto the chart shelf. 'That was stupid! How could I have missed that?' There's a long pause, a stunned silence prompted by my outburst.

Silence hangs in the air between us, broken by the sonorous radio voice.. NINE NINE EIGHT. FALLING QUICKLY..

I stare straight ahead through the windscreen, along the deck at the blustery rain blowing in every direction, taking in the implication. How stupid can you be? The continuing radio broadcast filters back into my consciousness. I listen again, faintly hoping that something in the redundant words might be of use.. RONALDSWAY. VARIABLE 5. EIGHT MILES. ONE THOUSAND. FALLING MORE QUICKLY.. THAT'S THE END OF THE SHIPPING FORECAST..

The irony strikes that we've only just passed one of the weather stations they name in the reports. And I stood there and waved at it.
Everyone is looking at me, unmet anticipation bouncing off the walls.
Eventually composure returns, 'I'm sorry everyone, my fault. I should have set the alarm. I can't believe I forgot that. I'm sorry. That was important.'

It was important and in the following hour became more so and, quite obvious that the early morning forecast has changed. Every so often the clouds build on all sides. The quality of light changes. Slate grey with a brownish tinge like you see before it snows. In the midst of one of these the sea swell rises, cresting so that we fall down beneath the wave heights. Spray flies easily over us with dramatic slashes across the window. It's changeable and we pitch and roll and then through a calm patch. I'm aware of our mood changing. Sally looking more uncomfortable, Pete is tense, Trevor more academic, pouring over the charts.

We manage lighter moments, spotting a school of dolphin about half an hour after missing the forecast. Trailing us for quite a while, they are pure joy that finds you. There must have been nine or ten of them running through the swell, leaping fully out of the water, performing through wave crests and rolling high in the air before spectacular splashing re-entries. Sticking close together like an inseparable family. Whilst we watched, in the far distance, twenty miles away north east, is a really heavy bank of cloud. Although we've been through squally showers since leaving Dowsing, the sky is still regularly broken overhead with blue patches. Under that distant cloud, dark translucent dust like sheets extend right down to the sea. It is still reasonably clear ahead but those clouds are thick, black and high. Ominous, for the moment quite far away but there is heavy weather all around. We all saw and noted it. We agree to wait and see. After all we're going so well, maybe even ahead of time, actually because of the weather. The wind, right on our tail, is as strong as we've felt it. Occasionally so much so, I worry about the sails, marvelling that the canvas, let alone the stitching can take it. Trevor calculates that the tide, still with us, has probably added as much as five or six knots to our speed.

But there is creeping ambivalence and over the next half an hour, it grows. Having missed the forecast we've only eyes and gut feelings. I don't like the feel of mine since seeing those clouds. A nagging sensation that horizons are closing in. The real horizons maybe but it's more like mine. The wind is stronger still, more gusty and fractious, Force Six North Westerly, maybe Seven. Heavier, dark clouds to the east are beginning to back behind us. They are building and the sea swelling, breaking more often, throwing white fringed crests high in the air to be blown across us. The sea has changed colour, now matching the sky. Cold and grey like menacing steel.

We are holding the course. With wind astern there is little weight or force across the beam and Cirkus rolls only a little, riding it well. When I'm sure we are all feeling the ambivalence I decide it's time to talk more seriously.

'What are the choices?' said Pete. 'Can we turn round and go back?'

'Trevor? What do you think?' I want to hear what everybody's got to say. We may be democratic but it will be me who makes the decision.

'I'm not sure,' Trevor begins. 'We could turn around. The tide'll be coming up for slack now. There's nowhere to go though but back into to the Humber. The tide would turn in our favour in an hour or two, but we'd have to beat it straight into that wind and it doesn't look like it's going to get any less.' He pauses for a long time, staring at the chart. 'The wind might keep the tide out. We could be out here for a long time trying to get back in that way.' Rubbing his forehead, his eyes are closed.

'We're about forty five miles out from the mouth of the Humber.' He continues. 'At a conservative guess, against this wind, it could take us nine or ten hours to get back into the estuary and up river. That takes us to midnight, one o'clock. I can't think it'll be much before that. The tide will be well on its way out by then, so we'd be going against the wind and the tide for the last few hours. That means when we get there, we'd have to find shallow channels in the dark and then find a mooring.' He pauses again and then begins to shake his head.

'We don't know what the weather's going to do. If it builds any more, when we get into that shallow water at the mouth of the Humber, it could cut up really rough.'

In my concentration on Trevor and the chart, I miss a larger cresting wave coming at us. Two waves from different directions collide directly into and over us. They topple and foam hitting us broadside, pluming in the air and covering the deck in a blanket of spray. Everyone grabs at something to hold. In that one pitching wave an edge of fear rises. I switch on the wipers, clearing the screen. Pete expresses the edge.

'Shit, we're not gonna stay out here if it gets any rougher, are we? I say we head for a port right now.'

Trevor taps the chart, maintaining business. 'We're off the Mabelthorpe coast and it's all flat sands and dunes. There are no ports. The next obvious port is Kings Lynn.' He picks up the Reeds, flicking through to find the page. 'High tide at Lynn won't be until.. yes here it is, eight-fifty five.' Licked finger peels the pages. 'It's very shallow in there through the Wash and it says here you can't get in more than two hours either side of high water. Along the coast a bit, Hunstanton, no, Wells,.. Blakeney maybe, but no I think it's the same story for all of those little ports along that north Norfolk coast. They are all shallow, with only enough water on the top of the highest tides.. We've got one of those but it's still touch and go whether there'll be enough water until you get near the top o' the tide.'

He stops again, cupping his nose and eyes, as though waiting for inspiration.

'Well that's okay, isn't it? What's wrong with that?' Pete interrupts, eyes fixed on his watch. 'That means we can get in there by sixish. That's only three hours and a bit. How far is it?' He steps up to look at the chart. 'Looks about the same distance to me. How long will it take us to get there, Trev?'

'Well it's over five hours, actually, it's high at eight-fifty five not eight and, at our present speed,.. yeh, I should think, five hours.'

'Well at least that's getting us off. That's it then. That's perfect isn't it? Let's go there.'

Trevor is calculating. 'Wait a minute, Pete.' I say watching Trevor's eyebrows rise. 'Let's hear him out. Go on, Trevor, got any more?'
'Well yes. I don't think that's a very good idea..'
'Why not!.. You said..' Pete interrupts, instantly combative.
I stop it. 'Pete, let him speak.. And pull on that rope will you, the sail's feathering.'
'..Because it's going to be really shallow in there for the next good few hours. With this wind across that shallow water,.. and we'll have to go through it to get there. It could really whip it up into a high sea.'
Pete is holding the rope through the half closed door. 'It's getting pretty high out here now isn't it?'
'No it isn't, not yet. This is nothing, Pete. Not compared to how it can be. This is just a bit of swell and a bit of wind and the water here is deep enough. If it picks up anymore and we move into shallow water, you'll see..'
'So, Trevor,' I intervene for the sake of calm, with an eye on Sally who is beginning to look decidedly unhappy. 'What do you think?'
'I think we should stay on course and ride it out.'
'But look at those clouds, man.' Pete is at him again. 'We're in for a fucking storm. What then?'
'Pete. Please! Let him finish.'
Trevor, quite purposefully calm, turns to me. 'I think we should stick to the course as best we can. Stay in the deeper water out here. Make it to Yarmouth and see if we can get in there. The approach is deeper, there's a better harbour, it's designed for big ships so the entrance is nice and wide and, you can go right inside,.. there's more shelter.'
Pete is about to react again. 'Look!' I say, cutting him off. 'We are not going to argue. As far as possible we're going to try to agree. And if we can't, I'm going to make the final decision.

Okay?' I wait for him to cool. 'Now, Pete. What do you want to say?'

'I want to say.. I want to get the fuck out of here as fast as possible. This is no joy ride anymore and I don't like the look of this weather.'

'Yeh, okay, understood. But have you got a proposal as to how we might do that?'

'Yes, man. I say we go for the nearest port whatever. And right now that's Kings Lynn.' The sail is feathering again and this time he slides the door back and climbs half way out to pull the rope. 'By the looks of these clouds.. Here come and take a look at this fucking' lot..' It is raining quite hard. 'I say we either turn back and take our chances or go to the nearest haven and get the fuck out of here.'

'Okay,' I say. 'That it?'

'Yeh, it fucking is, man.' He brings the ropes back inside and stands silent and rigid, staring at his hands.

'Okay.' I try to say coolly. 'Sally? Do you want to say anything?' She looks uncomfortable, staring into Pete's back. 'You know I don't know anything about it, Will. This is rough enough for me. I go along with what Pete says.'

While we're speaking heavy clouds are building around us. A dark one ahead looks absolutely full of rain. As we enter it the base appears almost to be touching the waves, a solid curtain of water falling. The sea is made quieter in the rain but as we hit the middle of the squall the wind swings around in gusts catching the sails from different angles. They rattle loose, flapping wildly, alternately feathering and snapping taught. Cirkus heels over against the weight and as we hit a wave awkwardly the deck and wheelhouse are covered in foam and cascading spray.

'I want to go out and fix that rigging.' I say steadily. 'Will one of you take the wheel? I'll come back in a minute and we'll carry on talking.' Trevor takes over and Pete holds the ropes ready to pass them out.

I step out of the starboard door. It's more sheltered this side in the lee of the boat. But outside it's obvious that the wind is howling now from different directions. Air is stinging cold, filled with flying rain and spray. Instantly soaked, I clamber back to put on my oilskin, adding the safety harness. Without looking at anyone, I step back out into it.

Hand over hand on the rail reaches the front of the wheelhouse and I clip my shackle on to the safety line. Cirkus, with little power and steerage is turning awkwardly in the swell. Pitching into waves, the sails flap wildly. Gathering ropes I signal to Trevor to open the throttle, he does and we settle back to the line. Then the pitching is suddenly violent and, the deck swimming in water, it's difficult to keep my footing. I make it up to the foresail and begin tying it taut to the mast. If it's going to be like this there's no point in relying on it for power. If we have to steer in different directions to meet the swell, it'll just be more trouble than it's worth to keep coming outside to change tack. I reef it to reduce its size and then pull it in hard so that it forms a taught straight line between the mast and the bow. It's a steadying sail now and may help with rolling, beyond that it's useless. Hanging tight to the mast I stand up to watch the mainsail feather and flap. If I can organise the halyard ropes and thread them through to the wheelhouse we might still get a bit of help from it. The gaff and top halyards, in fact all the ropes, are loose and flailing. With stiffening cold fingers, fumbling one by one, I shorten and tie them off. Whilst there I check the dinghy, ducking down as heavy wave crashes into us.

I crawl hands and knees back along the deck, the wind whipping spray to bite my face. The safety line is good but it's a light cord and doesn't give you much to hold onto. I need more practice from skidding and slipping every few steps. Back by the wheelhouse the roof rails provide a better grip and it feels much safer there despite the incoming water. I have a hand free to thread the boom halyards through the blocks and eyes into the cabin sides.

One of my funky adaptations is going to pay off. You normally have to be outside or with the doors open to work this old rig. By threading the boom halyard ropes through eye holes into the wheelhouse, you can work it from inside. Sure, you can't get much movement with it and you can't work the foresail, but if this wind keeps up astern it should work well enough. I hadn't been thinking about this kind of weather but staying dry and working it from inside makes luxury sense. If it gets much stronger we'll have to take the sail down anyway. Then it's just a big piece of canvas and with that limited movement in a high wind, if it came from the wrong direction, could push us over. Until you get used to a boat you have no idea what it will do. No idea how far it will lean. Just stay your paranoia and be ready to act. There's much to be said for a proper test and I think we're about to get one.

I make it round to the back of the wheelhouse and slide open the stern hatch. 'Pete! Will you look in that locker and pass me the skylight hatch cover. Whilst I'm out here I'll put it on.'

He hands the rectangular red canvas with its little ropes attached and I slide the hatch shut. Luckily I still have hold of the handle as a large wave hits the stern obliquely, covering me in deep and heavy water, the weight and force of it makes me slip. Flat on my stomach, arm up to the door handle, I can feel the drag of the water as it drains over the side. Pete is at the hatch window yelling his concern at me. It must have looked like I'm going over the side.

'I'm okay, I'm okay!' A searing pain is throbbing through my knee clouted on one of the hawser cleats. Slowly I climb to my feet and make it back up to the deck and the skylight out in the middle. It suddenly feels very exposed out here. My knee is killing me and I lie flat for safety to tie the cover on. My face over the glass, I can see down into the saloon. It seems a shame to shut out the light in the middle of the day but if heavy water starts coming over it'll soon leak into the saloon.

As I lie there another wave breaks high over the bow, the weight of it hitting me full in the face. I'm suddenly more aware of the noise around me, rushing water, the wind whistling and howling, the boom rattling under stress and the sail alternately flapping and snapping taught. This not what I had in mind for the beginning of my journeys. I'm not sure what I'm going to say to the others. I don't see a lot of choice. Whatever we do, whichever way we go, we're in for 'a dusting.'

Eventually I get to my feet, the deck rolling under me and the horizon, when I can see it, rising and falling a little too much for my stomach.

Back in the wheelhouse I strip off the harness and dripping oilskin. Clothes underneath are soaked in rivers and patches. No one speaks but the atmosphere is thick. They've been watching me get thrown about but I know our expectations are going to be rather different. I rub my fingers to bring back the circulation and massage the pained knee.

'Okay..' With a deep breath. 'Well I'm sorry Pete, but I agree with Trevor. I think we've gone too far to turn back and I don't really think it's a viable option anyway. The choice seems to be between one potential danger and another. And in terms of limiting dangers, which I hope you know is what I want to do, if this gets any worse and it could,.. we don't want to be anywhere near the land or shallow water. In fact we need to stay out and maybe even go further out to find deeper water.' I let it sink in. Pete and Sally look horrified.

'We're going to stay on track.' I'm nodding to Pete. 'We'll take a look at Yarmouth later if we can. If not, if it doesn't look safe, we're going to have to ride it out as best we can.' I let it hang there, still nodding to him. 'The boat is strong and watertight. It might not be the most comfortable, but we'll survive it. If necessary we'll heave to and put out a sea anchor and then sit it out.' I emphasise the 'sit it out'. 'We've got everything we need on board, plenty of fuel, food and water. For several days if we needed it.' Pete's about to explode at that, but I stop him. 'Look, I know how you feel, Pete, but this way is much safer than trying to get in to shallow water when the weather's like this.' I keep talking through his objection. 'We're just going to have to stick it out.. What do you think, Trevor. The echo-sounder is reading twenty-five to thirty fathoms. Is that enough or would it help to go find some deeper?'

'Yes, maybe, but I think we're fine for now. I certainly don't think we should heave to just yet. I think we should keep going south and do that later round Yarmouth if we can't get in.'

I'm anxious to make a bit of a compromise to keep them happy. 'Well okay, but I still think we should look at the chart and see if there is an alternative course to take us into some deeper water,.. in case it begins to cut up more. Will you do that, please?'

'Sure,' Trevor agrees easily. He's a proper ally, immediately leaning over the wheel to study the chart. By contrast Sally and Pete are chewing something nasty. Pete turns away.

I sigh deeply. 'Look, I understand you being scared.. But we are quite safe. It is not that bad now. It may get worse. But we will make it.' I emphasise every word. 'Cirkus is a lifeboat, she can take it. She's heavy and strong. Even if we get thrown about, she can take it with no difficulty.' I look at Pete hard. 'Don't cut off, Pete. We need to stick together now. More than anything that's what we need.' I turn to include Sally. 'If it gets rough now, we must work together to keep our spirits up. I'm sure we can find things to do and it is quite important to keep occupied. If you can't handle it, don't panic, try different things. If we start to roll and you feel uncomfortable, then go down below. Get as low as you can in the boat and you'll feel it less. Lie on the floor and above all try to stay calm.'

They say nothing. 'Okay Sally?'

'I'll be okay,' she says stoically. 'I'm just scared that's all.'

We have to break this tension. Pete is staring blankly out of the stern hatch window.

'Look, Pete, why don't you go downstairs and make us a cup of tea. Relax for a bit, we're okay up here. I can take the ropes, Trevor's got the wheel. Go on, go and relax for a bit, eh?'

He looks at me, his expression blank. Maybe he doesn't know how to react. We stare into each others' eyes. Searching his distress for some clue how to reach him. After what seems like an age, he nods and a half smile breaks.

'Okay, man, you're right.' He passes the boom halyards.

I return his smile with relief palpable. He crosses the room, putting his arm around Sally and they go downstairs closing the door behind them.

'Phew!' I act limp, threading the halyard through the ceiling rail and hanging on it. Trevor turns me a wink.

'It'll be okay.' He's reassuring.

'You're a good man. I hope we're right. Anyway I don't see any other choice.' Looking up out of the windscreen. 'Look at those bloody clouds now. We're in for it, you know that don't you?'

'Aye, skipper, I do.' he says with a wry smile.

I guess we would all have been surprised had things changed for the better. I've heard some sailors say it's boring at sea, time can pass piteously slow. I couldn't say we were unoccupied. The swell is building, the wind and limited experience, finding yet more. The speed of the tide, previously favourable, is turning against us. Running in opposition to the wind, the effect on waves when the echo-soundings read shallow, is to make them twist and cross, mixing peaks and troughs unpredictably. We change from one course heading to another, trying to steer some easier passage. It's almost impossible to maintain anything like a straight line. Dark and gloomy low cloud, closing in, with screens of blustery showers beneath them. Rolling and yawing down one wave, at an awkward angle mounting another. Erratic movement is a constant, relieved rarely when the wind drops, allowing rain to fall so heavily that it briefly calms the swell.

We change around our jobs, Pete coming back to the halyards, me taking the wheel and for some reason known only to himself, Trevor decides he wants pictures of it all. Inspired by Turneresque visions of unfocused turmoil, he dons the safety harness and staggering about the deck, lashes himself to the mast, taking photographs of us through the rain slashed windscreen. Thank God for Trevor. One of us has some humour and he looks ridiculous in the midst of a messy patch, forcing me to wrestle the wheel, up and over waves coming in three directions at once. The boat pitches heavily, throwing a large amount of water high in the air. Trevor disappears, swallowed by the plume. On reappearing, the cheesy grin he'd been wearing to get our attention had slipped to more of a grimace.

I change the course to the east, easier to steer in the swell. From the look of the chart it will take us into deeper water. I hope that might make it easier. Sally appears looking very pale, saying she feels sick. She fell into Pete's chest as he stood arms wide holding the halyards and, hangs there limp. He doesn't react with anything like sympathy.

'Try some deep breaths, Sally,' I suggest and she raised her head wearily. 'It might help a bit if you can see it coming rather than feeling it downstairs.' There's not much I can do stuck at the wheel and Pete seems just to stare ahead.

'Try holding onto the hand rails, Sally. If you wedge yourself into the corner there with your arms up it might help you breathe too.' She didn't seem to hear me and we are interrupted by the hatch opening. Trevor arriving accompanied by a mass of water. He is soaked and peels off the oilskin giving us all a cold shower. Smiling and happy with his work, he sloshes downstairs to change. The atmosphere rapidly returns to tense.

We watch and wait, going forward and bearing it. Sally didn't bear it for long and after asking for a bucket, which she snatches at urgently, hurriedly disappears below into the shower, locking the door behind her.

Pete didn't seem to notice but as soon as she'd gone seemed to wake up and smiling broadly at me said. 'Is this the moment to crack open the rum, then Cap'n? What do you think skipper?' From somewhere he'd produced a bottle and held it out.

'Grog?'

'Sure,' I said. 'Why not. I can see a bit of a break in the cloud up there. We should celebrate it.'

He didn't wait for the answer and was gone downstairs leaving the halyards trailing and the mainsail outside immediately flapping violently loose. 'Pete!.' I yell after him, trying to reach the ropes whilst hanging onto the wheel. He returned immediately with the little snorter glasses and very deftly, took back the ropes in one hand, pulled them taut and managed still to pour the rum at the same time.

I think that was the only time I ever drank rum at sea and, so much for traditional sailing practice, I was as sick as a dog within minutes. I never get seasick. I'm always the one picking everyone else up. And I've drunk whiskey, gin and vodka to shameful excess and yet on that occasion, one small glass of his rum hit me like a train. Trevor arrived for his ration, allowing me to collapse in the corner. I had to jump twice to throw up out of the stern hatch. Maybe half an hour passed, I have no idea, during which time I traversed shades of green inside and apparently out.

By the time I recovered sufficiently to take over the wheel, we had hit another heavy squall. In the midst of it, Cirkus pitched and rolled with rogue waves now falling both over the bow and wheelhouse simultaneously. The sea and swell getting higher, the boat heels over hard as we climb awkwardly down one particularly steep wave and into the trough, swinging the stern around. I spun the wheel trying to anticipate it but got it wrong and she shook and rattled as we skated sideways and several more waves hit us at once. Practice would make perfect, but anticipation is all. Right now there's no shortage of either but for all the good my steering is doing, I might as well be back in the corner. With less and less control, we sail on.

Anyone who has watched the sea will have noticed waves appearing in cycles. As always there are lots of arguments about how many waves make a cycle, but I think I see them in sevens. The first three can be comparatively small and rounder topped. They rise in height and steepness for the next four until the seventh, which is often the big crested wave breaking before it arrives. That large wave is then immediately followed by three small beginners of the next cycle. In deeper water, every third wave seems to be larger than its two predecessors and every sixth larger still. The roughest ride can be so much smoother if you react in time, especially turning into the big ones. If you can put the bow square into it you have a chance to stay upright. In cross-seas like today however, there is little rhyme or reason. You think you see the cycle forming and get ready to anticipate the big one, then a rogue appears, cutting oblique across the swell. This rogue will then either smooth out a larger one or increase it disproportionately. In such a sea the largest are undoubtedly built when crests of crossing waves collide. You stand, rock and sway, watching, taking private bets that these two oncoming leviathans will meet with you in the middle. Sometimes you are all set to brace yourself for the pounding and suddenly, instead of the crests it's the troughs that coincide and the waves that looked so threatening all but blend and disappear, dissipated by unseen force. There seem no rule, no empiricism determining which. They happen with chaotic chance and you take it for good or ill.

I don't think there is any mistaking this is now a storm. The clouds are thicker and heavier than before, mounting with no break, in towering steel-grey distension. A constantly whirling deluge ominously relinquishing long travelled loads. As we ride briefly on top of a swelling wave, a dark bulbous bottom of one cloud seems to swallow us whole. Heavy sky squeezing the final few feet between heaven and earth filled with a veil of rain and spray.

'We're going to have to take in the rest of that sail. Anyone want to volunteer to come with me?'
'I'll have a go,' said Pete, rather too enthusiastically. And immediately, before I'm ready, he slides open the aft hatch door through which a respectable bathload of water erupts. The spray fusillade soaks everything, finding its way past the engine cover to produce load hissing columns of steam. Surprise mixed with a look of guilt, he slammed the door shut.
'Getting a bit hairy out there..'
'Yes, Pete. I think that's a bit of an understatement don't you? You pillock! Listen just calmly, eh?' I try gravity so he'll listen.

'It is very hairy out there,.. and dangerous. So we're just going to have to do this with a bit of order. Okay?..' I'm still putting on my safety harness. 'So,.. here put one of these on,.. and together this time. Right? We'll have to climb out of the side doors and clip onto the safety line immediately. It's on the roof. Don't forget. Hands on the roof rail above the door and clip on. Got it?' He nods assent.

'Okay, you ready? Let's Go!'

We step outside into a roaring gale. Spray is flying everywhere from the tops of waves that all appear to be above us. Down in the troughs, windswept crests topple and spill, blending with horizontal rain. The whole world is liquid chaos! Solid water is predictable in some sort of way, and then not. You see it coming, brace yourself, but until the impact, you never quite predict its full force and weight on your body. The deck is entirely awash, one cascading wave after another. I lose my footing completely and slip. Driven by the water, sliding on my stomach all the way back to the lower deck by the wheelhouse door. The stanchion rail stopped me from going any further, hung there by the safety harness between my legs. The boat pitched heavily again and helped by the rising momentum, I managed to stand up. Hand over hand hauling back to the forward deck and Pete already at the mast. He is saying something to me but the howling wind carries his voice away and with exaggerated semaphore I signal us back to the work. We attach our safety lines around the stout mast timber and by enormous effort with freezing fingers, haul the mainsail and gaff down until it rests on top of the boom. It's almost impossible to hold on and tie the sail at the same time. Clinging, arms wrapped in a bear hug around the mast just to stand still. I make the mistake of looking up at the swinging top prescribing unbelievable spiroscopic gyrations.

Somehow we manage to tie everything off and then hand over slippery hand again make our way back along the boom to the wheelhouse to fix it on the roof. Job done we stand gripping tight.

I drew back the stern hatch and swung inside. Accompanied by a wall of foaming water Pete jumped in after me, missing the steps altogether and collapsing in an exhausted dripping heap. I slam the door after him, shutting out the beast.

'My God!' he said, panting heavily. 'I hope I don't have to go out there again. That is really wild!' As he got up water poured from the creases in his oilskin. Hanging from the ceiling rail, recovering breath, he wiped little rivulets from his face. 'Shit! God, that was something, wasn't it?.' He began to chuckle and slapped my back.

'That was good, boys. Good spectator sport. Did you enjoy that?' Trevor exaggerates cool and dry.

'We're all right for the moment,' I say still breathless. 'But if it gets any worse we'll have to throw something out to trail behind us and break up some of those waves.'

'Yeh? Like what?' Pete is disbelieving.

'Whatever I can find. I'll take a door off or something. Something heavy that we can tie a rope to.'

'For what?'

'Oh god, Pete, I don't know. It's just something you can do. It just steadies you and breaks up the waves coming over the stern. It must make the profile of the boat longer. Gives you some drag. Lowers the centre of gravity, fuck I don't know.. Gives you something to do that makes you think you're helping.'

Trevor turns from an intense scan of the horizon. 'We should be coming up on the next mark. Here have a look.' He passes the binoculars. 'Over there, somewhere at about two o'clock. I'm sure I saw something a moment ago.'

I waited for the swell to part, for us to rise on top of a wave, before searching the seascape. At first I see nothing, the view only lasting a few seconds before we drop into another trough.

Up again and this time my eyes are more quickly accustomed. Looking for anything small in a wide expanse, you don't see it until you see it. Then it's obvious.

'There it is! A conical top, dead ahead now!' Passing the glasses back, I point straight over the bow.

He saw it too. 'You're a star, Trevor. That's number four. What's it called?' Hanging on as another wave hits us, I peer at his jottings. 'Slight Holme. With a bell on top. We're hardly gonna hear that. Well done you two!' And then to Pete. 'Are you all right?' He nods, shaking more water out. 'Okay, listen, I'm going to make a celebration cup of tea. Or attempt to, anyway. Haven't seen Sally for a bit.'

Peeling off my oilskin, tottering and bouncing off the walls, I clamber downstairs.

Chapter Ten
what good is this?   Oh? Go with sadist

It is so easy to say these things mean nothing. Life can be so mundane, caught up and consumed by every day. The going to work, grinding the gruel. Whatever stands for the normal code that conditions and obliges us. Most of the time we are completely unaware of anything else going on. It would be easy to say that dreams of something better or escape from mundanity, have lead to an untimely choice. A forcing of chance and nothing more significant than foolhardy haste. It would be easy, but it's not, not today.

The old seafaring manual imperiously states, no proper mariner should ever be caught in bad weather. That properly gathered and observed information is used responsibly. You may think that's transparently obvious and up to a point, I agree. But isn't even such informed and responsible life, whatever you do, whatever choices you make, a risk? Do responsible people never get caught, never go hungry or poor. Supreme sought after common sense should not only mean we always avoid disaster but implies I am somehow inferior if I suffer it.
And what about the idea that there are some things you can't avoid because for some reason it is necessary to experience them. Are we victims of fate or the creators of it? I have the

strongest feeling that we were going to find ourselves in this storm whatever we did.

Is that crazy? By all accounts to believe such things when reason reigns supreme is irrational, eccentric, even mad. But I do believe it.

Wasn't it Don Quixote, tilting at windmills, who knew madness is the only sanity? We are limitless not limited. Why shouldn't we seek experience. I see nothing conditional in nature. Pure instinct working random sequence of billions interrelating. Sure, there are trends and, if I had a better knowledge or understanding, maybe I wouldn't have chosen this one. But why not, I am part of nature. Why should I want to stay out of it? At home in the shallow water. With some conditioned illusion of safety.

I force myself at that thought to stop. Unfortunately it's not just me. It's Sally looking sick and terrified over there. The existential crap might be okay for me but I don't have the right to include anyone else.

Bubbles has managed to squeeze long legs into Sally's foetal shape. I knelt beside her, one hand brushing hair from her forehead the other stroking Bubbles who is rhythmically quivering.

'Sally?' I call quietly and she slowly opened her eyes. 'I'm going to make some tea, would you like some?'

She is very pale, beads of sweat on her upper lip. The bucket next to her stinks of fresh insides. I took it away, flushing it down the head. When I came back I think she is still answering the tea question. She raised herself on one arm, nodding, but as another wave rocked and shuddered us, she fell back limp on the pillow.

'I've got some Rescue Remedy. It might help. Just in a glass of water.' She stirred again but the rolling of the boat as she lifted her head made her turn instantly to the bucket.

'It's okay.' I said to cover her embarrassment, pulling her hair out the way. She looked up again, sluggish and wiping drool from her chin.

'Oohh, I'd like some tea but I don't know if I could drink it.'

I fetch the Rescue from the medicine cabinet. 'Well here, put this under your tongue first.'

Another wave hit us hard. I can feel the sideways motion as it skews the boat around. It's very disorienting down here. Thrown around for something unknown, sends your imagination wild. Sally slumped back on the sofa.

Everything inside cupboards is clattering as Cirkus shudders her way off another wave. A sudden free-falling sensation ends abruptly like being inside an elevator hitting the stop. There's a huge boom at the moment of impact, my knees buckle under me and I'm thrown headlong into the bulkhead wall. This is incredible.

A couple of books, the kettle and some cups on the table come flying across the room smashing against the wall beside me. Doors open and slam shut. When the motion levels out the galley air is filled with a confetti of herb leaves or something settling like dust. I lay on the floor in shock and caught myself. This is what it must be like in an earthquake. No it isn't, this is what it's like in a small boat in a storm!

I decide to practice my preaching. I'll be calm, make tea and clear up. How many times have you done that for displacement?

I collected everything from around the floor and made a stumbling circuit of locking the cupboards. I could wedge myself in the galley. A hand on the wall is enough steadying. But when I put the kettle on the stove gimbals, even though it seemed we were going through a relatively calm patch, it swung so much that the gas can only have heated it one out of

every three minutes. It took an age of rocking and rolling. Finally it begins to boil and I only took my hand off the wall to arrange the cups in the holder. As if the swell waited for me to move. I am thrown off balance by another heavy lurch forward. Instantly the whole angle of our world is suddenly steep and thrown up with a twisting halt. An exploding violent crash came from the bow, a volley of cracking, splintering timber. As fast as the rolling allows I run forward through the saloon toward more crashing and clattering. In fear of what might greet me, I fling open the fo'c's'le door to see the anchor chain, link after link tumbling out from its broken locker. The door has splintered under the weight and the chain is now falling in a constant liquid metal stream across the bed. I don't know what I expected. Gallons of water gushing in, but as it is there must be a hundred yards of chain gushing out, rattling and clanging heavily onto the floor.
'What the hell was that!?' Pete yells from the wheelhouse door.
'It's all right!' I shout back at him over the din. 'The anchor chain's burst its locker.'
'You, okay?' he calls back. I stood over loud clattering, watching it run out and raised a limp hand to acknowledge him. Eventually every inch of it is piled in a mountain of solid metal and it stops.
Sally is sitting bolt upright, rigid with fear. I take her hand and squeeze it tight.
'It's alright. It's just the anchor chain come out of its cupboard. It's okay, it's safe now. We're alright. I'll clear it up later..' I brush more hair from her face. 'Come on, I am going to make this tea if it's the last thing I do.' As soon as I said it I regret the inference. I still think she'd be better in the wheelhouse where she can see what's coming. She can't bear the thought of that either.

'No, I'm all right here.' she says weakly, unconvincing either of us. She lay down, pulling the blanket around and enfolding Bubbles for protection.
'Okay, I'll be back.'

There wasn't a great deal of tea left in the cups by the time I got up to the wheelhouse. We are rolling heavily to the sound of the engine racing as the stern comes completely out of the water, the propeller spinning in clear air. The atmosphere is tense. They are certainly ready for tea or something. Pete at the wheel looks ashen and Trevor, fixed jaw, is staring through the windscreen searching. Invisible buoys or marks, anything that might give encouragement, some connection to diminishing sanity.

Another messy wave, strewn in chaos, throws white water over the whole boat. She shudders violently, the wheel spinning uncontrollably out of Pete's hands. The bow rises high into the air and twists awkwardly before he can wrestle it back.
'Close the throttle a bit, Pete. That might help. Goin' too fast we just create our own extra swell.'
'Oh, yeh?' he glances at me doubtfully. He tries a wry smile. 'I'll slow down and it'll all stop then, will it?'

Down in the fo'c's'le, I manage eventually to get the anchor chain back in the locker. Unsteady work and every few moments I hang on to anything within reach to prevent myself from being flung around the room. Working so close inside the bow the noise of each wave and wall of water crashing against it is unnerving. The hull is thick but imagining only an inch or so between me and the force outside is not something to dwell on. I nail the door shut.
Sally looks really ill. Kneeling beside her, I pull the blanket up, taking her hand but she doesn't want attention. Embarrassment

on top of sickness, she's best left alone. Or maybe I can get Pete to do better.

Once upstairs again my thoughts immediately race with the action. The wheelhouse is sturdy protection but outside pure hell is breaking loose. What must it have been like in an open boat. Happy to be alive?
Our bid for deeper water has made no difference. We may even be further into the storm. Waves rising higher with increasing frequency, the howling wind blowing frozen rain and spray. Pete looks exhausted and I take over the wheel. No longer a sitting job, wrestling and holding on. The direction of the waves is cross and unpredictable. Wind behind us, opposing the tide, makes them roll and break in chaos. When the swell is more consistent the waves build in rolling ramparts, broad and towering as they bear down on us. If they stay unbroken we mount them, over the top, suspended momentarily fifteen, twenty feet high before falling, skating, careering down into the darkness of the trough. That's the easy ones, when it comes cross again we're struck by other waves on the beam. It's impossible to hold a straight line. Riding one then avoiding or turning into another. Every moment in deep concentration. Any error is compounded by running into more opposition that shakes and swings, rolls and skews us around. The bow lifts higher, the stern plunging deep to disappear beneath. In turn the bow and aft decks are covered in swirling, cascading water. As the next rampart builds, in slow motion on the way up and on reaching the top, we dive the slope, the propeller clearing water then accelerating us fast before I can shut it down. The bow is consumed, scooping huge amounts of sea across the length of us.
Pete is back in his favoured position, arms outstretched to the handrails bracing himself against the back wall. Either side at the front, Trevor and I maintain our stare through the

windscreen. We are silent. The longest moments pass marked only by another wave, a dramatic pitching, a roll. We are speechless, consumed by our thoughts. What is there to say? We are bearing it, holding on, each in our own way. Beyond our physical proximity we are completely alone, experiencing feelings impossible to communicate. No relief in sharing it. Some connective thought strays, maybe it would help if we share it but immediately my own fear is more than enough. How many ways can you empathise with that?

Suddenly an enormous wave appears. From twenty foot above us and along the whole length of the boat, it falls into and over us full broadside. We are pushed violently, the keel slipping fast away to the right, throwing the whole boat sideways. I see the mast top careering through the air in a great arc in front of me. We heel over completely to the horizontal, half of the deck on my side disappearing beneath the waves and, slicing right through the crests. The top of the mast dips, gyrating lower and lower until it is completely submerged below the water. For what seems like an age, I am acutely aware of my position, standing behind the wheel, knuckles white with the strain and tightening shock. I am horizontal! From the keel to the top of the mast we are precisely parallel to the surface of the sea!
She's Gone! Internal panic yells. We've capsized! We hold there interminably, the engine screaming its naked propeller. With equal force she twists and yaws and we are thrown back in the opposite direction, accelerating forward as the propeller is plunged deep and suddenly, we are out on the top, swinging hard upright in clear view of the storm all around.
Closing my eyes momentarily, waves of rushing emotion pass panic subsiding.
'My God', said Trevor in a flat slow murmur. 'That was close..'
I stood hunched over the wheel, braced for more. If I can take that I can take anything. Through sudden oblique confidence,

as we fall and rise again, I felt as though I were on some churning fairground. Riding legs wide apart, knees sprung, there's room for a carousel horse!

A long time passed. Tossing and rolling, climbing up the sides of huge waves. At the top there is nothing below for twenty, thirty feet or more. We topple and fall crashing into the troughs with the hull booming on impact, sending a numbing shudder through every cell. Time and time again we are shocked and buffeted, shaken and rammed by waves growing ever larger. Heaving under the pressure, Cirkus plummets then rears up and we are literally stunned. Again and again the top of the mast dips below the water and every time, our emotions stretched to the limit, she comes back for more.

Beyond the edge of unbearable but with stark and harrowing certainty that we cannot escape. Such bearing is not bravery, there is no choice. When it seems it will go on forever, there is no longer any complaint or resistance, only frozen acceptance. Riding it, rigid, mouth agape, entranced by fear beyond any known. Caught in some bubble of reality where any sense of time passing is utterly paralysed and suspended. A nether world with no connection to anything like normality. Linking threads long swept away. It's not that you don't have hope for relief, but you dare not believe in it. Feel so vulnerable and each time the danger increases you suspend fear in anticipation. As though there is no space for it. Will she come up? That wave now bearing down will surely sink us! Surface from another survivable wave and there's no time for relief as the inevitability of the next is a few moments away..

We are so alone out here. We've seen no other life for several hours. We are the only ones insane enough and, the least prepared. Sitting warm and cosy by the fire, moored quietly on the gentle river Ouse, I read with an academic interest the bit in the manual about heavy weather. Think beyond battered senses and I remember over and over those passages. The trailing sea-anchor, only recommended having given up making headway. I don't want us to stop, even though in trying to push through we are probably hurt more. Giving up the idea of even small progress, doesn't occur. What does a real sailor do? The thought haunts inadequacy.

Braced rigid, don't imagine how the hull is bending every time we fall to the bottom of a trough. The impact boom shudders, feel it strike and jangle every nerve. And any moment of relief is filled with straining for a solution. There is none. I am helpless precisely at the moment I have to use all my strength to stand up. As though your strength can never be enough.

Is there help out here? But what help could stay still enough to get close?

Do you ever decide something and then, through a mass of emotion within a milli-second, do the opposite? A combination relief of urged decision and damning doubt. A critical mass of confusion such that I will leap in any direction.

And in aberration, almost without volition, a cracked voice broke the trance. 'Trevor, take over, I'm gonna call the coast guard.'

It took him by surprise.

It makes no sense. What could they do? Though as I step back toward the radio, there is already therapy in movement. Slowly the Pye warms, valves begin to hum and glow. I flip the dial to cover Channel 16 and turn the switch to transmit.

'I'm going to report our position and ask their advice.' Looking to Trevor and the chart in front of him. 'Who is it now,.. Yarmouth?'
'Yeh, I should think so. It doesn't matter, we're near enough and we'll get everyone on that anyway.'
'Yarmouth Coastguard.. Yarmouth Coastguard.. This is MV Cirkus.. Come in.. Over..' Turning the switch to receive, there is a crackle of interference and white noise.

'Yarmouth Coastguard.. Yarmouth Coastguard.. This is MV Cirkus.. Come in.. Over..' Click.. White noise..
'Yarmouth Coastguard.. Yarmouth Coastguard.. This is MV Cirkus.. Come in.. Over..' Click.. White noise..
I leave the channel open,.. to nothing but atmospheric hiss.
'There must be someone there.' Pete's laden distress.
'Yarmouth Coastguard.. Yarmouth Coastguard.. This is MV Cirkus.. Come in.. Over..' White noise.

'Shit!' The bow rears madly against another huge wave and Pete and I are thrown onto the back wall. At exactly the same moment another wave astern comes up underneath sending us careering forward at a rakish angle, the bow plummeting down through clear air. As we hit the trough we jolt heavily forward to the sound of a mighty crash down in the saloon. Amidst all the noise up here we suddenly focus on a new sound down below. It's Sally screaming! Pete jumps up from the floor and at the same time the saloon door opens. Bubbles arrives like a jet-plane, feet hardly touching the floor. Sally, arms braced against the door-posts is crying and shaking uncontrollably. She is absolutely terrified. Pete is there instantly, gathering her up as she began to faint and carrying her back down into the saloon. His surprised, 'Fucking Hell!', reaches us from the room below. Trevor locks the wheel and is about to follow when Pete comes back, wedging himself in the doorway.

'It's unbelievable, man! It's just like a bombs hit it! Two of those army batteries that were in the galley locker have just smashed straight through the door and are in the middle of the floor. There's wood and bits everywhere. It's fucking incredible, the force of that last one just threw them out on the ends of their cables.' He jams himself awkwardly in the door frame as another wave pounds us. 'God, she's so frightened, man, I'm gonna to have to stay down there with her.' He turned and disappeared.

The radio is still hissing an open channel. I gather myself and flip the switch to transmit.
'Yarmouth Coastguard.. Yarmouth Coastguard.. This is MV Cirkus.. Come in.. Over..'
Nothing. 'Come on!' Suddenly urgent.
'Yarmouth Coastguard.. Yarmouth Coastguard.. This MV Cirkus.. Please come in.. Over..' Click.. White noise...
'Yarmouth Coastguard.. Yarmouth Coastguard.. This is MV Cirkus..
Come in,.. Over..' Click.. White noise..

In the middle of another hissing, the atmospherics change..
'YARMOUTH COASTGUARD.. COME IN CIRKUS.. READING YOU LOUD AND CLEAR.. OVER..'
'Yes!' Trevor, wide eyed, mouthed an oath.
'Yarmouth Coastguard! Thank God!' I forget my radio etiquette. 'We Are In Heavy Weather.. Thirty-Five Miles Due East Of Ingoldmells.. Course One Eight Five.. We Need A Haven From The Storm.. Repeat.. We NEED A HAVEN FROM THE STORM.. Can You Advise.. OVER!'
White Noise..

'YARMOUTH COASTGUARD!' The voice is wonderfully clipped and efficient. 'LOUD AND CLEAR CIRKUS.. YOUR COURSE AND POSITION HAS BEEN REPORTED TO US THIS AFTERNOON.. YOU ARE ON THE SCANNER..
WE'VE HAD OUR EYE ON YOU.. GLAD YOU GOT IN TOUCH.. STAY ON THIS FREQUENCY.. WE'LL CHECK OUR INFORMATION AND GET BACK TO YOU.. DO YOU UNDERSTAND.. OVER..' White noise..
'Understood Yarmouth.. THANK YOU!. Over..'
'BACK TO YOU IN FIFTEEN MINUTES CIRKUS.. OVER AND OUT..'

Head bowed and holding onto the radio casing. Eyes closed, the release flowing through.
'Well done, Will.' Trevor is saying, steady and calm.
'Amazing! What do you think he meant, we're on the scanner?'
'Radar, I guess. Either that or somebody reported us. They must pick you up and follow the track on their screen.'
'God! We feel completely alone, like there is no one anywhere. No one must know or care. And all the time they're watching you? That's a bit spooky, isn't it?.'
'Yeh.' We stare at each other. 'Well come on, we better look again at that other large scale chart?'
Hanging from the rail I pull the chart from the ceiling holster and unfurl it in front of us. We search in buffeted silence, then Trevor begins. 'I still say most of those small ports along this coast are going to be too shallow. Pass me the Reeds and let's knock them off one by one. We'll need to gauge the tide heights and times at each one and the time it'll take us to get there. Here, can you take the wheel and I'll start.'

Between crashing waves and intense concentration to avoid the next deluge, we work through the possibilities. Trevor is an acrobat studying precarious form. Hanging with one hand, book in the other, ruler measuring distance on the chart, working the calculator.

As before, none of the options work. At each one of those north Norfolk towns, three maybe four, there is a port but they are all small and shallow. Two have sand bars protecting tiny entrances and long channels across their marsh. They'll be no good in this weather. We've no knowledge of any of them beyond small scale maps and, it'll be dark by the time the tide is high enough for us to get in.

'They are bound not to be lit and in this weather it's impossible to even think of trying to find small marker buoys in the dark'.

'We're fucked, Trevor, just like before. I don't know what made me think anybody'd be able to help. I can't see us being able to get into any of these. And there's nowhere else.'

Another huge wave looms and we fall silent for the strike. In preparation, lanky-crab-like Trevor lies over everything on the chart top, gripping the edges of the shelf. I fail to steer enough into it and, waiting over, it arrives on the beam, pushing us violently sideways. We rise up and up and eventually over it, rolling crazily one way and then another. As it passes beneath and we are sucked down with it, the mast-top disappears plunging into the next. Everything held in dramatic suspension with more clattering down below, feel the surge of buoyancy coming upright again. If just once another wave hit us whilst we are over in that position, we'll capsize for sure.

After a few moments at attempted calm.

'It's the same choice, Trev. None.'

A dreadful decision. If only there were one to make.

'So we'll have to stay out.. Unless we can think about Yarmouth again? How long do you think before we get there?'

He sighs a long moan. 'It's so hard to tell now. At a guess I'd say about four or five hours. I've totally lost track of our speed over the last hour, it's been so erratic. I reckon we might have

done about six miles in the last two. I don't know. Say five or six.'
I look at my watch. 'So that would make it about nine-thirty. Jesus, I don't know we can take this for that long!'
'We could get to Wells, or maybe Blakeney in four may be. I suppose Wells looks the best of them. Those are the only others that look in any way reasonable. What'm I saying? They're not reasonable. They look bloody awful!'
'Maybe we just need to go back to plan A and go further out?'
We fall silent again, the options dreadful. Really,.. like the devil and the deep black sea.

We keep breaking off to deal with what's coming at us and, again we take another fall from the top of a wave. It seemed higher still this one, high enough to feel the force of the wind as we descend. Crashing to the bottom, every rivet and plank absorbs and booms the impact. How can she stay together under such a pounding.
Pete arrives, clambering and half crawling up the stairs.
'It's incredible down there, man. Fucking unbelievable, it's a real mess. There's stuff everywhere. I reckon just about every cupboard opened. I've pushed the batteries back and cleared up a bit. They look okay. They're still working anyway. I arced one with a screwdriver and got a stonking great spark..
Sal can't take any more though, man. She's in a white panic, keeps fainting. I'm worried about her, man. It's really getting to her. It's fucking hell down there, you just don't know what's comin'. It's really frightening.. We gotta get the hell outta here.'
Another wave forces us sideways, sliding and shuddering.
'We're just trying to work out where to go. But all the ports are too small or shallow and we'll never find our way in the dark.'
Trevor followed with a long sigh. 'We're talking about staying out again and maybe looking at Yarmouth. But that doesn't look good.'

Pete is immediately angry. 'What the fuck are you two talkin' about! There's no fucking options, we've got to get out of here, we've got to get off! You're fucking crazy, the pair of you, if you think we can stay out here!.. I can't take any more, man!'

He turns away, swinging on the rail as we buck again.

'Look at it! Look at it will you! We can't stay out here in this. We've got to get off!.. You're gonna fucking kill us, the pair of you!'

'Pete! Look there's no point in raving.. You've got to understand.. It could be far more dangerous nearer the land. We've no idea what it's like over there. In shallow water the waves are gonna be twice as high as this. We could get smashed to pieces.'

'No, man!' He spins around to me, his face contorted in anger. 'No man! We're fucking getting off!' He turns to Trevor. 'You gotta get us..'

He is interrupted by the radio crackling into life.

'MV CIRKUS.. MV CIRKUS.. THIS IS YARMOUTH COASTGUARD.. ARE YOU RECEIVING.. OVER..'

I trip headlong across to the radio, grabbing the mike as I fall onto it. They broadcast again.

'MV CIRKUS.. MV CIRKUS.. THIS YARMOUTH COASTGUARD.. COME IN.. OVER..'

My voice is trembling as I fumble the mike and switches.

'This Is MV Cirkus.. Receiving You Loud And Clear.. Go Ahead Yarmouth.. Over..'

'HELLO CIRKUS..' A disembodied jolly voice. 'WE'VE DONE SOME HOMEWORK CIRKUS AND CONSULTED WITH OUR STATIONS ALONG THE COAST.. WE SUGGEST YOU COME INTO WELLS.. WE CALCULATE YOUR ETA AT APPROXIMATELY TWENTY HUNDRED HOURS.. WE'VE ADVISED THE RESCUE SERVICES TO STAND BY.. IS THAT UNDERSTOOD.. OVER..'

'Understood Yarmouth.. We've Also Been Looking.. But We've Got A Problem With That.. We Think Wells Is Too Shallow And Will Be Difficult To Locate In The Dark.. Do You Have Another Suggestion.. Over..'

'NEGATIVE CIRKUS.. WELLS IS YOUR ONLY OPTION.. OVER..'

'Understood Yarmouth.. We Are Looking At The Option Of Riding Out The Storm.. Can You Advise.. Over..'

Pete becomes very animated.

'What are you doing, man?! They're saying come in and you're gonna fucking argue! This is our only chance! Sally's gonna fucking die of fright! You've gotta do what they say!'

'Shut up, Pete!' I yell at him.

'NEGATIVE..CIRKUS.. WE HAVE A FORCE TEN STORM WARNING IMMINENT IN YOUR AREA.. WE DO NOT ADVISE STAYING OUT.. REPEAT.. WE DO NOT ADVISE STAYING OUT.. OVER..'

Pete is vindicated. 'I fucking told you so.'

'Shut up, Pete.' Trevor hissed.

'Understood Yarmouth.. But What About Riding It Out In Deeper Water.. Over..'

'NO CAN DO CIRKUS. WE HAVE TO TRY TO GET YOU INTO WELLS... IT'S GOING TO GET ROUGH OUT THERE.. IT WILL BE IMPOSSIBLE TO MOUNT ANY RESCUE AT SEA IF YOU FOUNDER IN THESE CONDITIONS.. OVER..'

I look to Trevor. 'What do you think? Stand By Yarmouth.. We are Discussing It.'

'Well a force ten changes everything doesn't it? I've no idea what that'll be like, even in deeper water.'

'Do what they say, man! Why are you even thinking about it?'

We're exposed and another mass of water pounds over the wheelhouse.

'We've both come up with Wells as the only option, Will,' said Trevor, immediately having to grapple the wheel.

'Hello Yarmouth.. This Is Cirkus.. Are You There.. Over..'

'GO AHEAD..CIRKUS..'
'What About Coming Into Yarmouth.. Over..'
'NEGATIVE CIRKUS.. WE'VE ALREADY GOT SHIPPING QUEING IN THE ROADS.. WE CAN'T HANDLE ANY MORE.. WE RECOMMEND YOU COME TO WELLS AND WE'LL BE READY FOR YOU WHEN YOU ARRIVE.. OVER..'

'What do they mean, they can't handle any more? Are we doing this for their convenience. Jesus, I don't know what to do.'
'I think you have to go with them, Will.' Trevor is saying. 'It doesn't feel right to me either but it's a fait accompli..?'
'ARE YOU THERE..CIRKUS.. WHAT'S YOUR DECISION.. OVER..'
'What about the ETA at Wells, Trevor. Is that right?' I know the answer but I need more time, some help or diversion. It feels wrong and we've already made this decision.
'Yeh. I mean it is a guess. It's going to be difficult to be that precise but it looks about right.'
I have to decide now and the spotlight is blinding. I feel completely wretched and stand swaying to the motion, the mike in my hand. It's impossible to think it through to any conclusion that works. My head is spinning with agonising 'can't'! Blocking all others. I can't.. Something must break or surrender..

I give up and flip the switch.
'Hello Yarmouth.. This Is Cirkus.. Are You There.. Over..'
'READING YOU LOUD AND CLEAR CIRKUS.. GO AHEAD.. OVER..'
'Okay Yarmouth.. We'll Come Into Wells.. Repeat.. Will Come Into Wells.. Estimated Time Of Arrival.. Twenty Hundred.. Over..'
'WELL DONE CIRKUS.. WE'LL BE READY FOR YOU.. DON'T WORRY..' He sounds like he believes what he's saying.

'EVER BEEN TO WELLS, CIRKUS.?. OVER..' Like it's a chatty question.
I look to Pete and Trevor, shaking my head.
'No Never Yarmouth.. Over..'
'WELL YOU'LL HAVE A BIT OF FUN GETTING IN THERE.. GOOD LUCK.. STAY OPEN ON THIS FREQUENCY.. OVER AND OUT..'

Chapter Eleven   what good is this?

The looks between us share disbelief. Was that nonchalance or confident privity? I take over the wheel and in dark emphasis another massive wave, crest breaking and foaming high above, comes flooding and cascading. In the moment I react, spinning the wheel, the wave breaks crashing across us. For an agonising age, we are completely blind. The wave forces us under as though we dove from a great height and plunged deep into boiling confusion. Striking the windscreen with such force, you cannot believe the glass will take it. The wipers stutter to standstill. We buck and wheel around until the spray clears and we are up again. Out and with clear sight toward the next advancing wave, I have only a moment to turn the wheel hard. We slice its cresting top and are scooped up fast as the bow crashes through. We descend, accelerating wildly into the next trough, the engine whinnying the propeller's freedom. No sense or consistent direction, no course I can hold. Before, as we ploughed on, maybe there was some underlying order. Now everything is speeding up, messy, crossed and awkward. One wave across the quarter, immediately one in the bow and then in the next moment a giant catching us from behind. In my desperation to get it right I think maybe there's still a pattern. Every five or so a huge one looms. I try to steer into it but with others and the previous ones knocking us away from any purposeful course, it's complete chance if we come through clean. On the chart shelf in front, the compass veers chaotically as we slew one way and then another. Forget which way we're supposed to be going, it's all I can do to steer in one direction for more than a few seconds.

Maybe the sea state is worsened by passing shallow water. The echo-sounder's wavering red lines are bouncing around so much. Darting glimpses at it every few moments I do feel like I'm getting some cogent picture. Every time it calms relatively, I think the joining dots are making a longer line. Deeper water, I'm sure it's the answer. Suddenly the red line shortens and we are off again on a violent roller-coaster. If it were a fairground ride you'd know you were getting off. No such glorious abandon here. At each moment I doubt I can hold on. And then I do, in time for the next.

'I've got the course for Wells. D'you want it, Will?' Trevor is still stoic, thank God.
'Yeh. Give it me.. What I'm gonna do with it, I've no idea.'
'One Nine Five.' He continues. 'That'll keep us out and then we go in from the North East, which is where the Reeds says the fairway to the channel 'll be.'
'Okay.' Numbed by anything beyond the moment.
'So, Wells then!' he shouts above the noise. His nose inches from the book he pins to the chart-shelf. 'The Reeds says, buoyed channel approached from the North East. Three fairway markers and an occulting green light on the first channel buoy.' Holding on and reading is as difficult as it looks. Standing on the engine cover, leaning over the chart-shelf, he can hang on to the inside of the windscreen. Checking his watch at the end of an outstretched arm. 'It's just after four-thirty, so we might have to hang around a bit. High tide at Blakeney, just along the

coast, is nine. It says you can get in only two hours either side of high water. There might be just enough by the time we get there.'

'I've two marks to find on the way. These two buoys, here look.' He's shinning a little torch on the chart, drawing a line with the beam. From his lying across it position, he twists his head to smile at me. 'Looks good! If we can make them?..'

'Yeh?'

'We're gonna get into some shallow water, though. Tide'll be coming in against the wind.'

'Yeh.'

We bounce around more heavily for a few moments. I glare at him. The echo-sounder dots over his shoulder, shrink to a short burst.

'Yeh! You wanna tell me that again.. about the shallow water.. I don't want to go anywhere near it!..'

Pete chimes in. 'It'll get us off, man. That's what we want!'

'Get us smashed to pieces!' I let it out angrily. Not at him but in frustration. 'This is not the right thing to do but now we're doing it. Because a disembodied voice in Yarmouth said so.' Which is worse, a voice of reason and safety or my inability to come up with a better plan.

'Let's just get to the marks!..'

I've no other answers. The argument goes round again. I don't see anything new. Like it's some sort of payback. You're gonna get what you're going to get. Face it and surrender. That's what you'd be doing which ever direction you choose. No certainty of anything that's right. You'll just find a whole other stream of paranoid arguments.

In this wind, blowing directly into the oncoming tide. In shallow water, it will whip up huge waves. With nowhere to go but hit the bottom. The chart shows no rocks, just sandbanks and shallows.

Safe in the shallows? Safe in shallow water..

I want completely the opposite. Without huge waves crashing over us and the danger of going aground, we might be able to ride it out. It's not safe in the shallow water. Why are they telling us to go there?..
Because it's not safe out at sea and too far for a rescue.

Pete arrives back from another staggering visit down below. 'You gotta get us out of here, man. She's in a really bad way down there. I don't know she can take it much longer,.. it's like she's hardly conscious.. Get us outa here, man!' His face is ashen. As he shouts the last sentence but the noise drowns him out. Another heavy wave breaking over us, crashing into the wheelhouse windows.
I am responsible for lives too..

'Let's get to the marks.' The boat spins again. As though flipped away by some giant's brush. Before sense makes anything of it, the top of the mast is under again. I'm upright, everything's upright, but now that means more than ninety degrees to the world. It's not going to come back. It's gone too far this time! We're going to capsize! Hold on, hold on. It's stopped..
No, it's coming back. We're up and over the top again!

This happened ten or more times before we got to the first mark. Another hour for the ship's log but I'd completely lost track. It got worse and seemed to be without end. We bucked and breached, one moment the engine screaming acceleration as the propeller broke free from the whipping strain. The next like some submarine, under it and gone. When you're under the water, it doesn't matter how deep. You throw your whole will at getting to the surface. When you reach the point of maximum displacement, new buoyancy drives you up so fast you leave half your being behind. The waves are higher. Grooved walls as they plough into us. One way and then another. One coming on top of another. Crashing over the wheelhouse. Rushing liquid pouring, the deck submerged, over the windscreen, over our heads, off the back deck in flooding rivers. The deck disappears completely. No more than a yard beyond the back-door, the stern is gone as the bow flies skyward. Over and over again, higher and faster. Falling endlessly off the tops into dark trough pits, booming at the bottom. Certain each time that she must surely shatter to pieces.

We are not hitting the bottom. The echo-sounder reads a hundred feet and then seemingly nothing as we fall from the top of a wave. It might be twenty, thirty or more feet into the trough. It opens up beneath you and you dive through clear air. The solid water at the bottom is soon rising up to meet us. And you hit. Seventeen tons at forty miles an hour.. The boat must be incredibly strong and takes it each time. We though, are shaken senseless.

We're going too long and must make the mark soon. Every so often one or other of us yells out. 'I thought we'd gone that time!.' Amazing that nobody screams when it's happening. The concentration, anticipation blocks it out. You brace yourself, wedged in a corner or gripping the wheel. Alone in blood-draining fear.
Red line dots bounce around. It's impossible to know how much water we're in. Is it twenty fathoms? Is it five? It's probably both within seconds.
Long before we sight the first mark Trevor demands, 'It's here. It should be here!'
We are only up at the height to see for a few moments then consumed in water mayhem moments from impact. That next one is cresting. It's going to break over us! We're gone again. This is it! And suddenly we are thrown up again out on top.
Collect yourself immediately to look for the buoy.

'It's an Occulting White light in threes every two seconds.'
We are sucked side-ways, the keel slipping like some giant carpet being pulled from under. We tip for another striking the bared hull. Violence shoots along the direction of the mast. In seconds we are flung up again, glaring through the sight of an angry sky, searching in every direction. The sky is getting darker. It's coming up to six, in April.

'There's a light! There!' Pete points to the right. We plunge down again. The rakish angle means we hit the wave bottom and are jolted upright. Both Trevor and Pete are thrown hard against the wall. As they recover and climb back to their positions I see it. 'Yes. I saw it too! Something like ten o'clock. I saw it, just out the corner of my eye.'
If the identification sequence is more than the briefest moment, we'll never get to see it. We each strain to catch it and count.

I try to aim directly for it. We must be sure. Trevor's navigation is fantastic but we must be sure. Getting there takes an age. One moment we are facing a tantalising flash almost long enough to count, the next veering away, plummeting down out of sight. After what seems interminable inch upon crest upon swirling maelstrom hindering, we are finally close. Close to it and for a fleeting moment we all count and agree. Trevor, pinned to the chart shelf, measuring, checking again the next course, eventually decides. 'One seven-five. That's it. That'll take us onto the next. The tide's running really fast. We should 'ave come at that one way further over t'East. We'll really 'ave to keep our eyes peeled this time. I've no idea if this is gonna get us there!.. If we miss it we can't be sure of the Wells fairway after that.'
I turn the wheel hard and spin the red needle on the compass to one-seven-five. That's nice, steady. Now try and get it to stay anywhere near! Each time we slew and veer, I wrestle us

back to the course. It's practically impossible and the question of how long we are actually steering that course, gets banished to inane fatalism. Only a short time ago I was yelling at Trevor to give me the luxury of a better one, a more comfortable course to steer through the crossed swell. Now it makes no difference. The only driver, that we must not lose our way. I grapple the wheel and watch the needle swing crazily.

The waves are getting higher. Down in the troughs we're dwarfed. On and on amid the noise of buffeting wind and crashing water. We are silent, hanging on for dear life. What does that sound like now? Every moment seems like an end. How many times can you anticipate it, thoughts racing to conclusions interrupted. Numbed confusion must move on, though all stability, every coherence is redundant.

The light fades with an ever diminishing sense of ourselves. On top of the waves only a faint lighter strip marks sky at the horizon. It's impossible any longer to make out any shape to the cloud. Dark closing in, we ride an even tighter world of boiling proximity. I switch on all the lights, mast-top, spotlight on the wheelhouse roof, the navigation lights. As the lights go on inside there's the briefest warming sense of normality. Perhaps inside our lit cocoon we are safe. The feeling lasts mille seconds, the lie revealed as we roll again until the light at the mast top disappears, extinguished by the abyss. We squirm and skew upright and the little point of light is reborn to career, spinning wildly in the air above. After a while I have to turn the spotlight off. Pointing straight ahead across the deck the powerful beam just seems to magnify the mayhem. Every sparkling drop of flailing highlit rain, spray and crests brought too much into focus.

After what seems a tortuous age we spot a tiny pin-prick of light way over to the East. 'That's It!' Pete yells. Trevor is more circumspect. One arm lashed by a piece of webbing to the ceiling rail, with the other he grabs the binoculars. 'Where?'
'Over there!' Pete still hasn't quite got the idea that we can't look at him and for the buoy at the same time.
'Pete! Tell me where on the clock!'
'Oh fuckin' hell, three o'clock then! No! Nine o'clock! Over there for fuck sake!'
Trevor is scouring the moment we get up on top.
'No! Can't see it,' he yells. 'Where?'
'It was there!' Pete yells back. But the search curtails as we are swamped and dive beneath another breaking giant. We are gone for an age before getting another chance, the pitching and tossing making it impossible to keep your eyes on any one point.
I saw it next. 'There, Trev! Nine o'clock! White flashing! It's a long way off! I'm gonna turn and go there! Jesus! We must have drifted a long way West!'
I turn us towards the light. It's our only chance. We must be sure. Forget any course if we don't make this one.

How long it took us to edge closer I don't know. Twenty minutes, maybe half an hour. I can feel the wind across us and behind. It's so strong that every time we get out on top I think I can feel it lifting us, surging us forward. Then we plunge backwards again and again into waves that are still growing. For a while they look like breakers coming in succession. From the troughs I can't see the tops, then we climb and climb, the engine deeply churning heavy load. At the top suspended, we get a view of the light seeming no nearer. I readjust the course toward it and we plunge again. Racing down, a huge force, the propeller out of the water and the engine screaming. Do I have time to cut the revs? No!.. We smash into the next trough, cascades of water until we are submerged and climb again.

Eventually we draw close to the buoy. We collapse together in exhausted relief. Of what I have no idea. Still I clapped my hand on Trevor's back. Pete throws himself across the room and in the attempt at a hug falls heavily, crashing into the step-well at the saloon door. For a brief manic moment we burst into stilted laughter. Pete scrambles to his feet, before trying to brace himself, clutching at air he falls heavily as another wave bursts.

Dead ahead, a beacon in the madness. Its flashing light willed by some all too temporary prayer. This tiny thing prompting such sanity. Or was it insanity matching the mayhem.
I am full of respect, a real heart surge. 'Trev! That's.. incredible!'
He is already clambering onto the chart-top for his notes. 'Okay, back to one-eight-o!.. Five, maybe six miles to the fairway.. Come On!'
It's a first. I've never seen it before or since. The compass needle spun a complete circle..

Chapter Twelve
what good is this? Wash hits it good..?

The first sight we get of the North Norfolk coast is from the top of an enormous wave we are surfing. A few momentary glints of light. As the waves get higher we have more time both above and below. It carries us aloft high above the normal sea-level. Down again and the water is pitch dark. Closed in, rain making alternately horizontal and vertical curtains to block the view and we spin and plunge off into darkness, claustrophobic and deep. The hull booms protest. We are almost used to it, braced and ready. The shock though, is still more than imagination.

'It's getting really dark?'

I look at my watch. 'Quarter past seven.' The sky is so full of black it's impossible to remember when it was not. A few moments ago I thought I saw some other lights. I'm not sure and say nothing. At only about two o'clock if dead-ahead is twelve. It couldn't have been lights on the land. They shouldn't be there. I don't see them again next time we're up,.. and too busy getting ready for imminent deluge.

It can only be a few miles to the Wells fairway. We seem suddenly close.

'How far are we Trevor?'

'I don't know yet. Four maybe. I thought I saw some lights just now. Like they were on land. I don't think that's right. Maybe we've drifted in. If so we need to turn left and get out further!'
'Yeh I did too. I thought I saw some lights. About two o'clock!'
The compass is all over the place. Trevor leans right over it, lying across the wide shelf, creasing the charts. We agree we're heading about one-eighty. But for moments only. It was me that asked for south I don't know how many hours ago.
'That could be straight into the land. The tide is coming fast now across us from the East. We could have been pushed further west.. Are we as far out as we thought.. Can you see a green light.. or the fairway buoys?'
'Let's turn left! It's the most obvious way. Coming back should be easier if we can't find it!.. We need to decide, Trev! If all we're going on is lights on the land,.. we're in more trouble than we thought.'
'Wish we had a GPS.' Was the first dumb thing I heard him say.
'Yes! That would be nice wouldn't it. We haven't. So let's work out where the hell we are shall we!'
'There! What's that?!.. Lights on the land!.. Over there, dead-ahead. There!' We all see it this time. It's only a couple of lights, side-by-side. Not that near. It's so hard to judge.
'Let's turn left, Trevor. Until we sight the fairway buoys. Is it me or did we seem to get here too quick?..'
Pete shouts. 'I can see more lights there. It's like a town, big town!'
Trevor is pawing the chart. Holding on grimly every-time it's bounced into his face.
I see the lights too. At about one o'clock. 'Yeh Trevor. It's only a few.' 'There's no big towns anywhere near with a sea front. Pete look through the binoculars. All of ours have a long channel before you get to the town. Those are still a long way off but they must be right on the coast'.

We roll and pitch violently at a crossed wave breaking over us. The world disappears again, the mast head plunging until another wave strikes from below and we are pushed upright through a dome of spray.

'Jesus!..' He recovers, 'No it's not that bad. We're just being driven there by the tide. We'd be close enough to see navigation lights. Whatever we've gotta get East. Maybe twenty degrees left? To make sure we've got plenty o' time to line-up. Right?'

'Okay!' I turn us as gently as possible, missing a broadside and diving through one a moment before it broke. The engine works harder immediately.

'We need a sail!'

'Yeh. What idiot's gonna go out and put that up then!'

'It was a joke, Pete!'

His reaction is perfect and it breaks the tension. I saw it and immediately thought about morale for sailors. Ooh Ay and UP She Rises arrived unwanted from somewhere. Should we be singing? I wouldn't have dared suggest it. Only the thought of it, one might have been braver? I bet it worked. Is it mad to say?.. But this time the enemy was huge. Down in the trough it was a roller as high as a house. Smooth without a blemish on its face as the curl bore down. Ooh Ay and up she rises faded away! Feel your stomach left by a wild elevator, through another crossed and violent on the way up.

There are lights blinking through the rain. Little pods of them, a few bunched together, then none. It's impossible to tell where we are in relation. Skirting the coast, it must be close. Maybe we're a couple of miles off. Trevor twists between the chart and the binoculars. As much as possible I'm keeping us due East parallel to the coast.

'There! A Green One! Two o'clock! See it!' I follow the line of his arm. We are about to dive! We dive and hold on! On the way up is the only time you can speak..

'There! There it is! Two o'clock. Green. Slow on and off. See it!?'

'Yes..'

'Keep on this course, Will, 'til we're well past it. Until it's about five o'clock. Then we should drift into it with the tide. Look out for the fairway buoys. There'll be a line of three, going away from it to the North east. We've got to get into the fairway first so we can line up the light and the entrance hole in the Bar. Don't drive into it from here. We're the wrong angle. Right? 'Cause we'll miss!'

'Yeh. Right.' It's painfully slow. Against the tide we're making almost no headway. Yet it seems to be getting nearer. I must try and keep us out instead of being sucked in towards the land. The light is almost dead ahead.

As we get closer the waves seem to come even higher. We are broadside to many, pitching and rolling hard. I try steer into them but their size is increasingly terrifying. We are flipped and deluged like some tiny pawn. Each time somehow we survive, out on top, immediately with a view of lights. The pull is intense but no sign of the fairway.

'We're bang on time! It's nearly seven-forty-five!'

'Nice to know we got something right!'

'If that's for me, Pete? I accept full responsibility!'

'Hold on you two. We're not there yet!'

The saloon door opens and Sally emerges looking incredibly sick. 'What's that? Are we there yet?'

'Just a bit more, Sal. Not much longer.. Why don't you do something useful and look after her.' I fire at Pete.

'No, Pete!' yells Trevor. 'Stay up here! We need your eyes looking out for the fairway.' He grabs Pete's shirt, pulling him back. Sally slumped to floor. He intoned. 'We 'ave got to find that fairway before we turn in toward the light. And look,.. it's almost dead ahead!'

The wheel spun out of my hand, wrist crunching fast. Both Pete and Trevor yell almost together. Too late, the wave breaks on top of us. Petrified, we are gone again. The weight of the water pushing us down and down. Nothing beyond the windscreen but whiteout and an agonising age. We launch upward and as we fly in clear air I see it. A buoy dead-ahead!

'There! Is that a fairway?'

'Must be! Look further out. Are there any more? Or in to the light. Look, there at two o'clock. Are there anymore that way?'

The echo-sounder reads only twenty feet as we are sucked into the same trough as a bright orange buoy. Swinging hard sideways we are up again. With a clear view a new cluster of lights on the land.

'Where are the rest?! I can't see anymore. It looks like that one's afloat. Look it's not attached to anything.' Trevor is spinning around with the binoculars.

'There's a building! Looks like a big searchlight on top! No buoys! I can't see any buoys!'

Trevor jumps down from the window to the chart. 'It could be the Lifeboat Station! There's that and a Coastguard building on the chart right next to the Channel!..'

Pete yells. 'That's it! That's gotta be it!'

'Can you see anything beyond the Green to get a sight-line on? Chart shows red and green all the way down the Channel. There must be a red over there somewhere!'

'Nothing!' Trevor replied to himself. 'Nothing! There's nothing to line up on through there. And there are no other buoys further out. Where's the bloody Channel then?' He yells out in the direction of the land.

'Here, man! You're fuckin' in it! This is the Channel! We've passed that buoy now. Get in it!'

'You're always the bloody back-seat driver, Pete! Shut up!' for the first time Trevor sounds angry. 'That buoy was loose..'

'You're in the fuckin' channel, man! There's the green light! We've passed it. Fuckin' turn in and lets go for it!'

'Look Pete, we've got to line up on something to find the hole in the Bar. That's where the entrance to the channel is! We can't see it 'cause there's nothing to line up on?'

'We're gonna be right in the surf in there.' Trevor hands Pete the binoculars. 'Look, have a look through these. You can see really big waves. Look!'

The next top catches us at an odd angle and we are surfing sideways, fast toward the lights.

'We might as well turn, Trevor! We've passed the only light we've seen. Is this the Channel?'

'The angle's all wrong! That Lifeboat Station's not gonna be in the Channel, but I can't see any lights!'

The tide is starting to push us in close. That last wave seem to push for an eternity. Do I turn in or wait?

'Wait! Wait! Not yet!'

But we are hardly moving, the tide so strong beats the wind. There's a lot of spray now and the roar of wind and bursting water is deafening. We get to the top of a wave. There is another clear view. A green light and no others. The building with its powerful lights, although still a long way off, every time we catch a glimpse it seems closer. We crash dive, booming flat into a trough. The echo-sounder dots disappear. Less than ten-foot beneath! The engine throbs on and on but there's no power enough. No headway but we are slowly drifting in.

'We're in the fairway! Turn, man!'

'He's right now, Trev. There's no more water! We've gotta turn in.'

'Do it then!' he yells back over the roar.

I feel I'm summoning every possible will. Desperately opening my own conduit to the light. I called on God or Nature or any being to help.

'God help us.' Trevor intoned on cue.

As we turn in we see another light. There's a new red light beyond the Green.

'This is it, man! We're in!'

'Shut the fuck up!' This time it's me yelling at Pete.

The first light, the Green maybe a hundred yards away, a red directly behind it. We are transfixed, staring through driven water. Willing the Channel to appear. We must be able to see a line? Cold, black nothing, strewn with confusion, no clues. I switch on the spotlight and see nothing but sheets of highlit vortices.

Suddenly all of the water in front of us is sucked away. Through the back window a very large wave is almost on top of us. I strain to look up at it coming. I can't see its top. It's too high! After horrifying moments of anticipation the grooved arch smashes over engulfing the stern, toppling and cascading above us the full length of the boat. We are thrown forward and submerged. As we rise quickly to the surface its overtaking crest is so close in front I'm sure we are going to fall off it backwards. It accelerates away toward the light. In the trough the boat heals and twists violently, we bounce and with a sudden long staccato shudder we hit the bottom and slew around. We hit so hard I swear I hear cracking and timber snapping above every other drowning sound. But then the noise of scraping on the bottom deafens all other. It could be rocks, it could be anything. Imagination runs wild. Do we smash to pieces now? The engine saves us, the prop bites and we surge forward again on another massive swell careering past at double our speed. As we lose momentum we ground heavily again, bouncing half sideways, the enormous weight

skipping up as if nothing, then landing, the keel broaching, digging in and tripping hidden wave-forms in the sand below.
'Where's the hole!'
Pete yells all the louder. 'It's there, man! It's there! Just go that way!'
'We're aground you idiot!'
Trevor chimes in. 'We've missed it!.. Look there's another light there now! Another red and it's the wrong side of the Green! We've missed it!'
'The Channel must be just over there!' A pathetic plaintive, surely it's still over a hundred yards away. How would you know from shadows and the darkest scattered gloom. A broadside wave crashes across us. The keel slips sideways and we roll almost completely over, the mast-head disappearing into deeper rising water. As it lifts us up we chop and yaw in a chaotic explosion of surf. On top again we can clearly see beyond Green and Red to the buildings with the spotlight.
Suddenly Pete is at the back-door, sliding it open. In his hand is a distress flare. He strikes the tape and like the best, most expensive firework you ever bought, it takes off with a huge rush, recoiling his elbow hard into the top step. I crane my neck to see it out of my window. The absurd thought that I had paid twenty-five quid and now I can't see it, got lost in my anger at Pete. 'What the hell do you think you're doing!? Who said anything about flares? What are you thinking?! What the hell d'ya think anyone's gonna be able to do to help us now, you idiot!'
He slams the door shut. We glare at one another. It's done and a more pressing deluge is about to strike. We breach and run aground again.
Trevor has the binoculars and shouts. 'It looks like there's a boat in the water over there!'

As a new wave boils behind us we are propelled forward into a clear patch of flat water that opens up in front. I accelerate toward the spot-lit calm.

'I'm going to come around and come at it again. A complete left turn will bring us all the way around and hopefully into some deeper water, right!' The clear patch is expanding. I know it won't last and begin to turn her.

The engine note has changed and there is a strong smell of burning oil. Blue smoke begins to rise from the engine cover.

'It's the sand!' Pete yells. 'We've taken up sand into the water intake. There's no cooling water! She's overheating!' A wave hits us broadside and we slew almost completely around, the bow pointing out to sea.

'She won't last long if she overheats. Do something!..' Smoke is rising to fill the room.

Our view through the windscreen is suddenly filled with a solid wall of water. I can just see its top, the crest breaking and blowing the fifty yards between us and over our heads from as high as a huge house. Its pace is incredible. It overcomes us, engulfing the mast top which precisely splits the wave in a widening groove. With the undertow we lurch forward sucked into it and then up vertically spinning at the same time at a rakish angle. With an almighty crashing just like an explosion underneath us, the hull broaches, hitting the bottom with such force it sounds as if every beam is cracking. With a deafening shudder the angle of the bow rears up almost vertical before us. The rudder is hitting solid ground. Violently the wheel spun from my hand. At exactly the same time a succession of loud mini-explosions, one after another, inside the lockers, spread like a circle ringing around the wheelhouse. From inside each locker a wood splitting clatter rattles as something hits the inside of the doors. The wheel spins violently. I let go before it takes my hand off. Pete half-diving, half-thrown, pulls off the engine cover, letting out a mass of steam and smoke. Then immediately distracted by the explosions he throws the cover aside and turns to begin ripping open the locker doors, sweeping cans and tools from the shelves and onto the floor behind him. Suddenly the whole moving floor is a minefield of holes and obstacles. The wave over us engulfs the whole boat and we broach again so heavily each of us is thrown to the floor amongst the debris. Pete is first to gather himself crawling back into a locker.

'Pete! What are you doing!'

He yells back, his head inside the pitching cupboard. 'It's the steering blocks. The cable's come right off the walls!' He is clambering inside the locker. I jump and grab at the spinning wheel. With a slap into my palm it falls completely slack. It's loose, limp in my hands, we have no steering whatsoever.

'Maybe I can nail them back on!'

'We've got no steering!' I yell over the din. 'We've got no steering!'

'We've got no engine either!' Trevor yells. You can feel the heat coming off it. 'We're gonna have to switch it off otherwise it'll seize up!' He turns to look up out of the windscreen at three star-shells exploding in the sky above us. As they fall the phosphorescence brightly lights the whole scene ashore behind us.

'They've answered us!' Pete cries out. 'They've answered our flare!'

The echo-sounder reads one dot. Past it and beyond through the side window another leviathan wave is looming. Bearing down on us deeply grooved, smooth and solid. It soon towers out of sight. The undertow sucking us, hurling us into its path. I try to accelerate with it as we spin to its direction. This might be the last of the engine and without any rational or real intent I pull the throttle lever fully open. We lurch forward as the engine screams. Like being plucked by some giant's hand we are thrown high up and under the wave's leading edge. Flipped in clear air, a matchstick insignificant weight. I feel us tumbling, falling and spinning, aware that the mast top light is describing an exact circle above and then below me. For an endless moment everything is suspended, time, emotion and fear. A void of anticipation moving at incredible speed yet frozen in incomprehension. Then it ends in a massive explosion of water, the spray cascade curtain parts and we land perfectly upright to surf down the face of the wave. Like a fast car suddenly accelerating, the inertia overcome, our weight shoots forward on the wave's momentum. There isn't the briefest moment to wonder how we got up here or where this is going now but, steady as a rock we surf incredibly fast. We get a last glimpse of the Lifeboat Station far away to the right. I'm sure I see people in the water pushing their boat!

Directly ahead in the spotlight is a long beach. We hurtle toward it high on the wave, upright and straight. The engine, smoke now billowing from it, screamed the acceleration then suddenly faltered, cut and stopped altogether. Its noise is replaced by an incredible roar of wind rushing and surf flying. How fast we are going when we hit the beach, I don't know. Fast enough that when the wave energy is spent, we continue to glide upright in shallow water. Spray flying up from either side, a very smooth hydrofoiled belly-landing, buoyed on a powerful wind. We travelled a long way before finally lowering in the water and coming to rest. Slowly as she stopped, she gently rocks and then heels over.

I threw open the door to let out choking smoke. Howling wind and rain arrived immediately. We've stopped! Our stillness is shocking.

Out on the deck Trevor is surveying the scene. It looks like some trees ahead a few hundred yards. There are a lot of lights a long way beyond in the distance. Rain is falling hard, slanting every which way in punching gusts. It's dark, the nearest lights on the Lifeboat Station now far away.

Pete arrives. 'Fucking hell, man! That was amazing!' Sally slips over the top step, landing in heap at our feet. I grab her arm as Bubbles stumbles over her. 'Are you alright, Sal?'

'Yes, I'm okay. What are we going to do now?'

I strain to see all around. My first instinct is to stay here and rest for a while. I am completely disoriented. The water lapping against the hull must be shallow as the boat is leaning over and rocking gently. We seem in no danger and but for the buffeting wind, the contrast to wild action a few moments ago is stark.

'Come on, man. Let's get off!' Pete is already half over the side with Bubbles ready to follow. Sally doesn't budge, slumped on the deck with her face in her hands.

'No wait!' I shout. 'Wait, Pete! We need to be more organised. We don't know what we're getting into over there. It looks like miles to those lights. I guess that's the town?' I need to think and Pete is rushing me. I don't want to go anywhere. I want to sit and let the shock drain.

'Come on, man, it's crazy to stay here. Let's get off!'

I hesitate then surrender again. 'Alright!. If we're going let's at least make sure we can be warm and dry. Everybody, go get your bags and chuck everything out. We'll just take sleeping bags and towels and blankets. Okay? No more than that. We don't want to carry it. Okay? We'll make for those trees. Perhaps there's a bit of shelter over there. Okay? Let's do it!' Pete helps Sally up and they go inside, followed by wagging Bubbles who now looks perfectly back to normal.

What's wrong with the shelter here?

'We should get the anchors out, Will.' Trevor makes sense. 'There's still over an hour to the top of the tide and with this

wind blowing we don't want her to be pushed farther up the beach.'
I agree and he goes below to get out the stern chain. I run the length of the deck and begin pulling the bow chain out and over the side. Once a good amount is paid out I jump off the front into the water. It's freezing but after the splash comes only just over my knees. Trevor is already in the water and we work fast together, pulling out chain, running back, getting more. Walking it towards the sea and eventually hauling enough out to make two good lines to seaward, with the heavy anchors on each.

By the time we're back up on the stern deck, Sally, Pete and Bubbles have gone. In the dark I can make out their fading forms wading toward the trees. I call out loudly over the wind. 'Why not get your stuff, Trev and follow them?' I still feel very reluctant to leave. 'Don't let them go too far. If it's no good we can come back and light the fire.. It'll just be on a bit of a slope. I'm going to lock everything up and I'll be there.'
Down inside is chaos everywhere. I ignore it and do the rounds, checking that everything is locked and safe. I must be in shock. My mind not working clearly. All I can do now, I keep repeating. I'll clean up later. I empty most of the clothes out of my carpet bag and stuff in a large towel, a couple of blankets and the sleeping bag. I thought about a fire and threw in the little axe, a couple of log sticks and some matches. It was completely mechanical. On my way out I locked the saloon door, put the engine cover back, closed a few of the lockers and switched off the lights. I stepped up to the deck, pulled the door closed and was fastening the padlock when I noticed over to the left two large lights low on the beach. The lights grow brighter and larger, very quickly approaching. It looks like something out of 'Close-Encounters'. Suddenly the twin lights, now very bright indeed, rise up sharply into the air. The wind is

howling so loud it's not until these floodlights settle directly on me that I can see and then hear the helicopter above them. I said I wasn't thinking very clearly and in that moment a panic came over me with a rush of thoughts. No! This can't be!

And then stupid guilt struck. Oh God! This must be costing a fortune! And I began to wave it away, frantically shouting. 'No, it's alright! We don't need you!' In the midst of my frantic waving I see a man at the door of the helicopter and now he's out in mid air and then coming down on a cable. The noise is suddenly incredible and the heat beneath this huge thing, now only thirty-foot above, is intense. In the wildly buffeting wind and rain this hovering giant is completely unmoving, rock solid above. The lights are so bright, the whole area around the boat lit up like day. The man on his cable is arriving on the back deck. A fantastically precise aim and descent but just as his feet touch the deck there's a blue spark off one of his boots and he jumps five or more feet into the air and backwards. He is gone over the guardrail and falling overboard! A surprised lightening reaction grabbed the scruff of his collar and hauled him back on board. Immediately he is upright he lifts his helmet visor to reveal a broadly smiling face and with massively over exaggerated gestures gives both thumbs up! I'm still shouting that we're okay, that we don't need them and waving my arms but even I can't hear my voice over the noise from above. He completely ignores my waving and with more grand gestures gives both thumbs up and then points both forefingers at the sky. Within a moment he has thrown something over my head and shoulders, swung on his cable to wrap both legs around me and we're up and flying fast skyward! At the helicopter's wide open door he pushes me hard onto the floor. Another helmeted man appearing from behind picks me up bodily, throwing me into a seat on the wall. The same man turns to grab something and turning back unceremoniously jams a pair of very large headphones over my ears. Instantly, the most archetypal RAF plummy voice is saying. 'Good Evening, Sir!' Picture the winged moustache.

'What!' The second man pulls down a little microphone on my headset and makes a sign like he's pointing to his mouth. The plummy voice continues. 'Bit Of A Nasty Old Night Isn't It, Sir?'

'This is surreal!' I must be in some kind of alternate reality and I'm going to regain consciousness in a moment.

'Are There Any Others, Sir? Do You Have Any Crew, Sir?'

'Yes.' I say falteringly. 'Three others and a dog. Wading up the beach towards the trees!' I gesture in their general direction.

'Jolly Good, Sir! We'll Just Go And Get Them Then, Shall We?'

Completely dumbed I say lamely. 'Yes, alright.'

I can feel the helicopter turning and the first guy is getting ready at the door. Above him are two lights, a red and a green. As we slow to a stop, the green light is on and he's out over the door-sill and gone.. After a few moments and in quick succession the green is off and the red light comes on. It occurs to me this must be the correct length of the cable to the ground. When he touches the ground he must be earthing some static in the helicopter. That was the spark as he fell over the side. So when the red light comes on, that's the very moment he's getting the shock!

Within a few minutes the light has turned green and Trevor arrives in similar fashion, thrown in and dumped in the seat next to me. We pat each others' knees. In more complicated but still quick succession, green light, red light, ouch!, green light, Sally, Bubbles and then Pete arrive in turn. We greet each other as much as possible over the noise. Pete looks like the cat who got the cream. Sally looks terrified hugging Bubbles whose tail wags out the back. The plummy voice is there again. 'Is That All, Sir?'

'Yes. That's everybody. Thank you very much.' I add meekly.

'Jolly Good, Sir!' He is so hail and hearty. 'All Present And Correct Then, Sir?'

'Yes, thank you.'

'Jolly Good, Sir.' And the helicopter is turning again.

'Just One More Thing, Sir!'

'Yes?'

'Where's The Life-Ring, Sir?'

'The what?!' Do I hear him right?

'The Life-Ring, Sir. Where's The Life-Ring?'

I have to think about it. Does he really mean the red and white cork ring? What on earth is he talking about that for? It's on the deck, tied to the stanchion cables.

'Hello, Sir. Where's The Life-Ring?'

'Yes. It's on the boat. On the fore-deck, tied on the port stanchion.'

'Jolly Good, Sir. We'll Just Go And Get That Then!' And off we go. As we swing around I see through the open door all the way back to the boat. She looks very small down there. Heeled over and abandoned.

The whole ceremony, green light, red light is repeated one more time and our man arrives with the life-ring and the same big smile under his flipped-up visor. He slaps me on the shoulder and sat down on the last vacant seat next to me with a few more exaggerated thumbs up and vigorous pointing. I still cannot believe that in this howling storm, he went down five times including the dog, and then put himself through it all over again for the life-buoy.

Chapter Thirteen
what good is this? Two aids to highs

We land in a field with goal posts and dazzling rainbows of blue and red flashing lights. Ambulances, police cars and a gaggle of onlookers. On touch-down an ambulance man rushes to the door, blanket trails in the wind. He takes the dog! Others arrive and enfold us. I feel acute embarrassment as my ambulance man is saying, 'Can you walk okay to the ambulance?' The blue lights, there must be four police cars! The beaming crowd all windswept and wrapped in bobble hats and scarves. 'Yes. Thank you, thank you. I'm perfectly alright really. Really I don't need an ambulance.' Please point me to a deep hole I can crawl in!

We have sirens and police escort for the procession into town. Along a sea-front quay, with another little gaggle sheltering by a gaudy lit chip-bar. We turn under a portico into a yard between the houses. My ambulance man is there, helping me down the step and around to a porch where a practically perfect looking grandmother is waiting for me. 'Here you are, dear,' she says, cuddling me through a door and down a hall. At the last door is a fluorescent bathroom. Inside, a steaming brimmed-full bathtub. 'There you are, dear,' she says in a wonderful mothering monotone. 'You get in there, dear and I'll bring you a nice cup of tea.'

Not only does she bring me a nice cup of tea but later, about half a pint of rum in a tumbler. She walks straight into the bathroom to place it by the tap. 'There you are, dear. That'll buck you up.'

After a while of staring at it, I sniffed over the top of the glass. Remembering this afternoon I was pretty clear what it would buck. I bathed and dressed in damp and salty clothes. As I finish, the uniformed cap of a policeman appears around the half-opened door. He asks that I come to be interviewed. He and a Coastguard officer would like me to make a statement for the record.

They are sitting around a gingham table when I arrive. It's very formal, name, address. I quickly get into the flow and tell how I had underestimated the storm, called the Coastguard for advice. They recommended Wells but that it was too rough to get in. I added that there was not enough water and, we could not find the buoys that would lead us into the Channel. I described that we got close but ran aground searching for the buoys and in turning away to try to come at it again we were hit by a wave as high as a house. As a result the steering broke so that we foundered. We were just getting off the vessel when the helicopter arrived. What I didn't say, that I wished later I had, was that I do praise the rescue services and sincerely want to thank them all for our safety.

But I still felt we didn't need all this. My embarrassment is acute. No doubt it will be said that I was stupid to be out there in the first place but we had in fact saved ourselves. I want to say that I feel completely disempowered by their authority. There will never be anyone else to blame but me. I wanted to say, that but for their intervention and my concern for my crew we might all be elsewhere. Tonight no doubt, in rockier beds.

The whistling wind appropriately rattled a door nearby. Of course I didn't say any of this because it would have been rude and ungrateful and perhaps not even correct. And for the record, I'm sure they would have been right to consider me an ungrateful wretch.

As I flag toward the end of the interview, the others arrive, Bubbles bounding up to greet me. They all look relieved, rosy and scrubbed. We ask what next and are told that we will be put up for the night. Did we have money? Then Mrs Abel and the Ship Wrecked Mariners Guild would offer us accommodation in their Bed and Breakfast. Mrs Abel arrives to move around the room tidying and offering sympathy and encouragement with more 'That's all right now, dear.' and 'You'll feel better now.' We smile weakly. Pete more in the spirit, shakes hands, nodding and thanking through the stiltedness. Finally we are left alone and agree to move somewhere else and come back later to bed. Whether quite the right venue for a recovery we agree to find a pub. I'm struggling with a mass of emotions. The others must be too. I said we should stick together despite wanting to get as far away as possible. Fortunately I suppose, I can't think sensibly anyway, so suggest nothing better. Somewhere around the middle of the bath, I surrendered the last finger to whatever next.

We are recommended a pub. The Golden Fleece, right on the quay, 'you carn't mess it', is where the men drink.

Under the portico and out in the street, it's immediately biting cold. The wind so strong, it's difficult to stand up through flailing torrential rain. Past a chip shop that almost grabs Pete, we scramble, blown huddled together. Only half way along the quay the pub is obvious, pools of light spilling out on puddles. Through the porch and double swing doors the bar is loud and abrasive. It's crowded with a TV blaring in the corner and something bouncy and banal from the jukebox. Quite a few heads turn but we are busy shaking coats and exchanging bath stories. Everyone seems in surprisingly good spirits. I offer to get the round. The minimum skipperly duty and I head to the bar. There's an empty table across the room and they make for it.

At the bar it's busy, one burly man serving all. The drinkers are deep in loud conversations. A few likely fishermen, waders and working muscles. I find my way through and eventually it's my turn. It's gruff and I give the order. Pete arrives and begins ferrying drinks. Then there's a heavy tapping on my shoulder. I turn around to face a small elderly man.

'You the bloke what come ashore tonight?' He wears a little blue bobble hat high on his balding head, very muddy wellies and fingerless gloves with little trailing threads.

'Yes.?' He stares at me from very blue eyes.

'Buy us a drink.' It's not a request.

My immediate thought goes something like, 'first night in a strange town. Do as the Romans..'

'Yes, of course. What can I get you?'

'Large Brandy.' And as he walks away, 'Come'n sit this 'ere window.'

Pete arrives back 'Can you take that as well Pete, I've been summoned over there.' I point to the bobble-hat, now staring out through the window. Pete cradle's his pint lovingly.

When the brandy arrives I pay and take it over to the window. I sit down opposite him and he parts the net curtain saying, 'See that ol' blue trawler o'r there?' Through the rain-splashed window, sparkling lights outside and the sheets of driving rain, it's not that obvious. 'There,' he repeats, pointing a stubby thumb. I see it, the gunwale just above the quay. In the middle of a line of working boats. Tide must be coming in high. They're all bobbing about, short masts waving frantically. This one is scruffy, the decks loaded full. An old blue trawler..

'I live a' Stiffkey, couple o' mile down the coast,' he says with a strong accent. 'I walk me dogs on the beach. An' every morning for ten years I pass 'er and you could see the top six-foot o' the mast.. One day I'm walkin' along and you could see 'er decks! So I went home and I got me spade and I dug 'er out.. And there she be!' He points a woolly finger.

'People'll tell you it's a graveyard out there. Hasn't been a boat come off there in twenty years.. Don't you believe 'em. You'll get 'er off.' He rests the blue eyes on me again.

'Thanks.' I said, trying to picture her over there somewhere beyond the dark. I've no idea how far or even in which direction. I couldn't speak or describe the race of images that flashed through. Or of anything else that made sense.

'Well yes, thanks for that.' I nod and get up. 'That was worth a double-brandy.'

It was a dark and stormy night. No really..

Next morning over breakfast, the howling outside still, we have our proper post mortem. Last night, by the time I got to their table we managed a second drink and fell silent just watching the comings and goings of the bar. I don't ever remember feeling so drained. We fought our way back through the wind, under the portico at Mrs Abel's and collapsed between clean sheets.

I'm pouring our second pot of tea. 'That bloke last night, Peanuts, said they'd measured it Force 11 in the car park. God alone knows what it was out there.'

Trevor said, 'Yeh, did you see those guys that came in just before we left?'

I remember them, a group of six, a couple of them still dressed in wet weather gear.

He continued. 'They were the Lifeboat crew. I heard them saying they'd spent over an hour in the water trying to get the

Lifeboat back in the station. They were pretty pissed-off. One of 'em said he'd like to get hold o' those f-ing idiots.'

I fed the momentum. 'Well, I think we've all got a right to be pissed-off. Mine says,.. if they hadn't insisted that we come in here, we might not have had any of this?'

Pete jumped in. 'Yeh and we might be fuckin' dead, man. It was the only thing to do!'

My reaction to the cue was probably too quick. 'No. Pete. It wasn't the only thing to do! You remember I wanted to stay out and find some deeper water. It's hardly any good saying it now but I wish I hadn't called them.. I know it was my fault to miss the Shipping Forecast but even then it was going to be too late to turn back. We'd never have made it. And yes, I did need to call them. I felt a real weight of responsibility and needed another opinion. A more expert one.. Sure, I was more concerned about you and Sally. I still disagreed with them. I thought they were doing it for their convenience. Which I know is reasonable,.. like it was their best way to ensure everyone's safety.'

'Yeh! Well they were right, man! We survived, didn't we? And thanks to them.'

Trevor, level as usual. 'We don't though. We don't know what it would have been like further out.'

I run through highlights in the silence that follows.

Trevor comes back sounding like he'd considered it. 'For what it's worth, I think we should have stayed out too.'

'Look, I know I got you into this. But the morning forecast was perfect. Force four to five North Westerly and a good tide with us all the way. And I know I should have thought more, particularly p'r'aps about Sally if it got rough..'

He interrupted me. 'If it got rough! Fucking hell, man, it was insane! I never knew it could get that bad.'

Sally still looks shattered, staring into her coffee cup. He looks at her and continues.

'You're fucking mad, you two. You could 'ave killed us all!'
That hangs nicely in the air for a few moments.
'You're right, Pete. And I'm very, very sorry. You're absolutely right.. I do want you to know though. Mostly 'cause I feel guilty about the whole thing, but I'm still saying we should have stayed out and not tried to come into this place with its shallow water.. Because it's far more dangerous! I think we proved that one.'
We stop. Pete and I both stare at our toast.
'I want to know about those buoys.' Trevor is earnest. 'Where were they? We couldn't 'ave missed them.'
I say, 'But we couldn't see anything for more than a few moments. I mean they could have been out there and we did miss them.'
'I don't think so. I think they weren't there. I think they'd blown away in the storm or something. I think we passed one of them adrift. I think there was only one left. The one furthest in. We passed it and, Pete, I reckon that's when you were right. We should've turned in immediately instead of going on further for the next one. That was it. There were no next ones. The others by that time should have been out to sea on our left. But they weren't there. I'm sure we'd have seen them.'
'So we'd got the angle wrong by then,.. and hit the Bar.'
I can conjure the full and colourful picture of that last wave. Surfing in.. 'That was incredible!' It was so shallow. 'And there wasn't enough water. We were only just inside the two hours. We got here too early.'
'Thank fucking Christ for that!' Pete was serious, but hearing himself say it made him laugh.
As we smiled, including Sally, who at that moment brightened, his volume increased. 'You're fuckin' nuts, man! The pair of you!'

They went home the next day. We walked them to the bus-stop early in the morning. We hugged and kissed goodbye but not much else. I imagined we'd talk about it later when the heat is out of it. I'll get their stuff back to them. Sally still looks quite ashen. I don't push it, they want to get away. What an amazing school holiday I gave her?

Trevor stayed for a few more days. The storm went on for almost two before finally blowing itself out. On one buffeted walk along the quay we spotted the Pilot mopping his deck. It says PILOT in big letters on the side of the boat and the back of his jacket, so we're pretty sure who we're talking to. He's surprises, the first in town that's not a scowl. Eventually I admit who I am. He smiles. 'Oh roight! Saw you in't Fleece the night you come ashore. Pretty rough, eh? Never gets that bad hereabouts.' Then he disappeared down inside and after standing there for quite a while expecting him back, we gave up and walked further along to look at the row of trawlers still bouncing at the quay.

We took another rain-lashed walk yesterday. I couldn't wait any longer. About a mile or more up a long road running alongside the Channel. At the top there's a deserted campsite and a sheltering pine-wood dipping and climbing over the dunes. The road ends in a turning circle and hidden in the dunes as the trees shrink to marram-grass is the Lifeboat Station and the Coastguard lookout. Beyond, a wide flat beach with the low-tide sea far away.

From the top of the dunes we can see her. Across the Channel as it winds its way to the sea. A wide and flat expanse of pale yellow sand as far as you can see. Completely dry and out there in the middle, half way between the Bar and a little stand of trees at the edge of a salt marsh. A long, long way down the beach, she's the tiniest toy in the distance. Far enough away that when we walked off the dunes and down to the Channel's edge you see her through a rippling mist. We can just make out the angle of the mast as she's leaned over.

The following day we passed the Pilot again all too briefly in the street. He said he saw her as he was coming in that morning.
'Still pretty rough it were, 's morning!.. She's a long some off i'n't she?'
'Yes. We saw the Coastguard when we were up there yesterday. He said he'd keep and eye on her for me.'
'Aye 'e's a good bloke, ol' Tom.'
'He said not many folk get over there?'
'No, well come summer, they'd be a few. When they's campin' up there. But not 'til May or June when they start comin'. Droves on'em up there then, though not many on'em get over that far side. We usually gets a few at Easter, but it's washed out like, this year.' He looks up at the sky. A few first bits of blue are appearing.
'You don't know where I can get a boat to go out there have a look, do you? You know, rent or borrow one?'
'No, Sir I doesn't.' He's formal and replies too quick.
'You wouldn't want to take me up there, I suppose. Would you?' The question hangs there.
'Well, I could.' He says slow and non-committal and then, after only a few moments. 'When would you wan' t' be going then?'
I laughed. 'Well right now, obviously. I need to get out there to my boat as soon as possible and, I need to see how much water gets in there on a tide.'
'Mmh. I can see youl'd wan' a do that..' He says, rubbing his chin. 'You can walk, look. Some goes across the marsh. You 'ave to watch out for them dykes look. Long stretch from here, mind.'
We can see where he points. Just visible away in the distance, the tops of the little stand of trees. To have got to town we

would have had to walk in that stormy dark, a mile or more across the marsh and dykes and then, to cross the Channel down here as it turns in front of the quay. You could only swim across, about seventy-five yards or so. And freezing too!
'How about on the tide in the morning? I can pay if you need.'
'Could do.' He drawls, like it's a question.
Let's do it!.. 'So what time shall we come then? Top of the tide'll be just after ten won't it? So how long will it take us to get up there?'
'Only just up and down the Channel, mind?'
'Up and back, that's fine.'
There's a long pause before he says. 'You come 'bout noine thirty and we'll see what's what.'
I'm sure that'll be too late to get all the way by the top but I think he means we're going.

We were hanging around the quay just after nine. A watchful coffee in the Milk-Bar, a bit of pacing up and down the cobbles. Looking at all the boats rising with the tide, some at the quay wall, fishing boats and trawlers with nets and pots. Others, a few small yachts and cruisers and a barge, moored out in the middle. We pass a redundant looking crane and big iron ship-sized mooring rings. The marshes opposite are beginning to flood. They are submerged only by the highest tide. On the top of the tide last night, lit by a bright big moon, a shallow rippling pool stretches away across the marsh to the island of trees and the sea beyond.

Just before nine thirty he arrives.
Up the Channel we pass almost sunken tops of the marsh. On the other side, a narrow beach stops at a flood defence wall with the Channel road on top. The launch engine chugs monotonously and at slow speed the Channel seems endless. There are a few boats moored on buoys at the edges. A couple

up on the marsh, just afloat with a few tops of plants peering above the water. The widening Channel snakes between green and red squat pylons and eventually past the Lifeboat Station. The marsh giving way to wide open water and there, some way out from the island stand of trees, we get a first glimpse of Cirkus. Though in miniature she comes into clear view, heeled over and motionless, the only visible object across the wide and flat expanse of still and reflective water. Further on is the Channel entrance at the margin of the sea, where the Bar breaks a line of waves stretching into the distance on either side. Inside the Bar, broad and flat for as far as you can see down the coast, is a barely rippled inland sea. The little island of trees looks solitary. Behind them the marsh is a submerged and unbroken shallow sea spreading all the way back to the town, lit in the distance by a splash of sun. The boat is right out in the middle, a couple of miles away at least, far and equidistant from everywhere!

I hoped we'd go out into the sea and skirt down the edge of the Bar until we got closer. Just before the Channel entrance though, the launch shipped a couple of wave splashes over the stern. They were quite tame but the Pilot immediately said it was getting too rough and turned us around.
Still tiny, she is heeled over, not floating. As we turn back down the Channel we passed a line of sight with her. She's in the middle between the Bar and the trees. You can see the water is very shallow. Here at the Channel edges I can see the bottom. There's maybe two or three foot of water. It could be even less where she's lying.

Over a lunch of fish and chips in the Milk-Bar, Trevor and I chew the detail.
'She was heeled over and nowhere near afloat today on quite a high tide.'

'Yeh, today's is an eight-nine. It's here on the timetables. On the night of the storm it should have been a nine-one. Up to a nine-three the day after that. It was probably a lot more than that with the North West wind behind it.'

'So we're not seeing it at its highest. What's that in? Points of a meter, centimetres?'

'I don't know. Metres I should think. This a local tide timetable, so it would be at Blakeney. Sounds a lot doesn't it? A height up the quay wall there? That 'ud be thirty odd foot? Too much. Oh, I don't know how they measure it.'

After a pause he continues. 'I couldn't see those buoys out there either could you? I forgot to ask the Pilot. He should know what happened to them.'

'She might float?'

'She might.'

'When's the next highest tide?'

He's reading the neat little timetable book and pointing it out to me. '..here we are, two weeks, look.. and then higher the next month, a nine-two. There's nine-two at the end of June. It's only a couple of months.'

'We need a metre and a half though. And if today was less than a metre, that's quite a lot more water that's gotta find its way in there.'

'A nine-point-five. That would still have to have some wind behind it.'

'Yeh but how much wind? That was a Force Eleven. Christ!.. I think I could be gone sometime, don't you?'

'You don't know. The weather could break for the next ones. You've got two or three days either side, when it's close and building up to the highest. If the weather breaks on any one of those days, it could do it. You're going to have to wait 'til it's right. And it might not need much wind to push more water in there.'

He pushed the optimism. 'I'm sure you'll get one soon. You got three or four chances every two weeks.'
'There was enough of a breeze out there today though, wasn't there. But not enough water. You saw how calm it was?'
'Yeh but we're talkin' about forty centimetres! And that wind today was right round from the East. You need a Northerly and forty centimetres. That's all!'
'Shit, it's not that much is it?'
'It's the difference between under ya wellies or in 'em!'
'It's not that much.' I said, low and slow and as determined as I could muster. And the pretence at determination made me think.
'I could chuck out some ballast. Hey, I could chuck out everything if that's what it'll take.'
'Do it, Will.'
'And I'll have to be out there on every one of those high tides to measure it. To move if it looks good. I'll need to clean up and get the engine running again. Maybe I could rig up some sort of little feeder tank for the cooling water.. Otherwise it'll just take up more sand immediately. Oh God. How'm I gonna do all that?'
'Well, perhaps you should just go and camp over there. If you made a couple of journeys with supplies, you've got everything else you need, water, fuel. What else do'y need?'

Chapter Fourteen
what good is this? Stood waist high?

The idea of being there formed the strongest urge but for the moment I can't imagine being there full time, stranded and out of touch. But I didn't know the how or the what of anything.

The Easter holiday over, Trevor went back to work in London. We agreed to keep in regular touch and pray for a nine-plus. The first few days I feel acutely alone and out of my depth. I need to get over there to see her condition. I need advice of every kind but see and can think of no one to ask. In the town I feel exposed. Everyone seems to know me and their attitude is a mixture of derision and disgust. They look over their shoulders as I pass in the street. The sympathy at Mrs Abel's, so prominent the first night and the next couple of days, has dissolved to formal greetings and requests. I had breakfast alone. It was deathly quiet. No-one spoke to me. I wanted to hide.

Early one morning, I went down to the Chandler's shop at the far end of the quay. I wanted to ask if there was a dinghy with a motor that I could rent or borrow. I have to get out there. I need to understand everything, the distance, the tides. To ride up the Channel in my own time and go out beyond the Bar.

Through a stooping low door, early morning quiet, no customers and no-one at the counter. Coffee smells drifted in from somewhere. I walked around aimlessly, looking but not looking at sailing clothes, ropes and packaged paraphernalia. Eventually, a tall, white bearded gentleman appeared from a door in the back. He smiled, his greeting bright. We started on the weather and then on to quiet Wells. He was very talkative, and with a public-school accent explaining he was a newcomer. Having retired and last year whilst on holiday with his wife decided to buy this shop. It had been failing, was scruffy and run down. He described in great detail as soon as he saw it he had a vision. By catering for tourists and the sailing set as well as keeping bait and essentials for the local fisherman, he could make a go of it. Then the down side. After six months, at the end of last summer, his first attempt at any kind of self-employed business, the weather had been so bad, the tourist trade had all but vanished and, this last winter incredibly slow. Optimistically he hoped now that Easter was passed, even though it had been a total wash out with that awful storm, that come next month, surely the weather would improve and the tourists will start appearing. He leaned over the counter to say confidentially, it was a funny town. Like a mausoleum in winter with only the locals for company and they were an insular bunch. He said it reminded him of some frontier town, lots of characters on the edge of survival. He and his wife hadn't socialised much. It was only during the summer season that the town came alive and then, if the weather's good, the tourists descend in droves and with them a more holiday-like atmosphere. He was genial and I felt the relief of a friendly conversation. Eventually, I said who I was and he said he had thought so.

'I already seem to have quite a reputation.'

'Oh you don't need to worry about that. It's a small town so you wouldn't expect anything else. Right now you're the local entertainment. They gotta have someone to gossip about. Frankly,' he said with a wry grin. 'They always need someone to deride and I'm just happy it's you rather than me for a change.' And then after a pause, 'You know what these places are like. You could be here for thirty years and not be accepted. Grockels they call us. We're lumped in with the tourists and any incomers. We're all idiots and not worth the time of day. They treat you with contempt. And you.. Well, they think you're just some irresponsible playboy who doesn't know how to handle a boat. And them all being professional seamen that's what they'd say about anyone like you and me. We're hopeless amateurs. Shouldn't be allowed on boats. And you could be here for years and still that's what they'd say.'

I could feel the question looming, '..so what did happen?'

I told him most of the story. He nodded and interjected sympathy concluding, 'God. I read the article in the paper and heard title-tattle from the Pilot but I didn't realise it was that bad. How dramatic. How embarrassing.'

'Yes. I feel I'm quite in the spotlight,' I said resignedly. 'Nobody'll talk to me but I get the impression a lot is being said.'

'Well yes, and you staying at the Abel's, you're right in the thick of it. They're the main family in town. Been here for generations. The old man died last year. He was the lifeboat coxswain and a stalwart in town for as long as anyone can remember. Like one of the founding fathers. But her and her two sons.. She's the matriarch and a lovely woman, but the twin boys, her two heavies you'll see on the quay. They work the crane and that dredger out there, they're like the local mafiose. Nasty,.. you won't get much out of them unless they think they can make money out of you. Haven't they offered you salvage yet?'

'Not yet.'

'You ought to get out of there.. I tell you what,.. one of the nicest I've met in town is old George Cole. He and his wife have a little B&B right down the other end of town. Little blue and white cottage on the left, you can't miss it. He's retired now but he does a bit of bait digging and fishing. They'll be empty this time of year. Why not go down and see George. He's got a dinghy and an outboard he'll probably rent you and he knows everything and everybody in town, lived here all his life. Nice chap.'

'My name's Phillip, by the way,' he said, holding his hand over the counter, 'If you need anything, I've got it all here. I've got a big diesel launch for example if you need something to carry gear. But I'll need some notice if you want it, ..and I'm a bit fussy about who uses it..' He chuckled and gave a little wave as I left. 'I'll be happy to make some money out of you. I could do with it if we don't get some tourists soon.'

The rest of the day was filled with a mix of encounters. I walked straight down to George Cole's and Phillip was right. There was the dinghy and outboard in the garden and the path was nicely littered with pots and netting. His wife showed me the room and it was perfect. Small but sunny with a view across the marshes and up the Channel road. She invited me for tea and we sat in their tiny cottage kitchen with the washing hanging around us. After a few minutes George arrived and we shook hands. He's very matter of fact and when we mentioned my arrival, all he said was, '..just one o' them things. We all got to 'ave a dustup sooner or later. That storm got 'em all ina roight panic.' He laughed, pointing a wrinkled thumb in the air. I was grateful for his seeming lack of a judgement. We agreed I would move down there the following day and rent his dinghy if the weather was fine.

I left feeling lighter but then came a difficult encounter. It was midday and mistakenly, I went to the Fleece for lunch. There were only a few in and standing at the bar I was in the middle of a pint and a Ploughman's when in walked the Abel twins. I greeted them as they came up to the bar. They are almost identical, both at least six foot, muscular and gruff. I've seen them a few times but I still don't know which is Dick and which Mike. One returned the greeting with a 'You'roight?', the other ignored me and moved to the other end of the bar. As he sat down on the stool he looked along the whole length of the bar and said loudly to the whole room. 'So, it's the fuckin' playboy sailor, is it?'
'Hardly a playboy,' I returned.
'Leave 'im be, Dick', said Mike.
'Leave 'im fuckin' be? I'll leave 'im be if 'e fucks off and don't cause me no more trouble.'
I should have ignored him but stupidly I said, 'What trouble have I caused you?'
'What fuckin' trouble? What fuckin' trouble?!' He looked instantly angry and his voice rose. 'D'ya know how long we was out there getting that fuckin' boat back in the station after you?'
'I heard it took you a couple of hours. I'm really sorry I put you to all that trouble.'
'So you fuckin' should be!' He shouted it, looking into his drink as the barman placed it. 'Wanker!'
'Look,.. I'm sorry. It's the last thing I would have wanted to do. I didn't want to come here. I was ready to go further out into deeper water and ride it out..'
He interrupted. 'Go further out.. Go further out! Then we'd 'ave 'ad to fuckin' come out there after you!'

'I don't think so. I think I could have ridden it out. It's a strong boat.'

'Don't talk bollocks, mate. You dunno what you're talkin' 'bout. You'd 'a' been stuck out there for nigh on two day and then we'd still 'ave 'ad to come out there and pick up ya fuckin' bits!'

'Leave 'im be,' Mike was insisting.

'I'm not gonna fuckin' leavin' him be. He's a fuckin' wanker and ought to be fuckin' shot, fuckin' wanker!'

'Look, I've told you, I didn't want to come here. It was the Coastguard that insisted I come here.'

'Course they did! Why should we wanna come out after you in that fuckin' storm!.. But fuckin' wankers like you wouldn't think o' that, would you?!'

'Look, as I said, I'm sure it's no consolation or help to you. I'm really sorry for your trouble but I think I could have ridden it out. Instead of which I took the Coastguard's advice and came in here,.. where the water was too shallow and there were no proper fairway buoys. And now I'm the one with the problem. My life is stuck out there and I don't know what I'm going to do.'

'Look mate,' he shouted the length of the bar. Everyone in the room now engaged in the argument back and forth like tennis. 'I don't give a fuck about your life. It's mine and our crew I cares about.. We 'ass to go out on the sea every day to make a living. People like you,.. go out there for pleasure.. Put all our lives at risk,.. fuckin' deserve everything you git.'

I don't know what I thought I was going to do but I put down my pint and turned to him. Mike immediately moved to stand in front of me. 'Leave it, mate. Ignore 'im. Leave it alone. He don't mean nothing. He's just like that.' He looked over his shoulder down the bar. 'He's just fuckin' mouth.'

I downed my pint and made toward the door. As I opened it I turned, addressing the whole bar, 'I'm sorry, landlord. I'm sorry everyone for causin' you any trouble. As soon as I can get my boat, I'll be away..' As the door swung closed behind me I heard Dick say, 'Fuckin' good riddance!'

The following day, early in the morning before another sullen breakfast at Mrs Abel's, I packed my meagre belongings. Thinking I would come back and pay her later, I tiptoed out and walked the length of the quay down to George Coles. He was stooped over the old dinghy in the front garden, tapping a repair with a hammer. I wove my way up the garden through the lobster pots and boat planking. He was instantly friendly and we stood looking at grey sky and the day's prospect. I asked if I could leave my bag and move in later and, would he let me have a dinghy to go up the Channel.
'Won't be much water up there, today,' he said. 'But you'm tak it steady and you'll get out. Toides 'bout twelve, I reckon. Be 'nough. You'm gonna need some wellies. Tak some outa that box. Pleny on 'em in nere for soize. Want the missus to make you a cuppa 'fore you go?'
I put the bag in my room and drank tea with them. They could see I was itching to go and George and I carried the dinghy across the road and down the harnser at the end of the quay. We paddled out to the tiny stream in the middle, all that is left of the Channel at low tide. He started the outboard for me, pushing off and giving an encouraging wave as I drifted slowly away. Up the Channel stream and interminably slow, I weaved through the low tide shallows. Down in the dinghy everything is bigger. Beached boats, anchor buoys and mud. After an age we're level with the Lifeboat Station and a first sight of the Bar ahead where the smallest waves are lapping. Far over to the right the island of trees mark the boundary between salt marsh and beach and there! There she is.

Gloomy but calm and hardly a wave breaking when I finally reach the entrance through the Bar. It's so shallow I can see the round humped rise beneath the water as we pass through the gap. I could have stepped out of the dinghy and walked on it. When the tides are low, if the weather is as calm as today, it's impossible to see which way the water is flowing. Choppier as I made the edge of the sea but still hardly splashing the gunwale. Once far enough beyond the Bar I turned right along the line of the beach. The real coastline stretching and winding far away. Over tiny wavelets, the sea and sky, the distance to everywhere, is huge. I can just make out the top of her mast through a shimmering haze.

About half an hour chugging along, on the water over there inside the Bar, barely a ripple rolls in. Half way along, the dinghy almost broaching, a couple of seagulls are standing on the other side. They are standing on the bottom, the hardly undulating veneer from my wake lapping onto their chests. I pass and nod to them as their heads turn to follow. Eventually, reaching a point in a line with Cirkus and the trees beyond, I clearly see the bottom. Switching off the outboard, I paddled with an oar until we ran aground and stepped out of the boat into the water over the hump. It came about half way up George's wellies.

'That's not enough to float a bucket.'

She's still a long way off and it's so difficult out here to tell accurately. Distorted by the haze still shimmering, I can see little detail. Maybe half a mile or more from here. Double to the island of trees beyond. There's reflective water around her but she's certainly beached, her mast leans at a rakish angle. Impetuously I started to paddle-wade and make for her. Even at four inches though, as each step parted water my wellies soon filled. I turned back to the dinghy and sat onboard. Taking off boots and socks I decide to look from here, over a cigarette. Some thought passed that with distant perspective, a truer picture of the enormity of it. The truth is my spirit sank and, after the second cigarette and an hour passed, I decide nothing is to be gained from walking there now. I'll do it dry in the next couple of days and see how far it is to walk. Against the tide and my growing impotence, it was almost three hours before knocking on George's door to ask him for help with the dinghy.

I walked up there every day, about a mile up the Channel road to the campsite and Lifeboat Station. Out through the dunes and onto the beach, I hardly saw anyone. At first I didn't go all the way. I sat on the dunes trying to comprehend the incomprehensible, flipping from optimism to pessimism in a blink. After three days I took the plunge, literally. Walking along the Channel at low tide to find a shallow place to wade across. It started off okay, hopping from sandbank to sandbar but then the last bit had no sandbanks. I looked everywhere, up and down peering into the water. There are no shallows so eventually I wade in and hope. It's only about three yards to the other side. How deep can it be? I took off my trousers and coat but the bottom shelved away quickly until the water covered my chest. So cold, it took my breath away. Making it to the other side felt like an achievement and dripping determination, I stepped out across the dry sand. After the water temperature, the air seemed positively balmy. Half an hour's steady walking and the boat and my anticipation grew dead ahead.

This vast expanse of sand is impressive. There are few undulations, higher and by some inches lower but mostly it's flat, flat and more flat. A world very particular to sand and sky. The sociable company are seagulls and peeping Oyster Catchers. They are all around, digging and prodding, putting up to unknown alarms. When the water comes in they hold little parties until the last moment, on rare sandbars that remain uncovered. Precious few features, odd rippled depressions that snake to nowhere, reabsorbed by consuming flat. Ripples in the sand are common, twisting patterned echoes of the water's action. Hard packed and dry, sometimes wet and soft and you wonder about quick-sand. It's never that bad of course but nevertheless, child like diversions, lightening steps until finding firmer ground. Near the hour with only a few stops and deviations, the boat rises out of the haze. I pass one hopeful depression, almost a channel in itself that ends not far from her. I say not far, it's a few hundred yards. Out here in the middle, nothing is near.

When eventually I got to her she is facing down the coast. The last few steps were stumbled and quite full of emotion. I clambered onto the sloping deck and crabwise up to the mast. Standing up and holding on, for the first time the vantage point takes it in.

The rush of feelings overwhelm. A cold shiver brings it home deep. Trying to control it I stare, sensing rather than remembering, it feels a heavy weight. Eventually, I jumped down onto the sand to walk around her. Let's be busy at this point.

The anchor chains are still two lines, now at right-angles away toward the sea. For quite long parts of their length, slack and buried surprisingly deep. In the middle of one buried curve, I pull at the chain but had to dig along a twenty foot length to break it free. I imagine quite a movement of sand with the in and outgoing wash.

Almost unbelievably she looks fine. The hull still quite pristine white, just a few sandy smudges. I crawled underneath the higher side, into a large pool of water, to look at the joints along the bottom. It's hard to believe that the keel could still be straight and attached. There is hardly a break in the paint. The rudder is not at all damaged. One of the anchor chains has rubbed and caught a piece of the red gunwale. It's pulled and scraped some timber away revealing board ends and a couple of nail spikes hanging. It's superficial, spoiling the lipstick stripe but the right piece of timber, less than three-foot, will repair it. I can find no other damage. After that pounding, it's remarkable.

Inside is like a bomb site but under the floor boards, when I lift them, there is maybe six inches of water in the bilges. That's about the normal depth in the bottom keeping the boards wet and expanded. About what it was when we left Hull.
She really is okay. Gratitude mixed with fading disbelief thanked God. She's lying heeled at an unlikely angle on one bilge keel, but survived intact and unbowed. Perhaps a little bowed.

On successive visits, my frenzy of cleaning keeps attention on the positive. I've left the engine for the moment and set to repairing steering cable blocks. I don't remember when the engine stopped, or did I stop it? I have no idea how seized it might be. That's still a worry that I can only check by turning her over. Whatever might be wrong and my imagination works overtime, I'll wait until there's enough water. It'll have to come apart and be cleaned. Can you wash sand out of engines? I'd be afraid to start it, for fear of sucking more. If she.. No! When she floats, I imagine walking in front in the shallow water and pulling her. Once you overcome the inertia she'll move okay. As long as there's not too much sand inertia! Slowly, perhaps over a few tides, we'll get nearer the Channel. She needs at least three-foot six of water to get the keel free. As she's slowly sinking in to the sand with water gathering in a depression below her, it looks even less. Whatever, it's not that much. That's become my mantra. 'It's-not-that-much, it's-not-that-much?' 'Come on just a bit more!' When the water does come, the middle of the month passive tides are so small. Plenty of time to prepare for bigger ones. Meanwhile, for days the weather is gloomy and calm. Surely they'll be one soon with a bit of wind behind it?

She's heeling over less by floating in her own new pool and I can move around more easily inside. A good tide is predicted at four in the afternoon, a little higher in the morning. I leave the dinghy under the Lifeboat Station on the return of each visit and when there's enough water. I launch her and cross the Channel. The water over the sand is paddling depth, half-way up my wellies when I step in to measure it. Near to four, there is plenty for the dinghy and optimistically I put up its little sail to get us there quicker. But there's not enough for Cirkus to float and once aboard and inside I light the fire and decide to stay and wait for the morning. Early hours creaking and groaning woke me. Up on deck I sat and watched every movement. A brisk wind blew up from the right direction and I wonder if it will help. The timetable says only eight-two. At the top of the tide there may have been eighteen inches. Our still heeled angle wobbles and shifts, slewing through sand but in reality hardly changed. At no time did we float.

I spend more time over there on each visit. The nights are cold but far too benign. I've begun to make a pile of heavy 'cast-offs' in the wheelhouse. I thought I could either tie them in bundles for chucking over the side or put them in the dinghy to take away. I had the floor up and carried ballast out to a pile on the beach. As far out of the way towards the trees as I can carry, Tom said there were four-tons and I might be half way. One of the fenders makes a little marker-buoy for the pile and I imagine coming back for it later.
In between bouts of work I pass hours sitting, fidgeting on the deck. Pacing up and down, leaning on the wheelhouse against the slope of her heeled over. Impatiently waiting and then

anxiously watching the tide come and go. An almost constant gentle breeze blows pathetic ripples on six-inch deep water. After each tide I feel like a tensile spring, weary of anticipation. A little every day, she gently rocks and shovels barrow-loads of sand along her keel-length. She is settling and slowly coming upright. The shallow trough fills and deepens until we float. Dark and brackish, when the rest of the beach is dry, she is lying in her own prison pool.

Shallow lapping water. Never a rush, just a trickle. Safe in the shallow water. Safe. We believe that don't we? But the risks of depth are jumbled here. In turbulent visions running over and over. The images and impressions, reliving minute detail, block out all others, coming fast like skating stones. Shallow water. A great metaphor to play with and too many hours to play and stare at the horizon or the bottom. Is this where it's safe? We are so conservative. Don't get out of your depth. Do what you know. My microscopic third-degree, some kind of contrast to the plain and uncomplicated vista. Fine and painful abstraction dissected, for pouring over hour after day, prompted literally by high and dry. Broken twice in twenty four hours by an unstoppable clockwork reminder of wretched fortune.

Just as the grass is almost always greener, my sea is almost inevitably deeper, just over there. The prayers and exaltations for deeper water begin to conjure dreams of lurid depths. Despite the constant ebb and flow, any of my movement is squelched by enveloping clouds of clinging sand. In deeper water, out of your depth, we know risk averse fear is imagined not real but just as if you had wished for it, irrevocably placed in the world.

The shallows are a barrier, fluid only trickling, fearful sand eroding grain over single grain. Constant, never rushing. Barely irrigating the most parched and unadventurous ground. The next will be higher, faster,.. it's-not-that-much, please.

Chapter Fifteen
what good is this? God a hit?.. it shows

Some sympathetic soul said, 'Well, you don't look very upset. If that was my life out there I don't know what I'd do.'

The days pass and beyond weeks and still no water deep enough. Frenetic activity covered the early shock. Now an odd contrast in distinct moods of hope and despondency. I calm panic by watching tides. There waiting, if not at the boat, somewhere at the water's edge. The enormity of it you can measure. Dimension, distance, weight. I've paced it, gauged in every direction. In the town library I found reference to lift and displacement. I've calculated it and still no water deep enough. Obsessive meandering wild geese imaginings that chase every lead or hair-brain idea. Every possible help gingerly solicited, every depression explored. Every tide sucked under the boat with a white-knuckle will power whose gravity must surely match the moon. In reality it's weak and wretched and still no water deep enough.

The local response is difficult. One lunch-time in the 'Fleece', two of the local well-oiled trawlermen who contribute to Wells' reputation as the Whelk capital of Europe, were propping up the bar. They work the boats, nets and whelk dredgers. Out in flotilla on one high tide, back in a straggling convoy the next. About two weeks a month with the Whelk sheds and smokehouse at the far end of town billowing black on cue. When they're not trawling for whelks, they're lifting sand and gravel or crane-loading coasters that arrive on the highest tides. Flour from the mill and grain in return. The hunky testosterone in town, almost always on the quay, regular noisy smoking gaggles. They are still quite purposefully ignoring me. Their sneering an awkward addition to my jumble of culture shocked alienation.

This lunchtime I try again at public relations, when George invited me for drink. He instantly betrayed my confidence to the assembled by trying to speak up for the number of trips I'd made across the Channel. I shifted awkwardly and trying to look cool my new waders got stuck over one another at the toes. They say walk a mile in another man's shoes. These things take some waddling.

Fair-minded George piped-up, 'No, that ain't so. Ain't just for fishin' or whelkin'. My boy goes out on them racin' bouts. No, you learns it different on 'em.'

The same implication every time. They are the professionals and any other use of boats or the sea is either plain foolhardiness or heresy.

'Don't learn different 'n the lifeboat, though do 'e? They all wants that when they's in trouble, don^ey?'

I've been copying the seagulls, digging Mussels at the margins. Yesterday on the long walk back from the Bar, I carried on to the little island of trees. Beneath the trees a silt edge before it becomes marsh, rings patches of succulent growth. Poetic Samphire, poor man's Asparagus. Waxing lyrically George said that when bait digging he'd often wander over to the marsh edge, pick a few fronds and eat them raw. His sophisticated recipe boils them in the pot with the mussels. Finding them is a true harvest of consolation. Dinner turned out like nectar.

I had called the insurance company on the first working day after the storm. They sent me the usual sheaf of forms to fill, describing the event in detail including precise time and map references. Last week they sent a curt letter saying they would be sending their local assessor on Thursday at two o'clock and I should meet him at the Pilot station on the quay. One might expect to have been asked for an appointment but in investigating a claim your status turns from valued customer to irksome burden. Since I want to get on with it, as it happened it wasn't inconvenient. The tide was right out so we, that is me and the at least twenty-stone profusely sweating insurance assessor, arrived to wade the Channel.

'You mean you want me to wade across?'
'Well, yes. I assumed you would have seen the maps and know the state of the tide. I guessed that's why two o'clock was chosen. If the tide was up we could have used the dinghy.'

He had no idea where he was going or that this was part of the journey. I warned you had to watch your step as it could be deep but he confidently took off only shoes and socks. He rolled his trousers just four inches and muttered something about knowing these waters intimately. He was about half way across when, concentrating on my own footing, I only saw the end of a large splash. Some serious gurgling and he completely disappeared beneath the water. His coat bobbed up on a huge air bubble, quickly followed by his head under it, gasping and writhing for air. Standing above him on firmer ground I stretched over and grabbed the coat, pulling it off his face along with a few lengthy strands of comb-over. Cursing through gagging mouthfuls of Channel, he swam over to the other side and hauled his enormous bulk onto the sand. Collapsed panting, a beached elephant seal he lay there. I fancy I even saw his nose dangle. From his prone beaching he raised his head to say angrily, 'Why didn't you tell me it was deep?'

The rest of the afternoon was little better. I warned him to be ready for a long walk. I said I thought it must be two miles plus and he sighed long suffering. Along the way he kept stopping to catch his breath, his clothes hanging ragged wet and sandy. He stooped, spreading arms around his huge stomach, so that he could barely touch his knees to lean on them while wheezing alarmingly. I kept asking if he were alright and he muttered curses and carried on wheezing. His face was so red I worried that he might not make it. I even thought on one particularly prolonged wheeze-break how on earth I was going to summon help for him. Visions sprung rather too easily of sticking him on a plank, dragging him by his comb-over to the waiting ambulance.

We finally got to the boat and he threw himself exhausted on the sand. He didn't move or appear to breathe for about ten minutes. I returned to him with fresh water and towel and with a gasp that sounded like it might have been terminal, he opened his eyes saying breathlessly angry this time, 'Why didn't you tell me it was this far?'

Too weak to move, his complexion oscillated white, red and green. I sat with him convinced that he was going to expire until he rolled painfully over on to his stomach and jacked himself up.

'Look at me?', he said. 'Look at the mess you've got me in?' And with a fussy finger-nail brushed at a small spot on the overall covering of sand, he walked off back towards the Channel.

'Don't you want to look over the boat?' I shouted after him and he turned, planting his hands somewhere around where his hips might be and said. ' For what? It's a wreck!'

His report arrived by post at George's this morning, completely condemning unsalvageable damage. That steering failure had caused the wreck, and quoting from the Survey, 'the steering wires and sheaves require maintenance'.. Going on to say in the accompanying letter, that whilst Eagle Sun had accepted the premium in good faith, it was obvious that the wreck was a result of negligence and poor maintenance. Therefore on this occasion they would be unable to assist. As if on some other occasion, no doubt with some other higher premium, it might be different.

'The baaastards.' George said, slow and drawling it. ' Can 'em do that?'

'It looks like they have,' was all I managed.

Composed, I telephoned and spoke with my Claims Adjuster. He seemed to be saying that it was just one of those things, sometimes they help, sometimes it's more difficult-like. Yes, I said, it was! We wrangled. I said this must be the result of the huge premium I paid and the other letter I had in my hand saying Eagle Sun would be insuring the boat? He talked of company policy. I got more aerated and eventually he said he would look into it. He could do no more but that it did look like the letter would be their final decision. It would be much better for all of us if I shut and roll over. Not quite like that of course and so I thanked him as politely as I can muster and said I would appreciate his looking into it and letting me know something different indeed.

'Goodbye, Mr Hamm...,' he said as the phone clicked dead.

I've had no chance to think it through. At nine thirty on the quay this morning I met Brian Holt, designer and manufacturer of a odd product. These large rubber floatation bags fit, rolled up with their compressor, in much too small a van. We drove up to the Lifeboat Station and like a birthing, as Brian stood well back to open the van doors, the heavy elastic sausages sprung and flopped onto the beach. They are normally used to raise sunken treasures when inflated under water. I called Brian after seeing an article about him in the local newspaper. He'd salvaged a Roman galley. That was just below the piece headlined, 'Four and a Dog in Surf Wreck Drama.' After endless missed phone calls I finally met him a week ago in his factory. Our sausage use today will be to make a kind of life-ring under the boat. To inflate when the water comes and assist her to float.

Between us we hauled and toppled the bags into, over and flopped across two dinghies. Setting off across the flooded sands as the tide was going out we dragged and towed the dinghies and our giant jonnies through the last of the water. It was almost dry when we got there, the last half-mile dragging sand. After reviving ourselves with a cup of tea, we wandered around together to survey the task. Fitting the sausages around and under the boat, ready to inflate them on this evening's tide. It's almost exactly a month, tonight's nine tide being the highest since 'the wreck'. We finished all we could do and settled down to wait the five hours. I offered to cook him dinner and sitting in the saloon we happily chat. I'm pleased with how game he is for this. I'm paying him, we agreed three hundred quid for the twenty-four hours, and I promised that if it worked I would certainly get him publicity. Actually though, I think he's happy to find novelty sausage applications, seeing the potential of new business. A spirit of experiment and 'boy's-own' discovery, plus a few hair-brain stories and uses for his sausages were explored over my standard lunch of Mussels and Samphire. Growing more outrageous, washed courtesy of the Cirkus wine-cellar. He told me his life story, I told him mine. We are optimistic and the time passes quickly.

It's getting dark as the water arrives and we start the generator to inflate the bags. Charging my batteries at the same time, I rig the large spotlight and the scene is lit like a stage-set. Slowly the cradle inflates, hissing and creaking as the rubber grips the hull. She is sitting upright in her hole and we can feel little shifts in the weight while we peer over the side. The water is barely half way up the bags and we've no idea how much of them needs to be submerged before giving the lift. As they inflate it's obvious we are raising the boat, but the displacement stays the same. We fail to spread it any wider. The sausages add another three foot to the bottom and that might be the lift we're getting. We'd equalled it out.

On the top of the tide, in unspoken madness, we both had the same hapless thought and jumped over the side. With ropes on the bow and stern we began pulling for all we were worth. Nothing happened, a gesture nothing more. I thought a couple of times that she might just bounce over the edge of the hole but it wasn't deep enough. Hardly any wind, so there'll be no more water.

Out of breath and slumped in the wheelhouse, I switch on the radio for the morning weather forecast. Nurture vain hope that tomorrow's might blow a hurricane but more calm and grey is the prospect. I lit the fire and put the kettle on. Brian decided to stay and over more tea and bedtime snacks we post mortem our efforts. How could we spread the lift? We couldn't imagine getting four Jonnies over here, then the generator would have to be bigger. Such a major operation we agree is beyond us. Could you take a bigger truck in at Moreston down the coast and drive it along the beach? Someone has that kind of local knowledge. I'll walk that way at some point. We grew tired and the ideas more eccentric. I don't know which one of us mentioned helicopters but Brian remembered the US Air Force base at Sculthorpe, just up the road. They have those C-Sixty-Two, Jolly Green Giants that lift the Sherman tank. Perhaps we could borrow one of those for a couple of hours. Pick her up and plonk her in the Channel. It would only take them a few minutes.. And think of the great publicity..

Did we waste our time? I don't know. I certainly knew what didn't work. Whether we would try again with more sausages seemed unlikely, although Brian agreed to go away and recalculate the lift. I said I'd think again but have no idea of what. Meanwhile, it was hopeful for a short while and I enjoyed someone else appreciating the problem. I didn't want to let go of him and any possibility however remote. But by the morning Brian had decided it was a lost cause. After cramming them back into the van, we did thanks and goodbye at the Lifeboat Station. I said I'd walk into town. Instead I sat on the dunes and stared through the binoculars.

Sitting there for some time, a stronger breeze picked up, coming in damp and icy straight off the sea. How far submerged the sausages, that little prancing moment of possibility when I thought I might pull her free. There could be more water over there now. I would never know. I've no idea of the subtle impacts. How much wind, how much water, how much of any myriad of factors.
A melancholic uselessness overcame me. How could you ever really know about anything. Sure, accumulate information but how do you know you have enough. I know what I know now, in ten minutes time I might know something completely else. Please. Always short of a final jig-saw piece. Turned on by whatever it is, inspired and motoring, that level of engagement gives you an edge. But if you're anxious, stressing or frustrated, filling the space with undermined confidence.. I doubt my capacity right now to recognise a jig-saw piece if it came and hit me.
'Need to get motivated then..' said the gremlin.

'Oh come on?' I dropped the binoculars in my lap and stared long at the tiny shape and the tiny shape of my thoughts.
'I have to be out there more. Have to be more,.. there.'
The breeze blew in an icy squall. It whipped at the marram-grass, just to intensify exposure.
'All this must surely have some purpose?'

I walked to town and wandered empty streets aimlessly all afternoon. Like some unseasonable tourist, looking in darkened shop windows through yellow redundant filters. By the time I got back to George's, I decide to pack up and go out there tonight.

Chapter Sixteen
what good is this? Withstood A Sigh?

I wish I had done this before. It is so beautiful out here. This morning at first light the huge sky grew a spectacular colour. Thin strips of mackerel cloud turned pale puce pink, dappled by the hidden sun. Purple shot their velvet underbellies and the reflection bathed everything, sand, sky and me in orange pink glow. An all enveloping stillness, sounds floating, phasing in and out on far away wave gushing. Occasionally the breeze carries a hint of activity but it's rare. I drink it in like tea, warm and satisfying, coupled with a different detachment. Separate from the rest of world sleeping allows secret sentiments to breathe. Thoughts drift free uncluttered by the wide awake clamour. At the perfect moment, a party of Oysters Catchers put up together, pee-witting counterpoint, as if they couldn't resist saying something about it.

Want to design your life? Then you'll want it beautiful. And it is ever there right in front of us. Spend time being grateful and our part in it deepens.

In truth waking up every day out here throws into stark relief my pitiful antipathy. Back and forth through moods of inadequacy and expansiveness. Filling the time with cleaning, oiling and repairing and long thoughtful walks across the vastness. In one moment connected completely, inspired at the hip with circumjacent joy. In the next, utterly disconnected, judged hopeless.

Last night after a tiny tide, I sat until two in the morning by a camp-fire on the island of trees. Trying again a distant perspective, at least five hundred yards away, staring into the space it occupies.

What should have been sheer pleasure, cooking the Mackerel I caught with a line at the Bar and Samphire picked on the marsh. An uplifting meal adventure to savour but I was absent. Smoking endless cigarettes after dinner I drifted in and out of connectedness. Old backwater thoughts, like those in London, returning full of dumped detritus and deficiency. Ugliness and superstitious doubt mixed with guilt at my ingratitude for the boundless blanket of stars.

Why do we keep recreating the same reality? Why do we keep getting stuck in the same loop of thoughts and emotions that spiral in familiar patterns? How on earth do you break them? In a sea of infinite potential, how come we keep creating the same ones. Is it possible that so trapped by conditioning, we completely buy into the idea that we've no control. We believe the external world has all the power and don't begin to see any other.

Is reality what we perceive through our senses or do we create it? The truth is it's probably both and we can't tell the difference. Like a set of index cards, trying to cram new experience into the old, we only see what we believe is possible or can extrapolate from something previously understood. New experience is difficult to file and almost always denied. Is it really possible then, that if you haven't prior knowledge of something, you don't see it? It's a myth now that when Columbus's ships approached the Americans Indian's land for the first time, because the natives had never seen or imagined anything like them, they couldn't see the ships until the soldiers, men who they did recognise as real, disembarked and began killing them.

I don't sleep much but time out here has such a different rhythm. Early summer mornings, spectrum filled sunrises. At first light it's cold and I lit the arctic with a couple of bits of driftwood. As it crackled and spit, I search for an extra layer and the kettle boils for tea. Incongruously, I have everything here including a well appointed wardrobe. In warm jumper and jacket, sitting on the back deck, dreaming and drinking the brew, watching the chimney smoke snake slowly. A peaceful antidote to the wrangling inside.

The colours fade, leaving the sky cloudless and blue. A smoky sea-fret hanging over the Bar, blends out the horizon. After an hour or so and several more cups of tea, slowly the sun is beginning to warm. I turn my face directly, bathing in it until the faintest sting. Then something made me open my eyes. Away across the sand, in the far distance, a large flock of birds, indistinguishable but for their mass, rise like a swirling cloud and turn as one out to sea. Just visible beyond them, still and rigid, another shape, larger and black appears to be sitting, cushioned by the haze. I lean into the wheelhouse for the binoculars and almost before I've raised the glass to my eyes the shape is taking more distinct form. I twist the lens to focus and through it the shape, clearing the mist, becomes a low flying aircraft advancing directly towards me. As it looms now fixed in the centre of my circle sight, I recognise the shape. Engines high on the tail, short square wings, it's one of those American tank-busters. Low and slow, lolling wings dipping through the horizontal, only a finger's length above the beach and still making straight this way. Frozen in anticipation I glare through the binoculars until, within seconds I can see emblems on the wings, then features through the wind-shield and the pilot's face. There is no sound but it's closing fast. I stand up as though ready to greet it, feeling time accelerate its approach. At about a hundred yards distant and no more than fifty foot above the sand, the nose begins to rise. In a split second and suddenly upon us, the whole plane twitches, flips and turns, throwing itself dramatically upward, exploding the air with a deafening roar. The sound wave shudders the whole boat and I'm forced to protect my ears from the violence passing through every cell of my body. Gyrating an impossible pirouette, the wing tip whips through the air missing the top of the mast, I thought by inches. It whirls away and upward and the air turbulence hits me like a hot wake. I recoil and duck uselessly looking straight up into the engines as an aperture opens and short blue streaked red flame fires from both at once, unbelievably increasing the bellicose screaming. It banks hard, revealing a full profile. The twisting wing tip appears again to almost touch the ground as it howls away and across the Bar. I follow the line of flight out and over the sea, still waltzing and lolling, now looking like celebration rolls. Time returns to normal as the sound dies away, the shape fast receding. I slump back on my haunches kicking the tea cup off the deck and over the side.

'How unbelievable was that!? I've been practice attacked by the US Air Force! Who the hell created that?'

I sit, still shaking, straining to find the pinprick disappearing in the mist, then collapsed into dark and obstacled reality.

For the rest of the day, like many others, my resort is to cleaning and stowing. What else? I took more ballast to the growing pile. There are only the boxes under the engine to empty of a few hundredweight. The engine and the last of the outboard bits, injectors and pump are cleaned of sand in every crevice. Water filters are pristine and ready to do precious work. They were clogged with sandy goo, but not that much and, remarkably little had stopped the cooling water flowing. Is that a good sign, I've really no idea. Yesterday I rigged a water line from the bilge-pump and with some pressure passed it through the engine cooling jacket until it appeared from the pipe outside. I let it pour into a bucket for quite a while, waiting for sand to appear, until the waste of my fresh water got too much. Of course having done all of this, without sand free water under us I dare not start the engine. The water in the hole is too dirty and with poor knowledge, I'm trying to figure out how to set-up some kind of closed water loop. I could then at least try a test start but can only imagine it working.

Then, as part of the ongoing beating of myself, I go through all the guilt stuff about false economy and how, had I not been so cheapskate and paid the money for a modern radio, I would be able to summon help and advice and someone to talk to and would be sure about what I was doing and on and on.

Sometimes the gremlin makes sense. 'If the problem can be solved there is no use in worrying. If it can't be solved worrying will do no good.'

'It must be time for tea.'

I sat on the back deck to watch another pathetic tide. So low it practically exhausted itself before getting here.

She is upright now in her prison pool, deep enough to be afloat with sides too high to float over. Permanently afloat, tide or no tide, stuck below sea-level. 'Maybe I could dig a channel.' From here to the main channel via low lying depressions. Visions of digging fanatically all the way to the Lifeboat Station is instantly shattered. Apart from taking God knows how long to dig, on every tide it would fill, washing the sand spoil like tired sandcastles. You'd have to shutter it all the way, like navigating

your own canal. How long would that take, and how much timber would you need for such a long trench. 'Shuttering the beach against itself!' Like some insane Herculean task. How could you do that? How would you fix the timber so that it didn't float away? I'd need a lot of people to dig that far.
'Perhaps I should cost it out.. Don't be ridiculous. It would cost a fortune. But it is different?'
On my evening walk along the line toward the Channel, I chided myself with the pointlessness of even embarking on the thought. But by the time I got back to the boat, having paced sand for hours, I still somehow manage to feel heartened to search for some completely other solution. Something lateral. Anything will do, anything that doesn't depend on waiting and watching this pathetic amount of water.

Phillip had agreed to take my post and when I called in, a letter from the insurance company had arrived. The letter is formal in the extreme, full of legalese and gobbledegook that avoids naming anything. In the light of the 'difficulty', after due consideration and without prejudice they have decided to assist on this one occasion.
'...without prejudice they have decided to assist...' I read it out.
'I should bloody-well think so.' Phillip drawled. 'But does that mean they're accepting liability? Surely it must?'
'They say that I will be receiving a communication from J.Arthur Williams Naval Architects, in due course, to arrange the rescue. The Rescue?'
Phillip offered me coffee and we stood at the counter deciding what sort of rescue a Naval Architect might consider. As if perfectly on cue, the shop bell rang and our postman filled the doorway. In his outstretched hand were five letters. The one on top boldly announcing J.Arthur Williams Naval Architects.

Chapter Seventeen
what good is this? Ho Ho? Dig As Twits

Enthroned on a chair Phillip provided, J.Arthur himself was consulting a pocket-watch when I arrived only moments after the appointed time. His first word is, 'Punctuality.' Over my shoulder I wondered if he might be addressing someone else. He stared into vacant space somewhere near me as the word, clipped on its own, sufficed to convey his take. He stood to attention and then slowly sloped one foot away, at-easing himself.

How tall is a naval architect? I'd imagined him very tall and imposing. He is indeed way above six feet, dressed in a suit that could not have been tailored more like a naval uniform, double-breasted with ships on the buttons. He pierced through a magnifying monocle. There was no monocle. I imagined a waxed moustache on his stiff upper lip. There was none. His voice, commanding, stabbing staccato, revealed not a shadow of doubt as he described exactly how he proposed to affect the 'Rescue'. We would not use the word 'salvage', this was for lost causes and amateurs. Striding around, aloof and commanding the shelves in Phillip's shop, all would be accomplished efficiently. With pin point precision he pincered a speck from his cuff as Phillip and I nodded submission.

Instant dislike of him is too strong, he is extreme and full of importance. When I called to acknowledge receipt of the letter, the insurance agent had told me that this would be their only assistance. I didn't argue and agreed to faultlessly comply with the instructions given.

The plan is hardly naval architecture. On the contrary it's hilariously Heath-Robinson. He intends to build a raft under the boat out of forty-five gallon oil drums.
'We shall require at least fifty drums.'
'Right'
'You will secure these.'
'Right?'
'We shall require these in the best of condition.'
'Right.'
'We shall dig a trench under the vessel large enough to construct the floatation platform.'
'Right?' I wonder who this 'we' is. I can't imagine him doing any digging.
'The platform will then be lashed to form a rigid structure.'
'Right.'
'Thereby increasing its displacement, causing the vessel to be uplifted and towed inshore.'
'Right. I mean, good.'
'The Chandler here, will provide us with his launch for transportation. You will be in receipt of paper orders by Royal Mail within three days.' Phillip raised his shoulders and eyebrows in unison.
I almost didn't dare ask. 'Erm. Where do you think I might start looking for fifty oil drums?'
'Well that's simply a matter of searching,' he returned in impatiently obvious tone.
'Right. Of course. Silly me, of course I'd thought of that, hadn't I Phillip?'

He smiled benignly as though saying, 'Don't ask me.'

The threat of naval wrath is real.

'We shall also require labourers. I will make arrangements to engage some of these local trawler chappies. They will effect the digging.' He paused just long enough to indicate the end, the rest surely obvious to any damn fool. Phillip and I are briefly allowed to fill in the details for ourselves.. 'At o-seven-twenty on the fifteenth, the platform will float on the high tide; an eight metre seven according to the log timetable, and will then be towed, the vessel atop, using the Chandler's launch, into the harbour.'

'Very good,' I managed, more rights too flimsy a response. I only had a moment to shoot a quizzical glance at Phillip. Leaning on the counter staring at a spot just in front of him. He looked up, thoroughly unconvinced. I smiled encouragement.

'Didn't you try that with the floatation bags?' Phillip submitted daringly.

'Couldn't possibly have done it that way,' J.Arthur cut across my reply. 'The loading displacement of oil barrels will be far more reliable.'

'Do you think that'll be a high enough tide?' I found courage to venture.

He completely ignored it, leaving us lesser mortals floundering in his wake. He demanded of Phillip. 'So my good man. Where do I go to speak to some of these trawler chappies?'

'The Fleece, along the quay I would say, almost certainly.' A jaunty smile broke across his face. 'That's the only place. Of a lunch-time'.

J.Arthur brought out a pocket-watch and then turning to me. 'We won't wait for that. You will accompany me. I dare say you are familiar with these types.'

'Yes, I dare say I must be.' The idea of him strutting into the Fleece sends a shiver. Even so, let's imagine going for a drink and having a quiet word with the most likely..?

He led the way to the Fleece, striding through the door and before I could get inside was announcing his intention to an assembly that included the Ables.

'Any man who would like five days well paid work should muster to me on the quay in ten minutes. I shall make arrangements to employ them immediately.'

Harry, the landlord, behind the bar in mid glass polish. 'Yer roight. I'll be there.'

Work is certainly hard to find in Wells, more desperate than I imagined. Within ten minutes he had eight labourers marshalled. He inspected them on parade, looking them up and down for muscle and sobriety. Commanding the length of his nose at them, they would be expected to muster on the quay at o-seven-thirty each morning, be ferried to the 'site', and there to dig and shutter a trench to his specification. Amidst ribald muttering, cynical in my direction, to my amazement they all agree to start work tomorrow. He even had paperwork for them to sign.

Once the formalities of naval employment are complete and they're dismissed, he and I march back along the quay where I receive my instructions. I too will muster at o-seven-fifteen with Phillip's launch at the ready, to ferry the digging crew up the channel. There, if enough water is present I will take them all the way. If not I will drop them and their pre-prepared luncheon sandwiches and tea for the day on the other side of the channel. I will return the launch and begin my oil drum searching. My return time synchronised by tide, I will collect them at the end of the digging day. Apparently, there will be six days digging and one lashing, during which time I will somehow amass a pile of oil drums. I am to find these by visiting garages and local workshops, the oil-terminal at Yarmouth if necessary. For this it will also be my duty to secure a vehicle to carry them. The details of where the hell I'm to find a vehicle, is to be left to my discretion. He informs me that we have a budget of two-thousand pounds and therefore vehicle hire is out the question. I will have to borrow one and surely must know where that might be arranged.

'Right.' I said stupidly distracted by two-thousand pounds.

Dismissing me he strides off to a further meeting with Phillip, presumably to marshal sandwich marshalling. I hear the trumpet voluntary sounding muster at dawn as I slink off toward George's to plead for sanity.

I can't imagine who is going to lend me anything. I'm the playboy, remember, I'm sure they think I have loads of money. George though was reliably sympathetic, 'Well, youm gotta take this chance if it being offered, an' ee.' He suggested Stan who runs the Whelk sheds and smoke house up the other end of town. 'He's got that ol' Whelk truck they uses to ferry back and forth.' The truck does little else when the tides are low. 'They parks it up thar int' garidge. Even when they's Whelks to smoke, it don't do more 'an a couple o' hours back and forth.'

The smoke house is a famous sight and smell of Wells Next the Sea. For four days almost every month, black billowing smoke hangs over the edge of town. If you don't see smoke you'll know it's happening when an unfavourable wind wreaks rotting cabbage baked in gorgonzola socks.

George introduces me to Stan who, to great surprise, is persuaded immediately to open the little rickety garage and reveal the dead mollusc encrusted flat-bed Transit. 'Maybe yous can give 'er a wash,' says Stan as the opening of the garage door breaks a seal on the stench. 'Strong bain't she,' Stan remarks as I fail to hide my recoil.

Later that afternoon, after scrubbing desperately to wipe just the driver's seat clean of some fermenting goo, I decide to drive the truck to the car-wash on the edge of town. It's been a

hotter day and the only way round is up the narrow High Street. Past shops and gaggles of new tourists in their beachwear and flip-flops. Cruising at molluscs pace past the tea shop with its neat gingham clad tables outside, I smile a pathetic apology for the inconvenience to those previously absorbed in scones and jam. Seated at one table, a father, mother and three children, as if in tortured unison, each raise a hurried hand to their nose.
'My God!' floats a protest through the open passenger window. 'What on earth is that appalling stink!'
'Only me,' I say under my breath, turning a fading smile away to avoid future recognition.

That was five days ago. I've not done bad, though fear I may hold up the timetable. I've managed to assemble exactly thirty-one oil drums on the end of the quay, stacked as neatly and out of the way as I can. Only another twenty-five to go to meet the new target. Like some demented hawk, intuition has become finely tuned to their form. Never on my everyday shopping list I spot them in the most unlikely places. Drive past a garage or yard and half a dozen lie in a seemingly idle pile. How difficult can it be? I practice, ' 'scuse me mate. Are you going to use those oil drums?' Would you be willing to lend or give me them?' I've no idea if ever I'll return them but it sounded like a good line. Suspicion or a fob-off follows creeping inevitably and I had to explain why and how and where. Of course, within a five mile radius of Wells, they all knew every detail anyway.
'Naval architect?', they say.
'Couldn't a bit o' local salvage done the job?'
'Makin' a raft is it?'
'Sound a bit far-fetched to me. Him good is he this naval bod? Sounds a bit of a pratt from what I 'eard.' My act of standing there holds damning association.

After the third such encounter I started to answer back with something other than blush-saving, 'my hands are tied by the insurance company'. I would join in the condemnation but for fear of chancing fate or God or whoever might be listening. George suggested going straight to the oil terminal at Yarmouth, where I'd surely get 'undreds o' the buggers.

Meanwhile, each morning further embarrassment is endured as I dutifully ferry the diggers, Philip's wife's sandwiches, J Arthur and lengths of wobbling timber. The jolly jabs and snide remarks continue unabated. It's all pretty harmless low level mummers and behind-the-hand derision but I'm trapped. I suppose we all are. Frustration is perfectly humoured by J.Arthur's architectural glares at everyone. Yesterday he lost his patience altogether and threatened to fire them all before we'd got half-way. The argument continued through every inch and ripple, several of them about to take him on. There was even a moment when I thought they would throw him over the side.

After an hour or more arguing through the shallows, we approach her and I haven't got this close for days. They've made real progress. Excavations to one side of the hole making a substantial crescent shaped mound of sand. Submarine thick grey mud is slopped on top so they must have dug deep. Drawing closer, Cirkus is held in clear air by four upright beams supporting the bilge keels and driven pyramid-like into the bottom of the hole. As the pool under her drains away, the boat is dry with a growing space underneath. The hole will never drain completely, constantly fed by filtering tidewater but it looks already as if there'll be enough space under her for the raft.

'I've re-calculated buoyancy,' informs J Arthur after we unload and arrange ourselves around the hole. 'This means that we can reduce the floatation coefficient by eleven-point-five percent.'

'Really. That sounds a lot.' I say scanning the faces.
'Flootation coagulation?' Someone mimics.
'Does that mean we need fewer drums?' I say, trying not to sound hopeful.
'No, no. You can carry on.' He dismisses.

It's five days to the full-moon tide and for the last few I've been ferrying drums every time I collect the men. Just a few at a time and my collection is up to thirty nine. Driving miles to search for them is resolving, following George's advice, into one hopeful final trip. Yarmouth and the oil-terminal, an hour's drive away in my Whelk encrusted truck and the road reveals our favoured destination on the night of the storm. We called in here on Trevor's barge eighteen months or more ago and, like today, the sea was calm as milk. From a boat out there you see it very different. The wide sheltered bay is the haven. Further on you get a view of the harbour and its entrance. I imagine the difficulty getting through there in a high sea and then try to banish the thought.

A little way offshore a couple of small cargo coasters sit at anchor, waiting their turn. It's the queue I would have been happy to jump. I pulled over in a bus stop and stared longing out to sea.

After a few cycles of recrimination I fall to clichéd dismissal. No point again in dwelling, force the thought to override. Further along, I lean out the window as we pass safely moored boats at the quay.

Out of town the road turns along the sea-front and within a mile the oil-terminal comes into view. Arriving at a barrier gate, I get out and walk to a little office to explain my mission. I'm well practised but the security guards are surprisingly sympathetic, 'I'm sure we'll be able to fix you up, mate', a burly one smiled.

A phone call and I'm through to the operations manager who brushes aside any ideas of payment for shipwreck charities and within minutes despatches two guys out of the warehouse to load twenty drums on the truck.

Not quite believing it could be that easy, a day of mixed emotion resolves in a swaying drive back to Wells and small celebration of small success.

As ever fortunes and optimism come and go and this morning a meeting at Phillip's with J.Arthur ended in quite an argument. We were intending to buy the last few things. Not least the rope to tie the drums together. J.Arthur is there, inspecting shelves and barking orders. After greeting Phillip, I too take to slow marching up and down. There's a variety of different rope qualities, thick and thin, jute and nylon, high and low price. I pull out lengths, finger and measure. J.Arthur, naturally concerned about his budget, wants to buy the cheapest, which is a thin nylon cord. His moment and choice still took me by surprise. I have no say in anything anyway so I was flicking through some books over by the window when I heard Phillip ask if he didn't think that kind of twine would stretch. I moved quickly to the counter to add objection.

'I don't mean to interfere,' Phillip continued, trying diplomacy.

'Do you think that's the right choice?' I stupidly interrupted. 'I know you're concerned about cost but don't you think this brand new nylon rope will stretch when we put it under as much tension as we're going to?'

J.Arthur turned to me with a glare of disdain. 'Do you think I'm some sort of idiot?'

'Well, no, of course not..' I was about to repeat the stretching idea when he cut in, 'Mr Hammond, you will kindly leave the technical details of this rescue to me.' With that he spun angrily to Phillip. 'That'll be all. For the Eagle Sun account.'

Phillip was feeling dangerous. 'Yes of course, sir. You do know you should anticipate some stretching with this particular rope.'

J.Arthur exploded. 'Am I to be continually undermined?' Phillip is tall but J.Arthur drew himself higher. 'My good man, you are a chandler. I dare say you have some passing knowledge of your trade, but you certainly have none whatsoever of mine. Kindly keep your ill-informed opinions to yourself. I haven't gained an Admiralty rank by listening to the sort of drivel propounded by your ignorance.'

I couldn't hold myself any longer. 'Hey, now hold on. I asked and so did Phillip. That wouldn't you have thought it was blindingly obvious,.. that brand new nylon rope will stretch. That's no reason to have a go at Phillip.'

'Mister.' Here it comes again. 'If I have to tolerate any more insubordination from you, I will call Kirkham at Eagle Sun and have the whole rescue called off. Is that very clear? My patience with you is at an end.' And with that he about-turned, sloped his baton and moved to leave the shop. At the door he turned imperiously and fired at me. 'You will have remembered that you are to be on the quay at o-seven hundred tomorrow morning. Where I will expect that you to have completed your tasks. I bid you good day.'

'Arsehole,' Phillip said calmly.

'What is he on? And he must know that will stretch. He can't be that stupid. Can he?'

Phillip's eyebrows are bushy and one of them levitated slowly.

Next morning we're all mustered on the quay and marched to the slipway by his-navalship. The circle of men is mostly concerned about weather. Last night a brisk breeze from the northwest brought heavy rain and a mixture of what's good for the garden over safe on the sea. Just as we're loading the launch, old Ivor who turns out to be brother in law to George and one of the old school cynics, leans nodding to me with an arm-full of new nylon rope and says, 'I 'eard wen puttin' it together wi' plastic bands!' Over collective grunting grins. 'It'll go nice wi' that wankin'-plankin', won' it.' Ivor glares at me, pointing a shielded finger at J.Arthur.

Once we're up the Channel, the tide is well on the way out, making a long walk to the boat and plenty of time for polite discussion of the plan. The consensus is that the raft idea might work but tying barrels together with brand new nylon rope is for plankin' wankers.
The only reaction when I tell about the argument at Phillip's, 'Well, he's an edjiot then i'nt he.' And, 'it don't matter what you say, you can't stop 'im. He'n payin' for it and heen goin' t' fuck it up. That's 'is pergative i'nit. You gotta get on wi' it, boy. But don't you go countin' youm gettin' your boot back.'
There are two patterns to the morning's work. Their constant refrain of 'e's an edjiot', and mine every time I get near to a rope-tightener or an end, I heave and tug on it, stretching for all I'm worth. My vain attempts covered as they are by comments like, 'don't pull so 'ard there lad. You'll pull the 'hole lot over.' And, 'won't do no good 'owever 'ard you pulls it, lad. It's plastic-lastic i'nit,' And the best of all, 'you got the end of wankin'-plankin's jumper there.' I'm trying my best but grey defeatism spreads gluey tentacles. How is it that everyone else gets it but he doesn't? I share the deep sardonia and must sadly conclude that fate will take its course. A thin thread says so many opinions and amateur punditry could all be wrong. A smiling hand may be waiting, wanting to assist while we grind the grist. Or it might just give up the ungrateful ghost and go home. Go somewhere else and assist the faithful.

I daren't go to the Fleece with them when we get back. I can't stand to hear more and feel so impotent. I slope off to George's to avoid everyone and barricaded in my room, eventually fall asleep with a determined picture of her tied up against the quay.

After a night of tossing and laying awake, morning arrives with a surprising optimism. The first of three good chances. Not particularly high, an eight-seven. After next month's full-moon there's a nine-one. I stop a thought that I'll have to plan for that one. When we left yesterday with last looks at our handiwork, the drums tied together, planks across to give it rigidity. It looks like a raft. Please God it works like one!

Kirkham, the insurance agent, J.Arthur and I board Phillip's launch on the harnser and after the thin pleasantries fade, we head up the Channel. The sun won't be up for a while but the sky is bright and blue as we chug hard at the incoming tide. Unkempt me at the tiller and the allied antagonists, incongruously dressed in their suits, stand side by side imperiously in the front. I feel like a chauffeur, on route to a serious investiture. It's not a surging tide but still is against us and the little diesel in the launch struggles along. My usual interest in marsh inlets, searching the bubbling mud for flushed wildlife, is replaced by a fixed stare ahead.

As we approach the opening estuary, the sand on either side is covered in fast flowing eddies. The first of the Channel markers before the Bar and as soon as the water is deep enough, I pull the tiller hard over, turning us right to cross the shallows toward her.

I can see the bottom before we cloud it and often feel sand rubbing the keel. Soft broaching means our bit of sea is less than two-foot.

Beyond the Bar the sea is flat calm. Almost a glaze on the surface, thick like oil. Not a breath of wind to push the water. I drop the pendulum bob over the side and its string comes back wet to the length of my arm. It tells nothing. It could be deep here, shallow over there. Just something to do rather than invest in doubt.

'Get in closer!' Suddenly commanding, J.Arthur waves an outstretched arm toward the marsh. It seems pointless as we're still miles away but I pull the rudder and he's right. The tide flow full behind us, we speed up a little. Our gentle surge lifts the bow. Only half a mile an hour faster but we draw on and I can make out the shape of the raft underneath her. She might be sitting higher in the water. At this distance you can't tell.

The giant sun disk appears strong from behind the only dune-raised point on the horizon, its warmth an instant cure for anything. She does look higher in the water even if it is a mirage. Intense staring makes for any kind of illusion but I swear the flag I ran up yesterday is swaying slightly at her mast head. As once before, now a seeming age ago, I thought the Blue Peter, the sign of leaving port, might be a lucky omen. Before we left yesterday, I went to the wheelhouse and got it out of its cubby-hole. On deck with a derisive audience, I made a silent ceremony. It seemed like a vain entreaty but now I don't know. She does look higher.

As we draw near, low across the shallows a new sound mingles with Oyster Catchers and seagulls. A staccato snapping and whining like someone over there laying on with a whip. We draw closer and the noise defines into creaking and cracking. Rope on wood, rope on metal, even at this distance the air is alive with symphonic strain echoing through hollow drums.

With still a couple of hundred yards to go, J.Arthur is uncoiling the towrope. 'Pull around to the bow and we'll slip this over the winch-capstan and, as soon as that's done I want you to turn around and take the strain. Is that clear?' I nod assent. He doesn't have a single doubt. 'You will not begin towing until I give the signal.'

She is higher and as we get closer the whole raft shape is pulling tight around her with the outside drums rising upward like wings. The noise is now a continuous cacophony of scraping and creaking. I can see a few lengths of connecting rope stretched high above the drums, taut and quivering. Only minutes to the top of the tide, I chuck the bob over the launch gunwale. Hand over hand, pulling the string back, when the bob appears it's wet to three-foot. The water is flat calm, still not a breath of wind but the boat is rising and falling, the masthead swaying and her water-line alternately a foot above the ripples.

Finally, we draw up to her and J.Arthur is immediately animated, Kirkham sits down in the middle of the launch. Once our rope is over the capstan I turn the launch and hold her as still as I can with the rope taut. There's too much movement stirring up the sand so that I can't see the bottom or what's happening around the edge of the hole. The raucous strider of screeching and straining is getting louder by the moment and my worries over spoiled paintwork are lost in the clamour. J.Arthur looks at his watch. Still a few minutes to go and we stand, waiting on brimming poignance. An almighty crack booms an echo through the whole structure. I see no consequence and wait, my hand poised over the throttle lever.

The seconds ache as a gaggle of Oyster Catchers look inquisitive. Normally you'd hear their peeping cries as they take to the air but the hoarse squealing and twanging drowns them out. For a moment I'm distracted by them only to be shocked out of it by J.Arthur's high-pitched scream. 'Gooww!' With a reflex I yank the throttle hard against the stop and the launch lurches forward. Straight out of slapstick, as we surge forward Kirkham grips the gunwales and J.Arthur in fantastic slow-motion, topples, staggers and falls straight over the side, his naval cap flying like a frisbee. I'm so concentrated on steering the straight-line tow that I hardly catch the final comic splashing, until I turn to see his head and shoulders above the water, a lank of hair draped to his chin. He is sitting on the bottom. With an incandescent look he raises an arm out the water and angrily propels me on. He grabbed the gunwale and clambers in, his trailing leg revealing water knee deep.

I think he is about to scream at me when all is suddenly drowned by new cacophony. A sudden rasp, grating and crunch follow the loudest twang. The three of us turn in unison to watch a split plank cartwheel and two oil-drums one each side of her, catapult twenty foot into the air like depth-charges. Then, one after another, in the most dramatic sequence of escape, two, three, four, five oil drums are flying, spinning and careering, landing back into the water, booming on impact. From what was then obviously some elevation, Cirkus in a serene water-ballet, sinks gracefully into the hole. A billowing circled wave discharged by her weight, rocks us as it passes and her water-line disappears.

Ropes loose and floating free like frayed ends and, the rest of the oil-drums bob up in a forlorn circle. One by one they drift gently away toward the trees and Cirkus looks cosy, safe and stranded once more.

Nothing is said. In fairness we are together in being stunned by the comic apparition, let alone the failure. I'll remember that picture for a long time to come. The barrels launched from under her, high into the air.

It just blurted out I'm afraid. 'My God. They're going to love this in the Fleece.'

If looks could kill, J.Arthur's face is a fine weapon, contorted and dripping.

We drifted in a circle of clattering oil-drums. I grab the ones I can, looping trails of free rope around them. Some were long gone, drifting towards the marsh. I'll be able to collect the ones that don't end up in Stiffkey. I'll tie them to the pile of ballast to treasure even more evidence. Kirkham, mouth open, stared whilst J.Arthur sat bedraggled on the floor of the launch, tipping water out of a shoe.

The tide is ebbing and so before we strand the launch and have to walk back I make the unilateral decision. There's nothing else to do here except get maudlin or have a fight. I restart the launch and head for the Channel. By the time we get there Kirkham and I are already out wading and pushing us through clouds of sand soup. The water deepens at the Channel edge and we jump aboard to start a melancholy chug to the quay.

About half-way back, Kirkham tries reassuringly. 'We'll discuss our next steps when I get back and report to the office.'

'Okay.' Is all I manage. J.Arthur, fixed and staring ahead, says nothing and Kirkham resumes a position next to him in the bow.

From quite a long way off I see the twins Dick and Mike, standing on the quay edge looking out toward us as we approach. I don't understand it to start with, they are side by side making some movement in unison. As we draw nearer it becomes clear that they are signalling to us, miming between their legs, imaginary up and down strokes of two enormous penises.

Chapter Eighteen   what good is this?

What am I doing? Lurching from one hair-brain scheme to another. It doesn't matter, I can't stop. And it's not a question of hope. I can't see being released from it. What else is there to do? My gently wallowing, stranded life is out here.
'You don't seem very depressed.' I was told again.
I don't feel very depressed. Frustrated and obsessive certainly. Desperate to think of some way, some new dimension. How can it be hopeless? It's not some airy-fairy thing. This is measurable from every angle, the weight, draught, the distance from the Bar and the Channel. All aside from the towering fact that she is in perfect working order, complete and ready to go.
What am I doing? That's a different dimension. I've almost forgotten I had anywhere to go. I can hold to a simple purpose like floating the boat, that's mechanical. If I did manage to get going, the travelling money is showing a serious dent. I don't know how many more attempts that will float. And I daren't look any deeper.

Symbolic depressions? Plenty of those. I've been watching yet another form in the sand over there. They can get quite deep within a week. With the movement of every tide a hollow, maybe a hundred yards long gets deeper as it creeps tantalisingly close. Further away another is deep enough stretching almost all the way. I play hope-filled games of walking back towards the Channel, trying to connect low lying links with other shapes and changes. I've cut reed-sticks which now stand like little forest trails marking the most likely escape. What it significantly marks however, is how fast everything changes in shape and shallow. If you had all the time to watch it, you'd find profound rhythms and pattern. A life sentence out here perhaps. This nearest little valley I noticed only ten days ago and already it's getting closer. At the same time, wind direction and weather or whatever multitude of factors cause them, will also cause them to halt or change direction or disappear entirely. Depressions? The contrast between minute heaping of grain upon grain and my frenetic thrashing about achieving so little.

I'm tired too, of dubious celebrity in Wells. As if I'm not mad enough, I'm the target for every hair-brain idea that anyone may pitch. I dread the phrase, 'You know your boat out there..'
I've enough advice to last a lifetime of shipwrecks. Yesterday on the quay, noisy kids dangling bait down the wall to catch grazing crabs. I was in the middle of a long prayer to whatever forces might be listening, when someone tapped me on the shoulder. 'You know your boat out there..?'
His idea is wackier than most but I can't stop the thought that I should listen just in case.

They can be spectacular tangents. An ad in this weeks' Eastern Daily Press jumps off the page. 'If I had to design a new life, this would be it. 'The Happiness Purpose', an all day workshop at home with Edward de Bono.' Overtime scanning peaked and something struck a chord. The name is very familiar. He's the lateral thinking man. Those funny mind puzzles; there are three people in a lift wanting to go to different floors. How do they

get there without stopping? I could never work them out. I did read one of his books and remember that the idea was to resist going down the usual solution driven tunnels. You had to suspend judgement. Po he called it. Neither yes nor no, something in between. A device allowing new rationale to arise if you don't stop the solving process by deciding too quickly!
He is so close, in Fakenham about five miles away. I booked a place on the workshop. Maybe I'll get a chance to ask him for help. I'll make the opportunity to present him with the problem. Clutching at straws?

The saga grinds on, it's nearly a month since the insurance rescue. In a telephone conversation with Kirkham and subsequent letter, they say with the usual caring formalese that, without prejudice, this was their only attempt at assistance. In due course they would be offering me a settlement.
Like everything else, I'm waiting. Wait for the tide, wait for new ideas, wait for insurance mercy. And of course, I fill the waiting with the most incredible not waiting.

The day at Edward de Bonos' was a wonderfully distracting warm bath. In his workshop room at the end of the garden, he talked in assured tones and illustrating diagrams. All day, we engaged as he lead us in revealing intimate exercises. There were ten of us, four other smokers who sinned and talked long out in the garden during coffee breaks.
All made perfect sense as though it were already known. How to begin observing and thinking. How to look at the world as its own truth over the imposition of our view. We are believable and useful as long as we are part of creating it. Instead of judging and fighting it for what we think we need. Tolerance and humour rise. Rather than competitive, relationships are

enjoyed in respect for their contribution. A deliberate pursuit of happiness and dignity.

A journey of a thousand miles beginning with one step of my own. At the end of the day, I managed a few minutes with him. He was tired but smiled and invited me. I garbled it but he understood and all was perfect and, lateral. We talked about why we should wait for water and what meanwhile. I drew an A-frame, the apex of which was roped to the keel and a tractor that would pull and lever her forward. No water needed, just length by steady length. By the end of the conversation, my drawing had log rollers and boards and we could see it rising and sliding towards the Channel. If there should be enough water meanwhile, we're moving whatever happens. He wished me luck in finding a willing tractor.

I walked thoughtfully down the road from his house and having missed the bus to Wells, wanting to enjoy a reward for new ideas. 'I'll hitchike if a car passes.'

Three or four miles into the sunset evening, the road to Wells is a country lane and only a few cars ignored me. A pick-up sped past and I thought I'd lost another when the brake lights flashed. It pulled onto the grass some way ahead and I ran out of breath, 'You going to Wells?'

A ruddy face beamed red like it was polished. 'Nowheres else.'

He's a farmer at Blakeney and business is not good. So he's looking for other work.

'Got a brand new drot I bought t'other week. Five ton, caterpillar tracked she is. Could go over any ground. Gonna hire m'sen out to builders. Might even get a bit o' work off the Council.'

As obvious as can be, like the prize of the day. I could hardly contain myself. 'How about salvage?'

'If it can be towed, she'll do it'. His inflated red face gleamed through the window when he'd dropped me outside the Milk-Bar.

Sometimes you imagine you are being presented with some guiding. Coincidences skip you into another gear. Belief or disbelief the only question. It couldn't happen without the exact timing. You're so happy but then the doubt vortex sucks it down a black hole, bumping along in the dark until it fades. Every silver-lining had a cloud.

Endlessly walking the beach, mood matching depressions. All too literal and growing. Sitting for hours under the outermost tree, I've got up so many times and paced it out, stomping across the beach and then beyond to the Bar and the surf. It's about a mile, maybe a little more and she's somewhere in the middle, nine hundred and more stomping steps from nowhere.

We tried the A-Frames and the tractor-drot. He managed to get it off his low-loader truck within about three miles down the beach at Moreston. The caterpillar tracks rumbled slowly over soft sand. An hours' plus journey each time before we set up. And it was more setting up than hauling. Hauling, sound-tracked with creaking and screeching, we inched her out of the hole. The frames worked after a fashion, levering her up and forward. The angle is crucial and if the lever too shallow the drot is not strong enough. After each haul, I prop the bilge keels and we back into position. Sometimes a few feet, sometimes not. Each time setting up, making sure the rope held under her keel without damage. Rolling around in puddles to push boards underneath.

At a certain point after a particularly arduous few inches, some part of me woke out of the tunnel. We are playing some incredible beach game using the most impressive, dreamed

array of boy's toys. It's all shouting and waving arms and peering on your hands and knees at bits of wood about to take the weight. It wasn't how I imagined long hauls. Ours were squeaky jolts.
Six hundred and fifty pounds for the week equals thirty yards and my red faced co-hauler is frustrating. The drot is brand new, so he can't possibly get salt water on it. The sand is bad enough. In panic driven bursts of new energy every time the tide threatens, he gathers everything and he's gone. Over the rumbling and his shoulder he shouts, 'Don'e worry. Back tomorro'. We're getting maybe three hours work at a time. At the end of each low-tide day she's keeled over so that moving around inside is back to being impossible. Collapsing on the saloon sofa looking up at the table across the rakish slope, the sky through the opposite porthole. I stumble around, clearing up, pacing up and down sand, waiting for a pathetic trickle of water that doesn't even wash away our scars.

It's so uncomfortable. I am so uncomfortable, wretched and exhausted by painful progress toward a beckoning depression, maybe still a hundred yards off. 'Over here' it shouts. I'm hearing voices in obsession. I heard a seagull squawking it. 'Over here!' It's pitiful and will anyway have disappeared before we get there. I remember de Bono but my truth is arm-locked. Paralysed, it doesn't matter whether here or over there. Within a couple of weeks she'll have dug a new hole and we'll be thirty yards from the old one.

Once in a blue moon there are two full in the month and three or four more good chances. The first is tonight, a nine-one. Over the next two days it'll rise to nine-seven. The sea will cover everything to the quay. The Channel and the marsh will disappear and become one reflecting sea. Little sparks spring eternal. Phillip told me this afternoon, he read the forecast. Tuesday morning will be the highest tide of the century. The nagging gremlin says it's bollocks.

Like a ritual, do I ask again if I can use the launch without paying? Phillip will be encouraging. Early morning or evening I'll chug impatiently up the Channel. Waiting for enough water to cross the sand.

In complete contradiction to the forecast, perfect English holiday weather is raining horizontal. Driving us extra fast, veering through shallows, avoiding raised mud. Off the land, the brisk wind keeps the water out and it's surely the top of the tide before there's enough to get the launch out of the Channel. Making for the nearest of my reed forest trails, it's maybe fifty yards before I run aground and have to walk. Rain lashing my face, I sweat and pull-trudge the launch across barely covered sand. For the last five hundred yards, I left it, throwing the hardly necessary anchor over the side. For nearly three hours I waited, looking at my watch, wondering if the wind could make it so late. The enduring image of the highest tide of the century is that it didn't quite come over my wellies!

The next morning feeling detached, I work hard at the dawn walk up the Channel road. I'm sure it's as beautiful as ever but I hardly notice. At about six I sat on the dune by the Lifeboat Station to stare through the binoculars. The wind still blowing might have gone round a bit. It won't help a tide and I've abandoned the heavy launch in favour of rowing or walking with the dinghy. Thankfully the rain has stopped. I demand gratitude for that.

A weary ebb, any further descent is quick. It all seems utterly impossible and I curl up in a dune hollow, marram-grass shielding the wind. Echoing foetus-like, I feel very small indeed. A wave of emotion arrives. Impotent, lost and incapable of hope, I fall into exhausted melancholia. Staring at sand grains running away through my fingers. Between despondence and frustration an effort raised the binoculars and I gaze lazily through the hole at my illusion of intimacy. Its gnawing consequence brings on paralysis. Rigid like a stone, nothing beyond the very present. Nothing to do more than just be here. Can't let go, can't walk away. The only possible release, waiting for water that may never come. Down the tubular view, an unseverable connection, an irresistible stream of consequence. Clearly chosen yet now so tightly confined. It doesn't matter anymore what those circumstances were or are. They have simply served their purpose to get me to this moment. Smallest sensible impulse is lost in crossed conflicting waves and the view begins to blur and wrinkle. In a stronger surge, too heavy to resist, I begin to weep. I don't try very hard and the weeping grows to sobbing, the sobbing to quiet shaking, only pausing to check I'm alone. Permitted by cold wind and slate sky and overflowing in powerful surges, joining trickles of water filling shallows.

Like some awful drama, alternately melancholic and manic. In anger I got up and kicked sand flurries, ran down to the edge and slashed at the water. Then release filled waves of self-pity slumped back in the hollow. I lay there staring at blank holes. In a moment, guilt at stupidity strikes again, demanding some action or some giving up. In one bid to break out of it, I got up and pulled the dinghy from under the Lifeboat Station. The water's edge is close and it's easily launched. With only half a wellie-full I pushed it and jumped in. A little sidling with the current while I grab the oars and we're almost across. As it beaches the other side I step in shallow paddling. Pulling in the dinghy I sit grounded on the bottom. Crossed in a moment, not fast or wide enough. There's no point in struggling. Give up, she's not floating today or any..

A hypnotising mist blew over from the marsh on its way out to sea. Shrouded by the rolling bank of fret, Cirkus disappeared.
Rain began heavily and pointless discomfort won. I crossed back over and this time sat dripping under the Lifeboat Station, emptying wellies, leaning on the dinghy.

Falling deeper again, out of control and careening down a well trodden descent. It lasts as long as patience, which means within moments I'm up again and tripping over down the dune to stomp along the remaining spit of sand towards the Channel mouth. I sat on the farthest possible point near the Bar. Unimpressive tiny wavelets lap either side, slowly eroding the spit. Cut off from the beach, wet quickly soaks into my jeans and, just like Cirkus, I'm sitting in my own little pool. Blank psychosis returned, staring along lines of little wavelets rolling miniature, inch high crests over one another.

Concentrated on disconnected space I didn't notice the trawlers approaching until they were close. Three of them, in a line entering the fairway. Processing slowly, directly, offering a master-class in entering the Channel from the right direction. Gliding serene, they follow in one another's wake. I turned away, paddling the spit back toward the dune. I don't want them to recognise me and as they pass, kept my head low, pretending to be a beachcomber. Why anyone would go beachcombing in this weather, doesn't really occur. What does it matter what they think? It matters and it doesn't matter.

Their appearance broke the spell. I carried on walking through the dunes and out onto the road. Pulled in every direction, ambling under the weight, every other step in danger of tripping over myself. A few cars are on the road and it's time not to be visible. I pull over my hood and through drizzle and more head bowed tremors, I make the quay and along the road to George's. Once upstairs in my room, I barely get the wet clothes off before crashing face down on the bed and falling into exhausted sleep.

Chapter Nineteen   what good is this?

I've come to the idea that worrying is like praying for something you don't want. Choices have consequences and an odd familiar pressure. Right or wrong, surely the choice I make now is the only one present?

Decorating the blue Formica, on the table in front of me, at my early morning Milk-Bar sojourn before the crowds, is a dear letter from the dear insurance company. Enclosed is a cheque. In the usual style the letter speaks of without prejudice, in due consideration and with reference to the Assessor's Report. If I will sign and return this tear-off slip, pledging no further claim, they will say no more. The cheque is for fifteen hundred pounds.

Cup in hand, hovering over the saucer, a numb angry fret rolls over me. That they could think I would accept such a small amount when they took a premium for forty-five thousand. Unless they think they've got me by the balls, which, of course they have. Just now I called Malcolm, a lawyer friend and he says it's unfortunate. I will have to argue over the survey and the meaning of the word 'maintenance' and that will be expensive litigation. No court would take the booking without a surety of something like eight-thousand to cover cost if I lose.

Needless to say I don't have that or anything like it. I have only ever thought of them as help not replacement. And fifteen-hundred won't move shit. And then what. If it doesn't work, they are out? The cup doesn't get to my lips but remains hovering.

Someone else came in and the door slammed. Hypnotised by tea, I'm peripherally aware of the figure coming closer and then standing at the table.
'In'it 'bout time we got that bloody boot off the sand'? I look up through muddy waders, dirty duffle-coat, to frayed blue bobble-hat. It's Peanuts, the little man from the pub on the very first night.
'Buy us a cup o' tea.' He pulled out the chair opposite and sat down.
I look into the blue eyes. 'Haven't seen you for a while,' I say lazily and thought I should fold the letter away.
'So you ain't got 'er off.' He swivelled on the seat, resting an elbow on the table. I had asked about him a few times but nobody knows him or his ol' blue trawler.
'I've tried about everything I can think of, up to the minute.'
'Yeh?'
'Well, the only thing I haven't managed is to get another boat in there up to her,.. something with a shallow draft and enough power to pull and push. But I'll never get that, who'd be daft enough to get their boat in there?'
'Don''now 'bout daaft.'
'Well you wouldn't put your boat in there would you?'
'I moight.' He paused. 'Iffen the right price.'
'Oh yeh, and I wonder what that 'ud be?' I tried to picture his boat. I've only seen it the once, through rain slashed windows. 'And what if you get stuck over there?'
He broke a broad smile. 'We'll 'ave a party then won'we.'

'How do you think we should do that then?'
He swivelled waders around and leaned forward across the table. 'There's me and two crew for three days. That's fifty pound a day each and 'undred quid to me when we float 'er.'

He paused for impact, pushing the bobble-hat all the way back. 'These moons comin', roight. Next few days. They looks good. What 'ave we got, noine-three. That'll do 'em.. We take mine outside and run her level until there's 'nough to get across the Bar. We rope 'er up and pull 'er. Roight?'
'Sounds easy. But even on the highest ones we haven't had enough water since April to do something like that.'
He waved a hand in the air. 'Don't you worry, boy.' Is all the mollifying I'm getting.
'You meet me on the quay, 'alf-pass-five tamorro' mornin', and we'll 'ave a goo.'

Is there more to say?.. I couldn't think of anything beyond insurance companies and whether to send the cheque back.
'Alright.'
He nodded and stood up. With waders shlapping shuffled toward the door. As he opened it he turned. 'We'll get that boot off, don't you worry boy.'

I sat there for a few minutes, as though waiting for some other reality to dawn. One that would surely show I'd woken from another silly dream. It arrived with a large double family. A dozen kids with water-wings and lots of screaming. I got up and left.

I've mostly forgotten him. In a rare quiet moment in the Fleece, Dick Able and I were sitting yards apart on bar stools. Not speaking of course, until I said. 'D'you know Peanuts?' He didn't look up from his pint but stretched the back of his hand across the bar to a small bowl. He said nothing but brushed the bowl perfectly, sliding it the whole length of the bar-top to arrive with clink at my glass.

'Nothing ventured, nothing gained,' was Phillip's response.
'Yeh, but I seem to 'ave been venturing rather a lot to no effect.'
'But you can't tell. This could be it. The tides are good, weather forecast looks flat calm.'
'Exactly. What difference is that gonna make.'
'Well sometimes the high pressure alone holds it in. You can't tell 'til you get out there and see it.'
I wanted to say more about the effect on me but relations with Phillip haven't quite reached that level of confidence. I imagine I have to be grown up and get on with it.
A good sentiment but it didn't stick. 'Oh hell, Phillip. I suppose so. It's got to work sooner or later, surely? I'm not sure I can take much more if it doesn't. If it goes on through the winter, there might be storms, she might start taking all sorts of damage.'
'You'll keep going, Will. You have to be patient. Like the sea.. And in no time,.. she'll be moored on the quay and you'll wonder what all the fuss was about.'
I stopped the mealy thought before it went further, him pottering blithely about with his tackle and t-shirts..

Next morning early, the tide well advanced, we motor up the Channel. The marsh inlets are filling, boats dotted around are already free from mud and facing the flow. Peanuts at the wheel under a Heath Robinson canopy and the two mates coiling rope and fiddle-tidying. It's good to be on a large boat again. We hadn't talked much, there wasn't much to say. Leaning over the bow, watching the stem push the water apart, barely present, lulled by the engine vibration. The sky is almost clear blue and you only feel a gentle breeze once we're beyond the lee of the dunes. Past the Lifeboat Station, she's there, along with my usual first sight feeling. Maybe it sounds corny but every time there's a physical aching full of emotion. I try to keep the focus, a licked finger for wind direction.

'Wind's roight.' One of the mates says as he threw a bucket over the side for deck washing. As we pass between the red and the green channel markers Peanuts yells out from his tent over the wheel, "nough 'ere!'
Like the portal to change, at the Bar entrance, we're out and into the sea. He takes us on into the fairway before we turn right. Fifty yards beyond the Bar and hardly a swell or breaking wave, we rock a little and the tide soon pushes us closer. I catch sight of the bottom. We begin to skirt along the Bar edge and I walk back through scattered pots to stand next to Peanuts. He smiles an unshaven and black toothy smile. "nough 'ere,' and nods up towards the echo-sounder tied with fraying blue string to the roof of the canopy. The three dot red line flicks to four and back again. The engine drones above even rhythmic splashes and our wake soon settles in the calm.

It takes us maybe twenty minutes before we're level with her, the line clear beyond to the trees. "bout a mile I reckon.'
'Yeh. Not so much. 'Bout a mile to the trees and she's right in the middle.'
He rolls his hand over the wheel spokes, turning us slowly to face the land. He opened the throttle and we inch forward. Within moments we breach and the bow rises over the slope. 'There she is.' He spun the wheel back and opened the throttle some more. Moving against it, rocking with the power of the engine. We're not moving forward. He shut it down and the boat relaxed and swung a little further round. He let us drift

and we move slowly sideways along the edge. Every few yards Peanuts opened the throttle again, each time with the same effect. We broach and try to power through it. The bow rises and we're stuck.

'Ten past seven ain't she, top o' the tide. 'bout 'alf an hour then.'

Successive attempts find the same result until we stop to watch the clock. Dead on ten past he threw the life-ring over the side and we watched that too. When it no longer drifts back towards the Channel it has to be the top. He turned again and opened the throttle. Only a few extra yards but we had a run at it this time. We broach even sooner.

'Alroight mate. Now you get in that dinghy and you take a line out to 'er. We're gonna put a buoy on the Bar 'ere, so's I can pick it up and mak' off out. We get a good long rope on 'er, by the time I get a good 'ead up, we'll pull 'er off.'

Is that a sensible idea? I don't have a clue and start with the mates to carry the dinghy with its little outboard. There's no time to think about it. Maybe all the water we're going to get. We unceremoniously heave the dinghy over the gunwale and climb after it. They start the outboard engine for me while I grab the end of the thin rope coiled on the deck. I swap places on the little seat in the back. It's a simple twist on the outboard rudder to make it go and I accelerate away with the bow high in the air and the rope trailing behind me. At first it's easy, the calm water inside the Bar makes unhindered speed toward Cirkus. About a quarter of the way I can feel us slowing down though and twist the accelerator hard. For a while it helps but the rope behind is beginning to curve and slack its long way back to the trawler. The tide must have turned and steadily as it gets longer the rope balloons further away with the ebb. The dinghy slows almost to a standstill. Less than a third of the way and I'm stopped. Little trails of smoke appear from the screaming outboard and I shut it down to an idle.

I don't know what to do and drift on the end of the line now pulling me back toward the trawler. I'll try and leave it here, stake it to the bottom. I look around the dinghy for anything to help. Tied to an oar might work. I could pile it into the sand. We wouldn't lose it, it's tied.. I decide to do it and step out of the dinghy. 'God!' It's about a foot deep. I pushed the paddle end in as far as I can and it stands solid as I tie the line off. Running to catch the drifting dinghy I filled my wellies and clambered onto the seat, twisting us away. Circling the oar, lifting the line to get under, Cirkus is so far away. A familiar theme of anti-climax. What are we achieving by being here at all. I linger, waiting, wondering if something other will occur. Nothing does and no more to do, I head back to Peanuts.

As I arrive they are throwing an anchor and a very large luminous pink buoy over the side. I hand over the painter rope and climb aboard. Peanuts joins me and we stand, looking out to the stick and Cirkus beyond.

'Alroight boy. Now what we're gonna do is this. We're gon' get all the rope and line we can this af'ernoon. And you'll gonna lay it out dry. Then tamorro' mornin', we'll come along 'ere and I'll pick up that buoy and steam off straight out. Roight? A good 'ard tug and I reckon we'll move 'er.'

'Hang on, Peanuts. Why do we need more rope. What about all this stuff?' I point to the unused pile on the deck.

'Not enough there, boy and not 'alf strong enough. We need hawser or chain better.'

It's at that moment I realise he busks with such authority but I don't have a better plan. He's probably right. It's got to pull seventeen tons plus whatever extra weight is created by pulling it through sand. I imagine that first yank causing massive strain.

'Okay, so we get more, stronger rope. I don't quite know where from. I don't want to buy it. I suppose I could sell it back again, just a bit wet and stretched.' He grinned. 'But how are we gonna do this. How we gonna get all that rope out there?'
'Alroight then. You'll take that Chandler's launch and do it tonight, dry.'
'What in the dark?'
'It don't start gett'n' dark 'til hav pas noine, do it?'
'Alright. But you're gonna have to help me get all this rope and load it in the launch and unload it over there.'
'Can't do that. We got another trip out tonight. We'll help you 's arf'ernoon. And load up. But you'm 'ave to do the rest ya'self.'
'So, what? After this evening's tide's gone, I'm going to spend the night laying all this out dry. Is that right?'
'Roight. An' in the mornin' we come along 'ere and pick it up.' He waved a hand over his shoulder.
'Okay?' I'm unconvinced. The highest tide is tomorrow night, so we might only get a couple more chances. 'That's half of a mile of rope or chain. Over half a mile..?' Peanuts has a woolly fingered hand over his mouth and stares ahead, seeming not to acknowledge it.
'Okay.' I repeat, it appears to have been decided. As ever, what else is there to do but agree. I have no other plan.

Once back on the quay we agree to separate to search for rope. If it's going to pull her through the sand, it better be heavy. I hope I can find somewhere strong on the boat to attach it. Somewhere underneath perhaps, around her keel like we tried with the drot. I have no idea if we're making any sense. Beyond Peanuts' confidence I can't see it through. I'm not sure he can either.
We said we'd meet back here at one. Five hours to conjure a miracle. As ever my first call is on Phillip.

'I'm going to need about nine hundred yards of heavy rope, Phillip. With the two anchor chains and all the rope I've got on board, plus what Peanuts has got, I reckon I'm gonna need to find another seven hundred at least.'

'My God, you don't do anything small, do you.'

'We couldn't get there. Even on the top of the tide,.. it was a nine-one this morning.. He couldn't get over the Bar. There was just not enough water. And when I tried to get there with a thin line, even that was too heavy over that distance. By the time I'd got half-way it was ballooning out so much with the moving tide, I was going nowhere.'

'Mmmm...,' is Phillip's response.

'I don'know about Peanuts. I don't know what he's on. One minute we're doing one thing and the next he's changing the plan. I can't see it.'

'Mmmm...'

'I've got to go with it though, Phillip. There's nothing else to do. I've got to come up with this rope or chain. Then lay it all out dry on my own.'

'Mmmm...'

Phillip's ruminating is not that helpful.

'So..' I do a little pacing along the counter.

'There's some old hawser out the back. I don't how much but you're welcome to that. I've got a bit of anchor chain out there too. And there might be twenty yards in the launch locker, and p'raps another fifty yards of rope, but it's not that thick.' He paused. 'Oh hang on, I've just thought. There's a big pile of chain round the back of the Whelk shed. I don't who you'd need to ask for that. Maybe old Stan if you can find him.'

I feel pressure and check my watch. 'Okay, Phillip, thank you. Look, and I'm sorry to have to ask you again, but may I borrow the launch again tonight. I've no idea how long it's going to take me to do it. It's going to be all night. Of that I'm sure. I've gotta wait for it to dry out, so it'll be stuck there 'til the morning anyway.'

'Of course. It's fine. You take it.' I don't know what I'd do without him. He smiled, 'And, really, I'm not going to need it for anything in the middle of the night, am I. You take as long as you like.' He nodded affirming it.

'Fantastic, Phillip. That's fantastic. I'm so grateful. I don't know what I'd do without your help.'

'Well good luck this time.'

I borrowed Phillip's wheelbarrow, all morning up and down the quay and beyond. By one o'clock there's a large-ish pile lying on the harnser ready to go in the launch. At a rough estimate, guessing what we've got on each other's boats and walking round and around the pile, trying to measure with a finger, we're very short. When Peanuts and the mates arrive, they are carrying quite a length between them.

'We're still short,' I said to him as we tried to estimate again, circling the lengths and coils, walking with our fingers.

'Borro'd this bit,' he said with a smile that said he hadn't exactly. 'Better 'ave more though. Won't do to be short.'

'Phillip says there's a load of chain round the back of the Whelk shed. Who d'ya think we ought to ask for that?'

'Let's 'ave a look then.'

We walk through the yard and there's no one around. Phillip was right, in the farthest corner, welded with rust to the perimeter fence, there's a huge pile of light anchor chain.

''ere it is then.' he says like it's the final answer. 'Let's 'ave this lot.' He pulls out a length, rust flaking off it in a shower.

'Well, hang on Peanuts, we can't just nick it.'

'It's 'ere in'it. Ain't nobody gonna care 'bout this lot.' He's picking at it and found an end. 'Alroight. Now you go and get that launch an' we'll load up what we got an' come back for some o' this stuff after. Roight?'

There's just enough water to get the launch almost to the bottom of the harnser. Together we make fairly light work of loading rope. The mates bring another pile from the trawler and it's full almost to the gunwales without the chain.

A slapstick quartet with the wheelbarrow full of chain and toppling. We lose it every few steps and start again. Much to the amusement of a passing gaggle of gaping tourists, it took three of us to steady and stumble manoeuvre it, with Peanuts scuffing behind like an honour guard in waders.

The pile covers the whole length of the launch to a height of four foot above the gunwale. It looks impossibly precarious. Like a mirror image of the launch, upside down. Which is exactly how it's likely to end up. Patting the top of the pile one of the mates says, 'You'll be able t' sit up there. Noice and comfy.'
I didn't enter the spirit. 'You're joking aren't you? I'll be lucky if I get past the quay.'
Once they'd gone I sat and contemplated it, sitting on the harnser slope with a sack of cleats and a fag.
'I'll have to come back when there's some water and see if it'll float.'
There's no point in going before the tide is up. The launch will sit so low in the water, we'll need the top of the tide just to get across the sand. Four hours at least to kill, I decide to go and get something stodgy and sustaining in the Fleece.

Comfort food, bangers and mash and a pint of Guinness. I might even have another after that. I sat at the window, parting grubby net curtains. Across the quay you can see the top six foot of the old blue trawler mast. By the time I'd finished the second helping it was eight and rising. A little crowd of on-lookers gathered in a group on the edge. I can't see from here what they're looking at. Eventually, the top of a cabin appears, mooring next to the trawler. A rope flies up and an onlooker with a camera swinging into his face, grabs the rope and trips while tying it round a bollard. The crowd parted and I recognise a guy from the new art centre at the end of town. Having managed all his ropes he stood, hand on hips, looking at the cabin top. Answering questions, first one side then another, he's smiling and pointing. He checks the ropes again and then turning on his way with a couple of skipping twirls like an enthusiastic dancer. Crossing the quay, he bounces over the road and in through the pub door. Whilst his pint is being poured, he turns and smiles a broad smile across at me. He's a very happy man. I raise my glass.

'New boat,' he says, the smile breaking out again.

'Oh yeh?'

I'm not sure I want company but I gesture to the empty chair at my table. He paid for the pint and came over.

Immediately, he can't hold it in. 'Yeh, just picked it up today from Hunstanton. I knew I was early. I've been out there waiting for the tide to let me in. But it's amazing, it only draws about eighteen inches, so as soon as it began to flood I could get in. It's fantastic. It's got zed-drives that come right out the back. Two of them, so I can go in incredibly shallow water and it's really powerful.' He looked out of window. 'You can't see it. Well only the cabin, but it's like two big outboard engines, but their inboard if you see what I mean.'

'Yeh. I see what you mean.'

'I thought it would be great for fishing. You know? I've wanted one for ages and it'll go anywhere.'

'Yeh?'

He stopped gushing enough to start his pint. I held my hand across the table. 'It's Will. You know, I'm famous. The shipwreck?'

He pointed a finger at me, lowering the glass. 'Yes, that's why I recognise you.'

'We met. I came to one of your film-club nights.'

'Yes, we talked in the foyer, didn't we, about boats. Apart from the centre, I think that's all I talk about anyway. At least that's what the girlfriend says.'

'She's got a bit of a rival now then hasn't she?'

He smiled broad and barely contained and took a long gulp until the glass was drained. 'Can I buy you another?' He nodded at my empty glass.

'Yes. Great. Why don't we go and have a look at your boat first. Look, it's almost up.'

No other prompting needed, he is immediately up and out the door. I follow him across the quay and down the few rungs onto the deck. Wide open with a little half-covered cabin over the wheel, it's a day-boat, maybe twenty-five foot long and pristine.

'Flat bottom I guess?'

'Yeh, actually it's shaped a bit like a speed-boat, and it's fast. The engines really pump it out. Look you can see..' He's pointing down into the water over the stern. 'See the props. Those zed-drives really boil the water 'til you get going and raise the bow. Then it almost hydroplanes.'

'Amazing.'

I'm sorry, I can't stop the thought. But I hardly know him. Too rude. How can I say it? How do I ask? This boat is exactly what I need tomorrow morning.

I spend an age rehearsing it as we walk around in his excitement. Even when we finish the tour I still can't find the courage. On the way back to the Fleece I decide to do it over the pint I will buy.

'Look Mike. I need to ask you,.. need to tell you something that's happening, well, tomorrow morning actually,'

He smiles broad and unsuspecting.

'Look, I know we don't know one another and,.. I don't expect any sympathy. But. I've got something to ask you.'

'Yeh?'

'Your boat is almost exactly what I've been waiting six months for.' He smiles once more but I think that the next bit will wipe it off.

'I want to borrow your boat.'

'What?'

'I want to borrow your brand new boat and do something quite dangerous with it.'

That was shocking, his eyes widened.

'Look, you've seen it. My boat's stuck up the beach, right in the middle of Bob Halls Sand.' He nodded. 'The wind and the tide put it there that night of the storm in April. And I've tried just about everything, but there's not been enough water to float her since. Tomorrow morning the tide is a predicted nine-four. That's one of the highest yet.. And that old blue trawler out there, next to yours..' I parted the curtain. 'Is going to pick up a buoy on the Bar and steam off out to sea with a tow. If at the same time, I could get right up to her, I might be able to push and pull, maybe rock her enough, so that the tug works. If I could get inside the Bar, right up to her, whilst he's pulling, I just might be able to give it that extra leverage.. and,.. the sort of boat I need to do that,.. is sitting right over there on the quay. It's perfect. It draws next to nothing.. Your brand new boat.'

The silence is long. He stares into the pint, his smile replaced now by more of a taut grimace.

'Can I borro' your boat, Mike?'

Chapter Twenty   what good is this?

The launch is unbelievably unstable. I manage to start it, perched on the back gunwale, straddling the rudder and wrestling chain to find the button. Every precarious movement tips it frighteningly but the chain is so solid it doesn't budge. The balance critical point, according to my heart pounding, is reached and passed so many times just trying to find a driving position. I finally get it by facing the back, the rudder between my knees and leaning against the pile. If I stay very still and go like a snail, don't turn or rock. I have to correct a heart throbbing wobble when I stupidly tried to wave to a bunch of kids and their parents on the quay. I didn't quite hear anyone say, 'who is that bloke? He must be mad..'

'We're okay.'
Into the Channel and the tide is already well up, almost covering the marsh. A few tips of taller plants waddle on the water. It's tempting to think I could take a short cut and head straight for the island of trees. I daren't though and stick close to the deep middle. It's incredibly slow, so low that any wave arriving, slops over the gunwale. I hope we don't ship too much and I wobble and wrestle with more chain behind my leg, to find the bilge switch. It's a relief to hear the little motor start

and a squirt appears out the back. I steady the boat. It's impossible not to sway every time I turn my head to see where we're going.

'We're okay.'

With a couple more heart in the mouth wobbles, we make it up to the Lifeboat Station and then painfully slow to the first marker. The evening sun is still warm, with a scattering of clouds beginning to tint. A light but pretty constant breeze is blowing off the sea. I can't see the bottom and after lots of doubtful anticipation, push the rudder slow, slowly towards my knee and we begin to turn. Nerves and balance right on the edge, I try to lean with it. Just out of the Channel, no bottom. High tide should be soon. Thank God nobody came the other way.

'We're okay.'

It's easier in open water. No sign of the bottom and I begin to relax. Keep the engine just ticking over, no sudden movements and slow, inching progress. The sea is calm beyond the Bar, a few white tips splashing rhythm away off. In the other direction over hidden tracts of green and brown marsh, you can see the mile or more, clear across smooth water to the town. Over my wobbling shoulder, a long way ahead, the island of trees now completely isolated. It's too far yet to be certain, over flashing glances, but I think I see the top of the mast sway. 'Steady, steady, keep in a straight line.' Still no sign of the bottom. Slowly the Lifeboat Station shrinks and with regular shots of incredibly deliberate and slow motion turns of my head, Cirkus begins to grow. When we finally get there, I plan to step lightly into the water. It doesn't work and the whole thing see-saws to the critical and back. At the last moment I jump into the water. In over my knees and every ounce of rigid calming deployed, I just manage to hang onto it, spread-eagled across the pile until the wallowing stops. My cheek resting on cold rust I see Cirkus moving from side to side. She floats!

Up on deck, the launch cargo suddenly looks dispensable. I grab the boathook and plunge it upright into the water for a measure outside of her hole. Three foot, maybe more. It's not enough but if you were pulling really hard. It can only be the depth of the keel.
'Couldn't that cut through the sand if you were pulling hard enough?'
'Wait.' I have to wait. At least until the water's gone down enough to paddle. 'Hang on maybe not?' The idea of pushing the launch and using it to pay out the chain suddenly occurs.
'Why didn't you think of that before?' Surely it doesn't matter, I can leave the launch here. Here or over there.
'I can anchor it. And get it tomorrow.' It's not going anywhere. 'And that lot's got to come off.' Come on. How reassuring talking to yourself can be. I'm grateful for a better plan.

Wading up to my waist, lifting and paying out the chain over the back of the launch is by far easier. Even so it's slow, pushing the launch and avoiding the chain scraping varnish off the stern. I tie a fender over the back and find a kind of rhythm. A couple of hundred yards or more nearer the Bar and the precarious pile in the launch looks hardly different. After only about an hour's good work though, she grounds on the bottom.

Now it's harder. Pull a length of the weight you can manage, but it's not far and you go back and pull the next length, back and pull half of it. Back and forth, relays back and forth, pulling out lengths then back to pull half of that length a bit further, then back again. I pace myself. Not too much weight each time, more back and forth in manageable bites. Progress is

painfully slow. The gremlin pops up. 'If you were sensible you'd have got here and used the launch for longer.'
'If you were sensible you'd be somewhere completely else. Doing something completely else..'

Length after length, pulling and walking back, lifting bits that get twisted, pulling and walking back, untangling links, pulling more onto the pile, then back and forth. Each back and forth I can manage the weight of maybe twenty feet. It is so slow. Slow and very, very repetitive. I hardly noticed the sunset but as it gets darker I imagine I have all night ahead to steadily work. I decide to take a rest with the excuse I should pace the distance back to Cirkus for tea. It's three hundred and fifty, less than a third.
Vaguely refreshed, armed with a torch and a lantern hanging on the boathook, I retrace the steps. Only three-twenty-odd this time. Maybe I lost count or tripped. The launch is now well grounded and heeled over under the weight. I begin the piling and hauling and the back and forthing. As I get further away from the launch I have to go back further each time to pull out the next length. Back and forth in longer relays. Pulling and walking back. Longer and longer, back and forth, pulling and walking back. It's exhausting. I stop for cigarettes. The moon, huge and orange arrives, hanging, watching with cool and dispassionate luminosity. I need no other light. Bright reflections and long shadows on the water are intimate company. Pulling and walking back. Only inches deep, they neither help nor hinder.

After midnight the beach is dry. A lot of chain still in the launch but for the first time rope under it is visible. I spot an end and pull it out. Let's have a rest and pull rope instead. By comparison it's so wonderfully light, I pull and pull. When a good long length is free, I walk with it over my shoulder,

leaning into the weight. At the end of that length I return for more. Again and again. Sometimes chain, sometimes rope for a rest. Pulling and walking back. On the Bar still a long way off, the buoy becomes a gaudy pink target in the moonlight. Some good way over half, I come upon the oar, fallen but still tied to its cord. I turn to look back at the distance. The lantern light hanging from the boathook by the launch is a tiny twinkling spot. Cirkus and the trees are colourless minor silhouettes.
'Am I half-way? Maybe. It's so hard to tell. And this cord I pulled in the dinghy is still no good. I'll have to lay out this heavier stuff all the way to connect up the lengths.'

After many short breaks I eventually have to stop and properly rest. I walk deliberately back, lazily counting the steps to the end of the chain. I didn't believe the count and then didn't care. There's no more rope to reach yet in the bottom of the launch, so it's back to hauling chain. This time it's much harder. Further to haul, further to go back. Endlessly repeating, pulling and walking back. The time and everything drags so heavy. Often impatient, taking too much and regretting it. Pulling and walking back. One step forward in every ten. I'm beginning to hurt, arms aching and back complaining. Pulling and walking back. I take longer breaks. More cigarettes and determination. Pulling and walking back. I try over again to measure each carrying length to my capacity but now it seems that even shorter lengths are too heavy. My steps falter as the tiredness grows. Must stop. Cannot stop, yet. Pull some more, lift some more. Just one more time back before another break. Pulling and walking back. Carry and don't hurry but carry on still. It's only two o'clock.

It went on. Impossibly heavy work. I seem barely nearer and fight darker and even darker defeat. Frustration building on back and forth, back and forth building on impatience. Forcing each step with rising oppression. I can't anymore cries feeble indulgence. You must!.. demands the gremlin..

In a moment of pique, without much warning I tripped headlong over it all and fell in an exhausted roll. I lay as I fell, facing the very edge.

The moon high overhead, I got to my knees and slumped backwards, eyes closed up to the sky. In the pause every sound grew louder. All at once I sensed the most dramatic tableau of all around me. Right in the centre, infinitely small, the focus of the moon spotlight, every detail of utter pointlessness exposed.. A mass of emotion built uncontrolably. As it grew in pitch, crying objection and judgements, every nuance of fear and hopelessness appear.. I have nothing. Guilt and shame for emptiness and repellent weakness.

But then a rage built against it. Disgust and despair at all too familiar inanity and uselessness, rising fast and fed from a vast source. Containable no longer, it burst through the surface. I opened my eyes and yelled out loud.

'WHAT GOOD IS THIS?..'

It filled and overflowed. I screamed at the whole sky.

'WHAT GOOD IS THIS?..WHAT IS THE POINT OF THIS!..'

A hesitation almost brought back sanity but there was more. An immensely powerful and loud voice almost separate from me, screamed again and again in cathartic rage.

'IS THIS IS IT? IS THIS WHAT YOU WANT? WHAT GOOD IS THIS?..

IS THIS WHAT YOU WANT ME TO BE DOING?.. WHAT GOOD TO ANYONE IS THIS?.. WHAT GOOD IS THIS?..'

It carried on in wave after wave of screaming demand at the sky.

After I don't know how many times of screaming it, I believed I'd heard it echoing enough in the void and let myself stop. I fell forward, elbows on the sand, head on the backs of my hands. But the next act played out. The spotlight beam tightened and narrowed to a piercing shard. The Gremlin grown to a giant, bellowed back.
'NO GOOD YOU IDIOT.'
The dam broke and a lifetime of self-pitying tears flowed. Resistance plied back and forth and finally collapsed as I let go the demand. Slowly the torrent ebbs and I'm only aware of my heartbeat racing through strangled silence. After an age the breeze returns with a sound of the waves on the Bar. Some sort of half normal reality is restored and I slump flat on moonlit sparkling grains. 'What good is this' still echoing, more like a surrender to anything and everything, including the sand in my mouth.

Something like an automaton eventually got up, spitting out sand and pressed into hauling. I don't know who or what he is but eventually some other thought had to arrive and then he kept running it over and over in his mind like a mantra, 'No good unless you make it good. No good unless you make it good. No good unless you make it good.'

All night that mantra held and after the longest walk of my life I got back to the quay just before six. Sitting hunched on the cold concrete of the harnser, numb and blank, I was beginning to drift through another of countless fags when they arrived.

Chapter Twenty One
what good is this?   Stood with a sigh?

I had left it with Mike that maybe he should think about it overnight. And so I felt quite a leap when I saw him coming along the quay. The group of us stood admiring Mike's boat as the fast flow of the tide lifted it up toward us.
'Give us a roly,' said Peanuts, tapping my arm with a bent finger. 'So we gotta plan then?'
I pass the packet and papers. 'Yeh.. Okay.. I think it looks like this. We go up there together. You go round and pick up the buoy.. I hope it's all attached. I used all the cleats and checked the length so many times. I've no idea how many miles I hauled, so God help us,.. I hope I didn't miss any.' That's too horrible a thought to affirm.
'Gotta loight boy?' He taps my arm again, smiling broad blue eyed encouragement.
'Right.. So you go and pick up the buoy, and while you're doin' that, we'll go inside on Mike's boat and get right up to her. We'll get more ropes on her and pull and push and see if we can break her free.' Everybody's nodding.
'It might work. If this tide is as good as last night's, it's only the depth of the keel that we need. And if it's only that, it's only a couple of inches wide, surely we can get that to cut through the sand if we're pulling hard enough.'

'Sound like a plan.' Ash drops from the wobbling cigarette stuck to his lip.

'I'll sound the siren when she's ready for you to pull. Right? You happy enough with that?'

'Reck'n we're see wha' 'appen when we get out there.'

As he turns away he gives me a little wink.

The mates take the cue and Mike and I board his boat.

'Well you're here so I guess you're okay with this?' I said once we were untied and pushing off.

He chuckled. 'Reckon we're have to see wha' 'appens when we get out there?'

Up the Channel in convoy. This is nice, like friends along. Reassuring, two boats on a mission. What's that? Safety in numbers or just company. I'm incredibly wired and hungry enough to confuse the butterflies. I chat inanely and by the time we turn out of the Channel and wave to Peanuts, there's enough water and a bond like we're going out to play. And from the back deck of the blue trawler as it moves away up the Channel, one of the mates is waving us a thumbs up.

I'm surprised at the amount of water. I climb over the front deck and grab the boathook, plunging in until it hits the bottom. It comes up at least three foot wet.

Waving it at Mike. 'Look. This is good. This is very good. Hasn't been this deep out here for months.'

I jumped down into the well of the boat and knelt over the stern. The engines are whipping sand. We're leaving a dirty brown wake but nowhere near grounding.

'She's afloat, Will. Look her mast is bobbing back and forth.'

'Yeh, but it might just be in her hole. You can't tell 'til you get right up to her.'

We slowly cross the sand on flat water and behind us, half a mile away now on the left, Peanuts is out of the Channel and turned, coming along the edge of the Bar. The rising water of our inland sea, stretches unbroken all the way back to town. The sentinel trees in isolation. A big sky is beautiful unbroken blue and the sun already beginning to climb over a clear horizon. I don't know whether it's numb, immune or overtired but I feel light-headed.
'It's so beautiful out here,' Mikes echoes. 'When the tide's up like this, it's like there's so much sea.'

Unlike like the launch, we get there fast. Cirkus is well afloat, whether in her hole or above it is hard to tell. As soon as we touch I jump on board, running quickly across the deck and down into the wheelhouse. I switch everything on ready to start the engine if we need it. Dials and switches all respond and the echo-sounder springs the red dots into life. They jump between three and six foot, confusingly expanding and contracting. No matter, you couldn't trust them anyway in this shallow. I hurry back onto the deck and Mike is trying to manoeuvre alongside.
'Mike. Let's tie the ropes both fore and aft. We could tie them quite tight and put some fenders in between and then once Peanuts gets going we might be able to go forward and reverse and try to shake her free.'
'Okay.' He's flat alongside. 'I'll do the bow, you do the stern.'
In the distance on the Bar, Peanuts is at the buoy. Hauling it in, the pink balloon disappearing over his gunwale.
We finish tying ropes and meet together at the mast.
'Okay..?' I don't how good or confident is Mike..?
'I need to take charge Mike. Is that okay wi' you?'
'Sure man, whatever you need..'
It's so simple, isn't it?

'Once I give Peanuts the siren, let's both get on yours until we get going. If it starts to work I might get back on her and try to start the engine. But I'll wait,.. I'm afraid to start it too soon. If there isn't enough water, she'll just take sand up into the cooling water and overheat.'

He still looks clear and happy..

'Alright?'

He nods, smiling and raises a thumb. I reply signalling both hands with fingers crossed and thumbs up. 'All right..!'

Back down in the wheelhouse I decide to lock the wheel straight and after a final dizzying check of everything I can see, I'm standing at the wheel with my palm over the siren button.

'Alright?' Maybe, who knows?

In the straight line view through the windscreen and along the deck, I can see Phillip's launch a way off where I left it and the old blue trawler waiting on the Bar. The echo-sounder dots are still jumping around and the wheelhouse clock says now's the time. This time?.. Is there a question? Free choices made long ago. Free choices now. Whatever the outcome. Free. No more hesitation, no more doubts of anything lost. I press down on the button and the siren winds into life until it's wailing. That somehow now promising sound that nothing could ignore. I switch it off and grabbing the binoculars climb the steps up to the back deck. Mike has a boathook over the stern of his boat and it comes up wet to half its length. For a moment he stands holding the pole at the wet mark. Like a javelin, waving it into the air.

I hear creaking underneath and run up to the bow. I can see movement in the water along the tow line. At the Bar a narrow profile of the trawler and a trail of black smoke, says Peanuts is on his way. I tied rope rather than hard chain for the last bit to Cirkus. A long loop under the keel at the back and up with a

quick release on the bow cleat. Suddenly like some long tail of a sea-snake rising, from fifty yards away the rope breaks the surface and flies up, twanged taut, bouncing and slap-splashing the line ahead. To the sound of a loud crack, it snatches tight and Cirkus lurches forward. I fall back on my haunches with the shock of the movement and recovering, run across the deck and leap down into the well of Mike's boat yelling 'PULL!'
'PULL!'
A skittish shared glance of agreement and I sidled in front of him to the wheel, opening the throttle as far as it would go. We lunge forward, the line of fenders between the boats squealing squashed complaint.
We're moving. 'WE'RE MOVING!'
I yell across to the horizon. 'GO PEANUTS, GO! WE'RE MOVING!'
The zed-drives at full power are churning the water brown behind us. It's inch by inch, foot by foot but WE'RE MOVING.
We're crabbing and you can feel the sand resistant but it's smooth and liquid and giving way.
'We must be out of the hole by now. Here..' He takes over and I grab onto Cirkus, clambering over the guard-rail onto her deck.
'KEEP IT OPEN MIKE. PLEASE. KEEP IT OPEN AS FAR AS YOU CAN.' I run the length of the boat to the back deck. Over the rudder there's only brown water. I turn away and leap the steps onto the floor of the wheelhouse. We must be out of the hole but the echo-sounder reads five foot.
'That's amazing. THAT'S AMAZING!'
I slide the side door back and yell across. 'FIVE FOOT. ECHO-SOUNDER'S READING FIVE FOOT UNDER THE KEEL!'
'THAT'S AMAZING!' he yells back.
We begin to move faster.

I clamber out onto the deck again and straddle the gap, jumping down into the well next to Mike. We're making incredibly good headway, smooth and even as you like.
'Shall we untie and let her go it alone?'
'Try closing the throttle and see if we keep going.' He closes it down until we can hear the rush of water between the two boats.
We said it in unison. 'AMAZING!' And laughed the most releasing laugh.
'When we let go, will you grab Phillip's launch and tow it back in?'
We untied and as I leapt back aboard Cirkus she began to bob and roll a little with the speed. I didn't need the steps into the wheelhouse. Flying to a remembered place I unlocked the wheel and began turning it, making us veer a little against the tow. Six and then seven dots, there could be six foot of water underneath as we pass the launch. I pulled the seat down and with an almost relaxed hand on the wheel, my head out of the door feeling a new sea breeze. Just like a pleasure cruise really. Underway again, I don't believe it.

When we cross the Bar the echo-sounder dipped just one dot. There must be at least five feet before it drops off the scale over the much deeper water. Once we were fifty yards beyond I wound up the siren again and bobbing in the sea swell, calm but still the sea.
'Did you hear that? THE SEA!' I walked the length of the deck, stroking the mast on the way to the bow and untied the umbilical tow.

Epilogue   what good is this?

The experts said it was probably deep barometric pressure or Arctic wind-blown currents. I have no idea. It didn't seem like that to me. And in six months I'd expertly failed to recover her nine times, for the cost of almost thirty thousand pounds, including trying to borrow a Jolly Green Giant. The end result, some say had nothing to do with me. Afterward I searched every possibility and there was no sign or cause and effect and certainly nothing like the condition that put her there.

What good is this? I'm not sure but, I will certainly concede for the moment, that there are more things in heaven and earth than I know. Even that some law of attraction works beyond and through us. That choices have consequences and consequences have grief and sorrow, light and inspiration, chance and unknown futures. It's also possible, even probable that something further unknown drives absolutely everything inside us and out. In our unstoppable quest to engage, we and it cause effects good or ill. Perhaps as random as a butterfly alighting on one flower or tides filling and emptying.

The great psychologist Carl Jung once wrote, 'We are dark by nature and also the source of the highest good. Dark but also light, not only bestial, semi-human and demonic but superhuman and in the classical sense divine'. And what of nature inside us and out? It is ubiquitous consciousness itself, ready and waiting on our contribution from moment to moment, however we find the strength or confidence to attend.

..And if it appears to have a mind of its own to which we are only occasionally privy, we are surely released to call on intuition for the choices we think we may or dare..

'Know thyself,' said the Oracle at Delphi, a fairly sensible prescription for living wisely. But it wasn't until the last century that psychologists seriously experimented with the Oracle's advice. Pretty quickly they ran into a problem; they found that we are indeed mostly incapable of knowing our own minds. We believe our senses, we think we know what's happening inside our head, what makes us happy or why we hold certain belief. But in truth it seems not so. Isolated and separate we rehearse a dualistic game for which we only know half the rules.

Think too much about that and it gets depressing. A perfect argument for giving up any attempt to manage our affairs or, to make sense of any choice over another. If we don't know what's best or why, then why make any choice at all? Why not be buffeted along by circumstance, carried by the current? Patiently waiting for what the next tide may bring..

Perhaps some more appreciation for a creative life over the limits of self-knowledge might be helpful. Knowing how much we don't know about ourselves might be quite liberating. It may even loosen up gratitude. After all, once our fixed ideas about what we think we need are revealed to have such dodgy foundations, isn't that a recipe, not for resignation but engagement? For experimenting, for doing things not expected and discovering new oceans in the process.

Oscar Wilde, who was always good at debunking fixed ideas, had no patience with the Oracle..
'Only the shallow know themselves.'

Afterlogue   what good is this?

Who knows how it works and whatever next. Life goes on almost seamless and ridiculously unexpected. Give me lemons and I'll make lemonade. We had such a party that night. I invited everybody who'd helped and almost everyone else on the quay, most of them complete strangers. In the morning I awoke to a loud knocking on the roof. I climbed into jeans and a shirt and tiptoeing over post-inebriated bodies on the way to the wheelhouse, went out on deck. Dazzled by the sunlight and my hangover, I squint hard. Standing on the quayside is the Pilot, now promoted to Harbour Master, who pretends not to recognise me and, three uniformed officers, two of them Police, the other I don't know.

'Excuse me, sir,' said the other. 'We're investigating the illegal importing of contraband and we've received a report that you were seen yesterday beyond the Bar, picking something out of the water. I have here a warrant to search the vessel. May we come aboard?'

'Well, you couldn't be discoverin' new oceans, lessen you got the courage to lose sight o' the shore now, could you?'

..the highest tide of the century   *

* thanks Donald Fagan
and Ella Gower

and most grateful thanks
to all who encourage me

Keithx

if you enjoyed What Good Is This?,
do be in touch

- more beyond horizons -
The Garden Sanctuary
gardening to soothe the soul
Noble Truths
new interpretations of old wisdom

contact:
km4beyondhorizons@live.co.uk

©copyright wgit/kwm13